THE
THRALL'S
SWORD

ENDORSEMENTS

AN ODYSSEY OF ONE YOUNG woman's loss, revenge, and restoration, *The Thrall's Sword* is a captivating tale that left me pondering the true freedom of forgiveness. Bringing hope to those with deep wounds, this novel is perfect for young adult and adult readers alike. Caylor has done her research, pulling the reader into a time when Christianity altered even the darkest of Viking practices. A refreshing, encouraging view of what it means to be a true Christian.

HEATHER DAY GILBERT
award-winning author of *The Vikings of the New World Saga*

SIGRID IS SUCH A RELATABLE character! You'll cry with her, question with her, grow with her, and celebrate with her throughout this vivid and moving historical novel.

BRITTANY MENG
author of *Unexpected*, and blogger at www.thebamblog.com
and www.motheringbeyondexpectations.com

THE THRALL'S SWORD IS A powerful story of forgiveness, redemption, and healing. I love the Irish words, references to Norse gods, the characters' accents, but most of all, I am in awe of the weighty message this story shares. Iosa, or Jesus, can save anyone, and beauty can come out of brokenness.

OLIVIA GIORDANO
blogger at www.livforhim.wordpress.com

GRACE CAYLOR

THE
THRALL'S
SWORD

AMBASSADOR INTERNATIONAL
GREENVILLE, SOUTH CAROLINA & BELFAST, NORTHERN IRELAND

www.ambassador-international.com

THE THRALL'S SWORD

©2021 by Grace Caylor
All rights reserved

ISBN: 978-1-64960-087-5
eISBN: 978-1-64960-097-4
Library of Congress Control Number: 2020949526

Cover Design by Hannah Linder Designs
Interior Typesetting by Dentelle Design
Digital Edition by Anna Riebe Raats
Edited by Megan Gerig

Scripture taken from THE HOLY BIBLE, NEW INTERNATIONAL VERSION®, NIV® Copyright © 1973, 1978, 1984, 2011 by Biblica, Inc.® Used by permission. All rights reserved worldwide.

Credit for Viking Funeral knowledge: Ibd Fadlan's account of the Rus: https://web.archive.org/web/20080409203620 and http://www.geocities.com/sessrumnirkindred/risala.html

AMBASSADOR INTERNATIONAL
Emerald House
411 University Ridge, Suite B14
Greenville, SC 29601
United States
www.ambassador-international.com

AMBASSADOR BOOKS
The Mount
2 Woodstock Link
Belfast, BT6 8DD
Northern Ireland, United Kingdom
www.ambassadormedia.co.uk

The colophon is a trademark of Ambassador, a Christian publishing company.

For those searching for freedom, hope, and a reason to live.

GLOSSARY

Aegir: god of the ocean

A-viking: going on a Scandinavian raid

Folkvanger: afterlife for honorable warriors ruled by Freyja

Freyja (not the human one in this tale): goddess of love and beauty

Frigg: the goddess of motherhood and clouds

Helheim (referred to as Hel): the Norse underworld for dishonorable people ruled by Hel

Iosa: the Irish name for Jesus of Nazareth

Jarl: the highest Norse class; wealthy men who led their followers into battle and allotted out the plunder

Oceanus: the Latin word for "sea"

Odin: the god of wisdom

Picts: a tribe who lived in what is now Eastern Scotland

Runes: letters of the Norse alphabet

Saga: a Norse poem

Thor: the god of thunder

Thrall: the lowest Norse class; a slave, servant, or captive

Valhalla: afterlife for honorable warriors ruled by Odin

Valkyries: female warriors who transported the honorable dead to Valhalla

"When pride comes, then comes disgrace,
but with humility comes wisdom."

– Proverbs 11:2

ACKNOWLEDGMENTS

SO MANY PEOPLE HAVE CONTRIBUTED to the making of this book. First, I want to thank my bookish cousin, Amy, for all the blunt and honest feedback. You didn't skirt around what you needed to tell me, and for that I am humbled and thankful.

Thank you, Olivia Giordano and Katie for your valuable feedback. I listened and took into consideration every word. Thank you, Brittany Meng, for being such an amazing freelance editor. Your constructive feedback grew me as both a writer and a person. Thank you, Jen Cudmore, for the feedback about Viking history and for loving Jesus so well. And thank you, Megan Gerig, for helping my novel become a more publishable piece and for all your thoughtful ideas to make everything work together more beautifully.

Thank you to Heather Day Gilbert, Sommer Lehman, Austin Ring, and Lori Vander Maten, for gladly stepping up to be my influencers, and to my friends who have supported me and encouraged me in my writing endeavors and in my relationship with God. Thank you, Young Writer's Workshop, for the few months I found a writing community and helpful information. Brett Harris and Jaquelle Crowe—you guys are awesome.

Thank you to my parents for helping me lean on God's grace through this whole journey.

Finally, and most importantly, thank You, God, for being with me through all these years of writing this book. You are, indeed, far better and far more valuable than my passion for writing. Your grace and mercy poured out on me through Jesus Christ is really all I need.

ONE

TEN MORE DAYS UNTIL THE funeral. Ten days until a thrall girl would have to die.

The rain outside poured hard enough to shake the longhouse, and water dripped through the thatched roof. My mother's nearness filled me with warmth like the nearby fire. Without looking at her, I knew her gaze rested on me, her slender figure hovering over the pot of boiling stew. It gave me a sense of comfort.

I yanked the needle through the fabric. The sewing needle pricked my finger, and I winced. My finger started to bleed, so I pressed the wounded skin with my thumb. Then I resumed stitching a neat line in the garb with my other hand. Other thralls busied themselves with patching up old tunics, weaving baskets, and chopping vegetables for the great pot of stew over the fire. Their voices filled the longhouse with the usual quiet chatter that carried on when the master was not around.

Today, one of us would be chosen.

But I wasn't ready to die.

A scruffy-haired boy scrambled across the dirt floor. "I forgot to milk the old girl. Master's goin' ta kill me; he's goin' ta kill me." He dashed out the door.

The boy's accent was similar to Tyra's, my Irish friend, who sat weaving a blanket nearby. She smiled at me, to try to reassure me, but I could not return the smile.

Mum took advantage of the silence and asked, "Are you ready?"

"Yes, Mum." My voice trembled. I wasn't ready at all. "I wish he hadn't died. After all this time, I wish he hadn't died." The words choked out of me. I couldn't cry. But deep inside of me, that was all I wanted to do.

"Because of the fool who took his place?"

I looked up at her, wishing she hadn't mentioned my new master. Even when he was not drunk, he unnerved me. Though I shrank from the thought of death, the thought of living with him as my master terrified me more.

Mum caught my gaze and stirred the simmering pot of lamb stew. "No matter what he does, the gods would have you obey him, my daughter."

I drew out the needle and tightened the thread with unneeded force. The horrid gods. I hated them for making me a slave.

"Your father would've wanted you to obey him, and—"

"He killed Pa, when Pa was only trying to help him." I jabbed the needle into the wool cloth. My stomach tightened.

Pa had tried to fight that fire, but the fire had devoured the dry wood and left the barn in ashes. And how did Ragnar thank his father's loyal servant? He beat him to death.

"I know, Siri, but—"

"I hate him, Mum!" I snapped. "I can't stand him anymore."

Mum sighed. She left the stew and rested her hand on my shoulder. "I have something for you."

I raised my eyebrows. Her gentle voice and my own curiosity melted my anger away.

"Today, seventeen summers ago, you arrived into this world. I was the same age as you are now when I birthed you."

The thought of birthing my own children was beautiful and terrible all at once. Torture and love combined into one act. How was I already old enough for such a thing?

"You were a strong child, Siri Finnsdatter, the only one I birthed who has endured the fires of life to this day." She gazed off into the dancing flames of the nearby fire. "You are a woman now, so full of life. If it weren't for you, I wouldn't be here." Smiling slightly, she pulled something out of her cloak pocket and slipped it into my hand. "Thank you for giving me a reason to live."

A straw-stuffed doll sewn from wool cloth stared up at me. The doll wore a green dress dyed from onion skins and indigo, and yellow straw hair hung from her head down to her tunic. The doll's delicate stick hands were clasped together.

I swung my arms around Mum's neck and kissed her cheek. "Oh, thank you."

I felt safe in her arms. I felt home. She was the only family I had alive, and I burst with love for her.

"Do you like it?" she asked.

"She's beautiful, Mum." I turned to my friend Tyra who sat near me and showed her the doll.

"Oh, she is so lovely!" Tyra declared.

"What should I name her?"

"Siri." Tyra reached over and squeezed my hand.

Mum smiled, a red glow in her cheeks, a light in her eyes. "The doll is you, Siri. You, with your pride."

The doll held her head high with the help of carefully woven straw, her face marveling at the sky. I would call her Siri, but she was not me. I had no pride, no purpose, no reason to lift my head up high. She was the me I someday hoped to be.

Tyra continued weaving at her loom, but Mum stayed beside me, ignoring the pot of stew.

My lips parted, but Mum silenced me with a firm hand on my shoulder. "I'm looking for it, too, Siri. Freedom from the hurt, the loneliness, the shame. It is a hard thing to find, but when you find it, you will be like this doll, with your head held high. The gods spare little mercy, but whether you die on that longship or from old age—look, Siri." She lifted my chin up with one long finger. "Look for something that will keep your head up while the rain pounds you to the ground. Keep your pride above all else. Don't let anything defeat it." She looked me in the eyes. "Not even slavery, Siri."

Thunder boomed, shaking my core. I gazed up at her, a longing arising in me at the sound of the pet name from my childhood. *Siri.* I had worn it for so long, as if branded upon my forehead.

After a moment's thought, I stiffened. I placed the doll in my satchel around my waist. I loved the doll, but it was a mother's gift to a child, and Siri was the name of a child. I was not a child. After all I had been through as a thrall, I certainly deserved to be treated like a grown woman for once in my life. No more sweet pet names, it was about time I was called by my proper name.

I frowned, then turned to Tyra and Mum. "Call me Sigrid, won't you?"

"Is that an order?" Tyra chuckled.

"Yes. The only one I'll ever get to make."

The door creaked open, and Ragnar stepped inside.

Mum hustled back to the pot and dished stew into a bowl for him. The manservants removed Ragnar's cloak and ushered him to a chair by the fire.

Ragnar dismissed his manservants and Mum with a wave of his hand and strode through the longhouse. "I need a young woman," he announced, his chest thrust out as if he were some mighty Norse god.

Niels, Ragnar's head servant, directed him to the first young woman within his reach. The battle with the Picts had not only killed Ragnar's father but had also destroyed most of Ragnar's eyesight.

"Tell me about this one." Ragnar folded his arms across his chest and faced the young woman at her loom.

Niels shrugged. "Not too fair, a little round in her face. Don't recommend her, Master, if I may advise you."

Ragnar growled and swatted a flea out of his face. "Where's the next one?"

Niels led him to my end of the longhouse to a young woman only a few feet from me. My hands trembled as I endeavored to concentrate on threading the needle through the tunic.

"This one's good old Kail," Niels said gruffly. "You've . . . enjoyed her a few nights, sir."

Ragnar turned his head to the side and perused the young woman. "I remember. Pretty, but not pretty enough. Find me the best-looking young lady in this room. You hear me?"

I glanced up to find Niels's gaze on me. My breath caught in my throat as Niels led my master over. My heart pounded as my new master surveyed me from head to toe, as if he could see me as clear as day. My white-blonde hair hung to my waist, and I regretted not twisting it into a bun. Mum said my long hair added to my beauty; and, when faced with a jarl, a thrall girl loses all desire to look beautiful.

He narrowed his eyes and murmured something under his breath. A chill ran down my spine. I'd heard of the Norse rituals imposed upon a thrall girl at a high-class warrior's funeral. They were unspeakable.

Tradition dictated that the thrall girl volunteered to suffer through the rituals in order to experience the glorious Valhalla while serving her master, but last night, Ragnar had informed us that he would choose the thrall girl himself.

I stared at the dirt ground. I didn't know if I believed a glorious afterlife awaited me. I didn't know if I could trust the gods who had made me a slave.

"Well, what do you think?" Ragnar asked his head servant.

"She's as beautiful as a thrall gets," Niels replied dryly. "See for yourself, Master."

Ragnar ran his calloused hand down my tunic. I shivered. He caught hold of the funeral garb.

"It's for your father," I said stiffly. "You told me to finish it before the funeral."

He stared at me, his face so close that I could smell his rotten, ale-tinged breath. His nose almost touched mine.

"Well done," he growled. "The thrall girl is doing her duty for her master." He backed away, a cynical smile building across his face. "Would you like to go to Valhalla?"

I sucked in my breath, clenching the edge of my seat. How could I leave my mother? How could I leave Tyra? How could I endure such sadistic rituals?

I could feel my best friend staring at me from her loom. Tyra was Irish, so serving my master in Valhalla would seem to her as a death in the underworld. She had told me that I could experience a blissful afterlife only if I believed in her man-god Iosa.

"You'll serve my father." Ragnar grasped my arm and pulled me to my feet.

I screamed. Jarl Valdemar's funeral garb tumbled to the floor.

Ragnar handed me roughly to Niels, who tightly gripped my arms, ready to escort me to my doom.

"No!" Tyra jumped up and fell at the feet of Ragnar. "Please, sir, please, take me instead."

I caught my breath. What was Tyra thinking?

"Get out of my way, thrall!" Ragnar bellowed.

"Isn't the thrall girl supposed to volunteer herself? Please, I beg ye. I will gladly go in her place."

Ragnar kicked her in the chest. She yelped in pain and crumpled to the dirt floor.

"Tyra!" I reached out to her, but Niels held me fast.

Tyra ignored me. "Let her go, Master. In the name of Iosa, I plead with ye."

At her words, Ragnar fell silent for a moment, then he cackled. "Ha, I remember you!"

I squeezed my eyes shut. What could I do to stop her?

Tyra stood and faced the man, her clear blue eyes calm and unblinking.

"Niels, what about this one?" Ragnar looked her up and down.

My friend sank down on the stool she'd been sitting on. I understood her small act of defiance all too well. She would not stand before that man while he inspected her whole figure.

"She's—well, you know, sir," Niels said in an embarrassed voice.

Tyra glanced at me, but I couldn't read her expression. I ached for her. Tyra was only one of the many women Ragnar had forced into his bed on one of his weekly visits to his father. And if I was chosen, I'd become the most-desired wench in the village.

"Show some respect and stand, you vile woman!" Ragnar demanded.

With remarkable calmness, Tyra stood up.

Ragnar slid his hand down my friend's chest. He then toyed with her slender face with his rough finger. "Do you really want to go to Valhalla so badly, thrall?"

I gritted my teeth and pulled against Niels's strong arms. "Not her! By the gods, you can't take her."

Jarl Ragnar laughed, his gaze still locked on my friend.

Tyra pressed her lips together. Her wavy, black hair cascaded down either side of her pale face. My friend was the most beautiful girl I had ever met, and today, her beauty might cost her life.

How could she willingly put her life at stake for me? What had I done to earn such selfless devotion?

I strained again against Niels's grasp. "Oh, sir, please, you needn't consider her. I'll go, sir."

Tyra's lips parted, but Ragnar shoved her back onto her stool. She started to fall backward off the stool, but he knelt beside her and put his arm around her. "See, your little friend is perfectly happy to serve my father," he lulled loudly in her ear, twisting my stomach in a tight knot. "I think I want to keep you."

"But, sir, Sigrid is my dearest friend, ye couldn't—"

Jarl Ragnar secured his hand across her mouth, muffling her pleas. Before I could think to do anything, he shot a quick glance at Niels. "After she's finished with that tunic, take the white-haired rat to the stable!" Niels loosened his grip on my arms and nodded toward the funeral garb.

I moved back near the fire, lowered myself to the crude thrall's stool, and lifted the funeral garb to my lap. I glanced over at Mum. She stared at me from across the longhouse with a long, vacant expression.

"Mum, don't worry. I will serve him faithfully," I whispered, wanting her to believe that everything was all right, wanting her to not be afraid.

Bringing a shaky hand to her face, Mum let out a soft whimper and hastened out of the room.

TWO

I BLINKED OPEN MY EYES, gazing dreamily at the light that poured into the room. The sharp odor of death filled my nostrils and brought back the horrific memories of the previous day. I pinched my nose and held my breath for a full minute.

I let my breath out, panting and gasping, the putrid smell hitting me again.

Wiping my bleary eyes, I sat upright in the pile of hay. Where was that smell coming from? I looked around at the small hut Niels had locked me in last night. It was filled with hay and manure, and beside me were a few pigs nestled together, fast asleep. A few feet away from me, lay the open coffin of my former master. He wore the regal purple tunic I had finished last night and was adorned in fine jewelry. His skin was white and rotting and his eyes were hollow, staring into nothingness. My head pounded. I wanted to vomit.

The door flew open, and two young women were flung into the room. The door slammed shut behind them.

I quickly recognized Tyra's black hair and the skinny form of Kail. After a minute of stunned silence, the two girls sat up, their hair disheveled from their being thrown about.

"Why are you here?" I asked.

"We're supposed to help you sew the Jarl Valdemar's new clothes for the afterlife." Kail's voice trembled.

I met Tyra's eyes. The memory of her self-sacrifice the night before sent a stab of grief through me. "Tyra . . ."

She came and wrapped her arms around me.

I squeezed her back. "You would have died in place of me?"

"Only because Iosa did it for me, dear friend." Her voice hitched with tears, and she released me. "He did it for you, too."

I smiled, but I didn't believe her. How could a good man's death have anything to do with me? "Thank you for what you did last night. And for everything." A sob caught in my throat. My dear friend had loved me and cared for me through the harshest points in my life, and "thank you" was all I could say?

Tyra held my hands in hers. Tears streamed down her cheeks. "Oh, Sigrid, I love you. I'm going to miss you so, so much."

"I'm going to miss you, too," I said softly. It hurt too much to fully process that I would never see my dear friend again.

The piles of fabric behind Tyra begged for my attention. "Well, we better get to work."

The two girls agreed, so we set our hands to the task.

Niels swung open the door, carrying two large jugs of ale and barking, "Drink and be merry, thrall, as tradition demands." He eyed the women with me and snorted out a laugh. "And don't you let your friends have any!"

He set the jugs down, stalked back out, and slammed the door shut. But I could sense his presence still standing right outside the hut, guarding us.

Tyra stared at me. "You don't need to drink, Sigrid."

"No, I must," I said. "Tradition says."

"You could empty the jugs and—"

"Tyra—"

"Kail and I could help and—"

"Tyra, I have to obey tradition." My firm voice silenced her. I was going to die anyway. Submitting myself to the Norse rituals was the least I could do. The liquor would ease the last wretched moments of my life.

I found myself a comfortable spot in the corner away from the two girls and drank heavily. I let the liquor quench my thirst and seep into my body, fogging up my mind and filling my senses with strange delight. Tyra urged me continually to stop drinking or to take a break, but I refused.

When I finished the two jugs of ale, I raised my voice to sing a merry song for the Jarl Valdemar, attempting to bring life into this fetid room of death. Could a dead person still hear? I continued, long and loud, for the rest of the day as Tyra and Kail made clothes for our dead master.

Nine days passed in a blur. I drank a lot, forgetting everything and laughing at nothing. My mind fogged, disillusioned and helpless to the effects of the ale. By the tenth morning, Jarl Valdemar's skin had turned black from frostbite. I myself was a shivering, dying piece of flesh, never warm enough at night in this hut where we had no place to create a fire.

Niels swung open the door before I could start my day of drinking and singing, and I *knew*. I knew it was time.

Today would be the worst day of all.

Niels grabbed my wrist and grinned. "Remember the next ritual, thrall?"

I stiffened as he looked into my eyes, his own fiery with desire.

"Me first."

XXX

That day left me nauseous, broken, and traumatized. Every man in the village had a chance with me as Norse tradition insisted. The ale made it easier for them to entice me and harder for me to resist them.

I cried out to every Norse god I could think of, but none of them answered.

The men of the village whispered words of passion and lust to me. "We are doing this to show our love for Jarl Valdemar," they said. Yet I couldn't help but wonder if such traditions arose not from the god's ordinance but from man's twisted desires.

Later that day, the Norsemen brought me to an empty door frame constructed in the middle of the village for the next ritual. Crowds surrounded us, watching the scene.

My legs were weak, and I almost toppled over. Two men grabbed a hold of my arms to keep me from falling. Another man forced me to chug a half gallon of ale. My stomach sloshed, and I vomited, the taste stinging the back of my throat.

I swayed on my feet, the world tipping side to side.

Two men bent down on their knees and held out their hands. "Come on," one murmured. "Step on our hands, girl!"

Two others grabbed my arms and hoisted me up. My body trembled from the liquors. The two men raised me above the doorframe, while the other men supported me at the waist so I wouldn't fall over.

"What do you see?" Ragnar bellowed.

I squinted at the familiar view that was now a blur of blue, green, and brown. My head throbbed. What was I supposed to see?

I was tempted to tell them exactly what I saw, but I knew what they wanted me to say. Defying tradition would only bring trouble to the whole Norse village. "Behold, I see my father. His hand is reaching out to me as he stands within Valhalla's gates."

Oh, if I could only see his smiling face. Pa had taught me to swim in the ocean, he had always kissed my cheek goodnight, he had treated me respectfully and kindly like no other man. He had loved me, and I would forever love him.

The men took me down for a few seconds then lifted me up again. "What do you see?" Ragnar yelled again.

"Behold, I see my dead kindred, seated. My grandparents, aunts, uncles, and cousins who died before I was born. I see my siblings who died as infants, their perfect faces laughing in the sunlight." My imagination would have to do to satisfy the rituals, though the words came out in a strain against my will.

The men lowered me down again then raised me back up. My whole body shook. I didn't want to do this, but the stares of the men below bid me to raise my voice again. "Behold, the afterlife is beautiful. I see Jarl Valdemar seated in Valhalla. He is drinking and feasting merrily. The jarl summons me." Swallowing, I resolved not to burst into sobs. "Bring me to him."

They lowered me down, and I collapsed into the arms of one of the men. I wanted to fight. Wanted to force them to leave me alone. But I allowed them to carry me to the wharf.

The longship waited for me, the body of my dead master inside. My bones cried out at the thought of the fire and the arrows. The pain. And the fact that I, too, would soon be limp and black and cold like my dead jarl.

I removed my bracelets and handed them to the Angel of Death. The middle-aged woman wore a plain thrall tunic, but I did not recognize her. She scowled at me, forcefully narrowing her brows. I removed my two anklets and handed them each to Tyra and to Kail who stood nearby.

I tried not to make eye contact with them, or it would hurt. I tried not to think about what lay ahead, or it would weigh me down. I tried to shut everything out but the dreamy, light feeling of the ale. Nevertheless, everything inside me was an untamed ball of fire.

Niels and another man lifted my quivering body onto the longship, where a large tent was set, holding the body and possessions of Jarl Valdemar. The Norsemen marched onto the ship banging sticks against their shields. Niels grinned and handed me another mug of ale.

I surveyed the weeping crowds. Their loud wails clenched a knot deep inside me. They cried for the great jarl, but not for me.

It didn't matter what happened to me.

Lifting my chin proudly as Mum would want, I drank the mead in a long, desperate gulp, then chanted a high, wailing funeral song. The chant filled the air, dreary and somber. The people murmured along with me.

Someone cried out to me, interrupting my song. I found Tyra in the crowd, but I couldn't make out her words.

I searched for Mum in the crowd. I couldn't find her, and a sick feeling gnawed at my stomach. What if watching her daughter sail off to Valhalla was too unbearable for her? For all I knew, she might be plunging a knife into her chest this very moment.

I swung my leg over the side of the ship. I had to save her. The Angel of Death grasped my arms and pulled me back onto the deck.

Her nails bit hard into my arms, and I gasped at her powerful hold on me.

"I have to save her," I whimpered, my words slurred.

But the Angel of Death dragged me into the tent. Bags of riches, weapons, and food filled the stern. A cow sat in the stern, mooing impatiently in his tight space. Outside, Norsemen beat sticks rhythmically against shields.

What would happen next? No one knew what took place inside the tent while the Norse battered on their shields outside.

And I wouldn't live to tell the others.

Goosebumps ran up my arms as six tall sturdy men entered the tent, Ragnar, Ragnar's brother Joar, and Niels among them. Each one gawked at me like I was some wild animal they were ready to kill and eat. My throat thickened with dread. Hadn't they used me enough for one day?

One by one, they satisfied their desires. I screamed and wept, but no one cared. The men outside only beat their shields louder, overpowering the sound of my desperate voice.

At last, the men laid me roughly down beside the dead Jarl Valdemar. The Angel of Death bound a rope tightly around my neck, then handed the two ends to a couple men, who began pulling on it.

Panicking, I thrashed out, trying to get free, but the rope only closed tightly around my throat. Fire burned in my lungs. Oh, help me! I cried out in my mind. But I didn't know who I was calling out to; none of the gods would help me, for they ordained these rituals.

The Angel of Death brought out a broad-bladed sword and stared at me, her fiery eyes scorching my already-broken spirit. She raised her sword.

I almost pleaded to Iosa to set me free.

A woman burst into the tent and cried out, "Stop, in the name of mercy!"

The Angel of Death paused her sword.

Mum? The ropes loosened for a moment then grew tighter again. Tears ran down my cheeks. Somehow, I was hearing my mother's pleading voice.

"Spare my daughter, please!"

Ragnar seized the sword from the Angel of Death. "And defy tradition? This is for Jarl Valdemar's honor."

Ragnar gripped my mother's wrists and pinned her to the floor. *No.* He raised the sword above her. *No, Mum!*

I squeaked out, "M—m!"

Ragnar stabbed my mother's chest. A guttural scream burst from me. I clawed at the rope around my neck, but it only grew tighter by the second. Strength slipped from my fingers. My body felt weak and limp, ready for death.

THREE

MY VISION DARKENED AND VOICES buzzed in my ear.

Footsteps pounded around me, and the ropes dropped from around my neck. I gasped in breath after breath.

As air filled my lungs and oxygen returned to my body, the blur of voices focused into words.

"Fight the fire, fools!" Ragnar bellowed from outside.

I gasped and panted for a long while. Somehow, I was still alive.

At last, I turned my aching body over slowly toward my mother who lay near me. She stared at me, unresponsive. The gleaming hilt of the sword rose triumphantly out of her chest, the jewels flashing in the dim light.

I clung to her hand and looked into her wide, empty eyes. A sob caught in my throat. The horrors of today spilled over inside me. I screamed aloud, tortured by the real-life nightmares and the ever-increasing shame I felt for what I did not do. I would never forget.

The longship jolted and moved into the sea. I sat up and looked toward the door. Would they shoot the flaming arrows or fight the fire first?

The fire. A strange sense of understanding came over me. I hadn't seen Mum during my long chant. Had she started the fire to distract Ragnar and the men? And then, when they hadn't noticed the fire, offered her own life in my place?

I clutched my mother's clammy hand and wept. She hadn't needed to. I didn't deserve it. I was a worthless, hopeless, defiled thrall.

"Mum, if I can take revenge on him, I will do it," I choked. "I swear it."

Shaking violently, I drew the sword out of my mother's chest and wiped the blood off on a blanket. I touched the sharp blade. This beautiful sword had killed Lovina of Kaupang, the mother who'd birthed me, who had labored as thrall of Jarl Valdemar for thirty-four summers without complaining once.

Setting the sword down, I stared at it. Its blade was long and golden, and its hilt was covered in red and yellow jewels. Full, heavy tears rolled down my cheeks, and coldness spread through my body.

Something bulged from under my mother's cloak. I lifted her cloak to find my small satchel. I peeked into the satchel, and, sure enough, there was the straw doll.

Mum had brought the doll to me, even as she risked her life to save me from this horrid fate. This doll was a testimony of her faithful devotion toward me.

I set the doll before me and examined its tall posture. Proud. I had to be proud for her. I couldn't let the gods define who I was as a pitiful, worthless slave.

Swallowing tears, I grasped the sword and lifted it into the air. Nearby, the sword's scabbard rested inside a small, open rectangular box. Ragnar must have intended this weapon to sail off to Valhalla with his father. Everyone knew how Ragnar had slain the Pict man who had killed his father and taken the Pict's sword home as a symbol of his bravery. And now he desired his father to have the precious blade to battle valiant warriors in the afterlife.

No matter. I fastened the sword's scabbard tightly around my waist with the ropes, then I sheathed the beautiful weapon. The ropes hurt my waist, but they would have to do. After all Ragnar had done, he didn't deserve to give his father anything to bring honor to himself in the afterlife.

If I escaped, I would slay Ragnar with his own sword—for Mum's sake. I would repay that beast for all he had done to hurt me. And then I would kill myself, so I could see Mum again.

I stepped out of the tent and gazed back at the foggy wharf. A fiery arrow sped toward me. Terror shot through me.

The arrow landed a few yards away and ignited a portion of the longship into flames.

I squinted over the thrashing waves toward the shore beyond. The sword would weigh me down, but because of Pa's nightly swimming lessons, I could try to stay afloat for a few minutes—I could even try to reach land if I moved quickly.

As I tucked the doll back in my satchel, another fiery arrow soared through the air and landed close to me, setting a squealing chicken on fire. Soon the bed, the restless livestock, the gold—everything started burning and drowning all at once. I stumbled toward the side of the ship.

The ship turned over. I screamed, the dark mass smothering me and driving me down into the depths of the sea. The sea washed over me, muting my cries.

My instincts took over. I swam away from the ship, pushing against the sword's weight and the ship's malicious urge to drown me. The current whipped me about like I was a mere strand of seaweed. I kicked my feet and paddled my hands as my father had taught me.

A wave roared above me, so I swam to the only safe place, deep under the water, holding my breath and sinking down into the cold silence of the sea. I squinted my eyes open. For a moment I forgot I needed to breathe, and I stared at the murky ocean, the undulating greens and browns of the water. Then I saw the ship sinking slowly, and bright gold coins twinkling down into the water, journeying to the afterlife. And I saw Mum falling, her brown hair wild about her— her beautiful soul, no more.

Sorrow overwhelmed me. But I couldn't breathe.

My senses came to me, and I pushed my body upwards with all my might to overcome the weight of the sea. Saltwater stung my eyes. My lungs burned, aching in agony and desperation for the air that was just out of my reach. Though the sword weighed me down, my weary limbs fought to reach the water's surface. A current dragged me down harder with the sword's weight. I grit my teeth and strained upward with all my might.

A sudden calmness settled the ocean. With several last paddles and kicks upward, my head finally bobbed out of the water. Gasping for breath, I spotted a piece of half-burned driftwood in the distance. I swam toward it, the current helping me along. I grabbed the wood, clung to it, and sucked in a deep breath. The waves pushed me about, mocking me, whispering, "We could destroy you any moment now."

I squinted through the fog. The longship's dragon's head floated above the sea a moment longer before the emerald waves swallowed it whole. Quivering, I looked beyond the sinking ship toward the land, toward the town of Kaupang, my home, that was barely visible in the distance now. I knew the mourners couldn't see me from here, let alone Ragnar with his poor eyesight.

I am alive.

Breathing heavily, I kicked my legs and paddled to keep above the water's surface with the driftwood's support. The waves tore at me, but I grit my teeth and paddled in the direction of the shore. The waves continually knocked me back, and the waters rose until I couldn't see the shore.

A little brown boat bobbing up and down in the dangerous waters sailed into view. If anyone found out I survived, I would follow my Mum and sink into the depths of the sea. I tried to steer in the opposite direction of the boat yet still toward land. I would not let them catch me for the crime of escaping my fate.

A rough wave pulled me forward with the current, and I tightened my fingers on the driftwood. Another wave rose like a hawk ready to swoop down to its prey. Before I could catch my breath, it crashed over me with salty fury. The wave ripped the driftwood out of my hands.

I sank deep into the water. My lungs burned for air as I kicked my numb legs, struggling upward against the waves. But the current was winning.

Squinting upward, I perceived a large mass above me. After a moment's hesitation, I swam toward it.

Something hit my head and pushed me further down. I tried to swim upward again, but the numbness in my fingers and toes had spread to my arms and legs. The coldness seized my whole being. I couldn't move; my lungs were on fire. I couldn't take it any longer. I needed to breathe.

A huge net fell like a cloak about me and pulled me upward.

When I met the air, I sucked in frantic breaths. My body shook in the sharp wind as my thin thrall dress clung to my skin. Panting and coughing, I fell to my knees under the weight of the sword strapped to my side and the drenched cloak overtop of the sword. My eyesight clouded so I could hardly see my rescuers.

"By all the gods, it's a *girl!*" exclaimed a good-natured voice with a familiar rugged Norse accent. The tangled fish net was torn away from me.

"Are ye all right, lass?" a young man asked in a similar accent to Tyra's. His green-gray eyes widened when they met mine. "What were ye doin' in the water?"

I gazed up at the Irishman, who looked to be in his early twenties. An unfamiliar face. Good. In fact, as I blinked the water out of my eyes, his was the most exquisite face I'd ever seen. His gentle features contrasted with the rough features of the Norsemen, and his hair was a wild crimson, like no shade of red I'd ever seen.

The Irishman wrinkled his brow and wrapped a woolen blanket around my shoulders. "You must be mighty cold."

The blanket was damp, but so much warmer than my shivering body. I wanted to sag into its warmth, which reminded me so much of Mum's woven blankets. The memory sent a stab of grief through me.

The Norseman behind him, who looked to be in his mid-to-late twenties, grinned at me. "Well, aren't you gonna thank us for saving your life, girl?"

Thankfulness and anxiety fought within me as I stared at them. Men were awful. I held the blanket tighter around me and shivered.

The only good and peaceful man I'd ever known was my father, but maybe such men didn't exist anymore. How could I trust them?

Yet these two men had saved my life. I owed them something.

So, I plastered on a smile and lifted my chin, just as Mum would have wanted me to.

FOUR

"LARS, THERE'S NO NEED TO demand her gratitude," the younger man rebuked the Norseman. "The wee lass nigh' on drowned her skull!"

"I'm Lars," said the older fellow. "Sorry if I was a little rude. I have a habit of saying exactly what comes into my head."

The younger man grinned. "As soon as I got to Norway, everyone's called me Erik," he said. "'Tis a pleasure meeting ye. Is that blanket comfortable?"

What was happening? After escaping death, I'd landed straight into more trouble, with two strange men staring openly at me. Panic gripped me; I couldn't speak, I couldn't do this.

I covered my head and pulled the blanket more tightly around my chest like a shawl. Chill seeped into my bones. I didn't want to imagine what they could do to me.

"Ye don't need to be afeard of us," Erik said. "Lars and I here are thralls, like you. Ye are a thrall, right, lass? Don't mean to be rude; your clothes give ye away."

My lips were unable to move. I couldn't tell him. I couldn't tell either of them anything.

"All right, enough jabbering," Lars declared. "What in the name of Odin are you doing out in the ocean like this? And what happened to your neck? I see rope marks. Are you . . . ?"

I stiffened, shame washing over me. I hadn't realized the marks were so visible. If I told them, they'd think I was a fool for escaping my duty of serving my master in Valhalla. Even still, it seemed they'd already guessed who I was.

The men stared at me.

"Ye look to have a hard life." Erik dipped his head in acknowledgment. "Mighty sorry, lass."

I did not know how to answer. That a stranger would sympathize with me, a mere thrall girl, was new and unexpected to me. Nothing but the wind and waves filled the silence for a long moment. I cleared my throat. "Where is your master?"

"We're escaping this monotonous life and going on an adventure!" Lars murmured from two seats in front of me.

Glancing at his friend, Erik leaned in and whispered something to him.

"What is there to hide from a thrall girl like her?" Lars shrugged one shoulder and lifted his hand.

"You must tell no one of this," Erik said through clenched teeth.

Lars nodded. "You are welcome to join us, isn't she?"

Erik's hands clenched the oars, then he stared back at me so intently, as if he could see right through me. I quivered.

Lars continued, "We might need a woman to help with the cooking and such. If you don't tell anyone about us, we won't tell on you about escaping some honorable fate, if indeed you *are* that girl, as we suspect. We aren't great supporters of the Norse traditions—that's one reason we're sailing away from them. Will we let her join us, Erik?"

The younger man cast a tentative glance at me again, then at Lars. "I don't see why not. But would ye like that, lass?"

It was hard to think of an adventure after all that had happened to me today. Everything in me wanted the overwhelming burden of those horrors to fade away. But I couldn't seem to get rid of the memories, no matter how hard I tried. They flashed through my mind, consuming me.

I muttered out a question in a faint voice. "Where are you going?"

"The question of old!" Lars cried, leaning his head back in laughter. "We're off to a green little country I like to call Ireland." He spoke with a mix of grandness and mischief, but his eyes darkened as if the place was attached to a distinct emotion of fear.

Ireland. Why would anyone want to go to a country our people hated? Two men wasn't enough to plunder a village over there.

"Why Ireland?"

Lars ran his hand through his dirty blond hair. "Jarl Ragnar plans to plunder and kill them. We want to help the Irish. To warn them of the oncoming raiders." He gestured to Erik. "He's Irish, so knowing him has gotten the sense in me that it isn't right to terrorize anyone, neither Norse, Irish, nor thrall."

Pa had believed that, too. Though we were of true Norse blood, all my family was destined to be of the lower class, along with captives from other countries. Many of the captives were Irish, like Tyra, and some were from Pictish tribes, others Slavic, others French, others German. But there really was no difference between us. We were thralls together, laboring long hours together, receiving lashings together. There was no point in causing divisions between us.

I didn't know what my parents and the other thralls would say to Lars and Erik, or what they would want me to do. Would they call these men traitors or heroes? All I knew was that Jarl Ragnar would never vanish from my mind.

Mum was gone because of him.

A plan started burning in my mind. Since Ragnar had been preparing to ransack Ireland, maybe joining these strange men on their journey was the only way to find and kill him. Then, I would kill myself and join Mum. Though she had likely gone to Valhalla in my place, I would take the risk. It could be that Valhalla wasn't real, or that the gods would finally show favor toward me. Would killing a man who deserved death not be an honorable feat?

The pulse in my veins livened at this thought, and that first spark of hatred grew into a flame. I'd have to work on blowing it into a fire if I was going to bring that man to his death.

"Well, what do you say, lass?" Lars finally broke the silence.

"I'm eager to see Ireland myself," I found myself saying, the lie flowing easily.

Still, I was baffled about why anyone would go there. Even more so, it was a great risk to escape one's master; a friend of their master might see them and turn them in.

"Very good. It seems fate has led you to us . . . " Erik gazed out at the sea. "After escaping the afterlife, you planned to swim ashore, I suppose?"

The fact that they were so sure of who I was unnerved me. I wanted to forget all that had happened. I wanted the past to fade away completely out of sight beyond the horizon.

I followed his gaze toward the sea. "Yes, I love the ocean."

Lars shook his head. "Why escape the glorious Valhalla? You love the ocean *that* much?"

I lowered my chin. I didn't want to answer any questions about the mysterious afterlife. The truth was, I didn't know how I felt about Valhalla. "I admire the feeling of the ocean current pressing against me."

"Ye've got to be jokin' me," Erik said. "I'm afeard of the ocean."

His confession surprised me, but by the look of his pale face, it wasn't hard to believe him.

I gave a tight-lipped smile. "I like to think of the ocean as a good place, if you only embrace it."

Each summer Tyra and I had plunged into the water together, our whole beings absorbed by the salty sea as if it was just as much our home as the land we lived on. It was in the big, wide ocean that I found a freedom which I found nowhere else.

"What's your name, lass?" Erik asked me.

"Sigrid," I murmured and avoided his penetrating gaze.

Lars raised a brow. "Ah, the name that means 'victory'! Nothing can stop us now, eh?"

I nodded faintly. What a cruel joke. Today had been a day of utter defeat. Only when I killed Ragnar would I find true victory.

"We better be goin' quickly, Sigrid," Erik interrupted my thoughts. "We're on this journey to save souls, aren't we?"

I frowned at his choice of words. Maybe he shared the same religion as Tyra. She often proclaimed that her God Iosa had come as a human to sacrifice His life so that all souls might be saved from death and given a new life. It was nonsense. The only way to save one's soul was to fight honorably in battle.

Was Jarl Valdemar battling other warriors behind the golden gates of Valhalla, enjoying himself in the fields of Folkvanger, or lying down in Hel, in a pit of nothingness, cold, in the dark? The last possibility struck me. He could have failed to fight bravely enough for both Odin, the god of life in Valhalla, and Freyja, the goddess of love who chose warriors to ascend to her afterlife, Folkvanger. My former master could be in Hel, the icy underworld for dishonorable fools.

And poor Mum could be with him. My chest ached. She couldn't be. She deserved Valhalla.

But the only thing I knew for sure was the new Jarl of Kaupang deserved death more than any other human being. Destroying that fool was my only solution to set things right again.

FIVE

"A STORM'S BREWING." LARS STUDIED the dark clouds that flashed with lightning. "We best get to shore. Erik and I thought we'd travel by land to Bergen, since this old rowboat is good for nothing. Don't want to get drowned out at sea."

Shaking off the chill, I settled deeper into the large bag I was lying on. My eyelids drooped as the rowboat surged onward in the tempestuous waters. My weary body could rest at last.

The two men silently directed the boat to a shore a safe distance from Kaupang and about a half mile from where we were paddling. The trees on the land stood far enough away for us to have a full view of the vast mountains. Snow graced their peaks, though it was still summertime.

As we neared the shore, the men instructed me to step out into the shallow water. I slipped the blanket off and climbed out into the frigid seawater, my bare feet hitting the ocean floor. I stumbled toward land as the waves crashed at my ankles, until at last I made it to shore and collapsed into the soft sand.

Once the boat hit ground, Lars and Erik clambered out and heaved the wooden vessel onto the shore. On the sand, Lars lit a fire with soapstone, and Erik cooked some fish over the fire. These men had come prepared.

Relief swept through me. I was safe. Could this be real, or was I in a dream? Was I really still alive?

Lars offered me an empty sack, which I wrapped around my shoulders over the warm blanket they had given me. I smiled stiffly in gratitude. I would never have expected such a horrid day could end with good people around a warm fire.

If only Mum were here, everything would be all right.

Erik laid damp layers of parchment on a few flat, large rocks. I must have looked astonished, because his emerald eyes twinkled with mirth. "Scrolls. They tell about my God."

"Your God?" I arched a brow. "It isn't that Irish God Iosa, is it?"

"Aye, it is," he answered.

Memories of Tyra tore at me. Dear Tyra. Everything she did reflected her devout belief in Iosa—pouring me a bowl of soup when I was ill, comforting a widow, or even smiling at Jarl Valdemar. She claimed it was all because of the love of her God that she was able to love others without any expectation. I did not believe a word about this Irish God, but she loved Him, and that love defined her entire existence. It fascinated me in a way I could not understand.

Hunger gnawed at the pit of my stomach. Finally, the men finished cooking the fish. When Erik handed me one, I bit off a chunk and chewed slowly, savoring the crisp, juicy flavor and the warmth that spread inside me.

Erik flattened out the last scroll to let it dry. Sometime, when I wasn't so hungry, I'd have to ask him more about how he obtained these costly papers and what exactly they held inside. Today, my stomach ruled over my mind.

"In Bergen we can buy a boat and sail to Ireland." Lars jingled a small bag of coins.

I stared at him as he brought out a gold coin that glinted in the firelight, almost speechless. "How did you get that?"

"I pillaged it awhile back. Not that I believe pillaging is right anymore, but it's here!"

Erik rubbed his hands together near the dancing flames, grimacing at his friend. "I know Ragnar's gathering more men in Bergen. I hope we reach the village before that feller does and get to Ireland first as well."

"We'll be fine. He's busy becoming the new jarl and mourning his father." Lars sneered, shaking his head. "He's sad about *that*, I'm sure."

"Of course, he is," I said seriously. "He wept like a babe when his father died. He better not find out."

"He wouldn't guess a thrall girl would shirk from her fate," Lars said. "Besides, we're free now, and we don't need to worry about that old life anymore."

Erik nodded. "Aye, which reminds me, we need a plan. We might be a measly three pints, but I think we can warn the Irish village of the attack and help them prepare for battle. We'll need some more men to help us paddle the longship, though."

"Perhaps we could purchase some Irish thralls," Lars suggested. "And when we get to Ireland, we can set them free."

"As soon as we get to shore, I can talk to the chief, while you two and the Irish thralls move the boat ashore," Erik said. "Once the chief knows everything, he'll send out the news about Ragnar's oncoming fleet."

I murmured my agreement. Would Tyra be on that fleet? The thought gave me hope of seeing her again but also dread. The memory of Ragnar's sudden interest in her filled me with disgust. No doubt she had become his favorite thrall girl for a while. How would she stand subjecting herself to the cruel man?

She had lit the room with a calming peace every day I had known her, and she had offered to take my place, even though she didn't believe in Valhalla. If it weren't for her endless kindness, I doubt I would like her. She had strange beliefs, and she was Irish, after all.

If Lars were a regular Norseman, he'd be wary of the Irish too. What was it about this Irish lad that had inspired Lars's loyalty to him?

I turned to Lars, curiosity overtaking my anxiety of speaking with strange men. "Why are you doing this, sir?"

He glanced up from the fishbone he was gnawing, his eyebrows pinching together. "Doing what?"

"Going to Ireland. You're Norse, like me."

Lars slapped Erik on the back, causing him to wince. "Erik is Irish, and he wanted so badly to go home, so I thought we'd brave together to save a few souls as he says. I have nothing left in Kaupang. No honor. No family."

So, he had nothing better to do. It seemed he had a thirst for adventure.

"Do you think your master will send search parties to track you down?" I asked.

Lars and Erik glanced at each other.

"We can only hope and pray we are safe," Erik replied.

"Our master Joar is undoubtedly busy being jealous of his brother for taking command as the new jarl. There's no point in worrying about it. I know these lands, and I can get us far away from Kaupang in no time."

"The Lord will take care of us," Erik said. "He already took care of our need for a woman to help us out with the cooking and cleaning."

"I—I am glad to be of service." I gave a tight-lipped smile.

Their stares made me want to shrink away and disappear. I hoped the thought of me being of any other service to them—whether as a wench or a bride— would never cross their minds. The thought sickened me.

I studied the redhead from across the fire. It repulsed me to think of wedding him. But something else drew me in, a desire to understand his character. Erik's strong jaw was set, determined, as he stared into the curling flames. Would he approve of my plan to take revenge? Was I even capable of it?

I realized that he was staring at me, not the fire, and my stomach churned. "Well, I better get to sleep. Thank you for saving my life."

The thought of sleeping near these men made goosebumps surface my skin. Nevertheless, sleep beckoned me. The day's troubles had exhausted me. I would settle behind the large pile of supplies in hopes it would ward off any temptation they felt toward me.

"Goodnight, Sigrid," Lars replied.

"Goodnight, Lars. Erik."

The Irishman said nothing.

Behind the large sacks of belongings, I nestled under my cloak, which had dried out for the most part. Fatigue weighed me down. I would have to trust the sacks to keep me safe at night. These men were my only hope to survive.

I fixed my thoughts on Ragnar, the man I had to punish for his many murders, his endless rapes, his ugly tantrums, and for slaying my dear mother.

Yet how could I defeat such a powerful warrior? I was only a thrall girl. Carrying this sword in its sheath was heavy enough. How could I wield it against a more skilled man? And what would Erik think of me if he knew what I planned to do?

I laughed silently at myself. After all I had endured today, this Irishman should be the least of my concerns.

SIX

I PULLED THE BLANKET TIGHTER around me and exhaled deeply, drinking in what warmth it provided. Still, my legs were restless.

I ached, not only from the bruises, but also from the memories of the rituals. I attempted to block them out, but they slipped into my brain, nightmares that would forever torment me. Closing my eyes, I thought of Mum—of her singing softly in the night or jesting that I ate my supper like a pig. But the evil memories of the men's leering faces crept in, gradually overpowering every shred of goodness I could think of about my mother.

I forced my attention to listen to the men beside the fire, thankful for the sacks that hid me from their view.

Erik spoke in a low, hesitant voice. "I am beginning to fear that this was all a terrible idea. Maybe we ought not to have run from our duty."

"But we are leaving for a noble reason. We are saving the Irish."

Erik sighed. "Aye, I know I am. But what of ye? I was thinking of what Sigrid said—she asked why ye, a free Norseman, were doing this. Why are ye doing this, Lars?"

"What are you talking about?" Lars asked. "I admire the Irish, because I admire you, my friend, and I know that they are only poor countrymen who cannot defend themselves."

My breath stilled so I could listen more closely. Lars was an amiable fellow, who I couldn't help but like. He seemed good and honorable—qualities that were rare in most Norsemen—and he was a man of peace, as my father had been. I admired his desire to bring honor to himself by saving the Irish. I only hoped I could trust him. While rape was noted as dishonorable in talk among Norsemen, it was regarded as an accomplishment in practice. Who knew if Lars truly was honorable enough to spare me from that?

"Ye don't even know what yer talkin' about," Erik mumbled. "Ye've hated the Irish all your life, until ye met me. I don't understand ye, Lars. How can ye truly change?"

A light breeze curled under my cloak, and I shivered.

"My eyes have opened to the truth, that's all."

"But what of Iosa?" Erik asked, as if a tense struggle was mounting up inside him. "What of *that* truth?"

"That man has been dead for hundreds of years."

A long, painful silence descended upon them before Erik raised his voice in desperation, "He's alive, I tell ye! He's every bit alive. He saved us from death by dying, and He offers us new life, by living. He lives in my heart, Lars. Don't ye see? He *is* God. How many times do I have to tell ye to get ye to understand?"

"Calm down, Erik, or you'll wake the girl," Lars whispered. "It's a ridiculous legend from a faraway land."

I bit my lip. So, Erik claimed that this long-dead man was God and that He lived in his heart. It sounded familiar to Tyra's Iosa yet somehow different. Why did the boy act so afraid and desperate when telling Lars about his God?

"I tell ye, it's the truth. Why can't ye see it?" Erik pleaded.

In the hush that followed, I stared up at the cloudy night sky, which was bright as an afternoon day. In the summer, these north lands were dark for only a short portion of the night.

At last Erik spoke again. "Dear God," he whispered, "why is Thy will so hard? Please, Iosa, help me." His voice was strained, distressed, waning. Who was this God he cried out to?

"Calm down, Erik," Lars repeated, his tone steady. "What's so awful that you have to talk to your God right now?"

"I don't understand," Erik said, his voice cracking. "I don't understand why God has me here, and why He kept me alive. I'm sorry for tryin' so hard to get ye to believe—or maybe I'm not sorry at all. It's not like I even wish to preach to ye. I just feel like I must. And may the God of Heavens curse me for it!"

He began to weep.

I frowned. What was the matter with him? Every word he spoke was stung with self-loathing, as if he were filled with tremendous guilt. This didn't sound like the same God as Tyra's. Tyra's God was merciful and loving, not harsh and condemning like Erik's seemed to be. I had never heard anyone hate himself so deeply, like he was going mad. Hatred was for battles, for Norsemen burning with bloodlust. Hatred was for one's enemies.

Curiosity surged through me, but I didn't sit up to speak. Perhaps the air was too cold, or I was too tired.

Or perhaps I was just afraid.

SEVEN

I'M FREE.

I sat up in the sand and blinked at the sun that blazed above the ocean's horizon. The tide rushed in and out, inviting me in. Eagerly, I rolled up my cloak and set it aside. I untied my sword and satchel and buried them underneath my cloak. Then I stood up and soaked in the morning rays of the sun. Freedom was mine at last.

I found Lars's knife in a sack near last night's fireplace, along with a piece of flint. Striking the flint with the knife, I lit a small fire like I had done so often as a thrall in Jarl Valdemar's longhouse. Soon, three small fish sizzled in a pan for breakfast. Despite the noise, my new friends still slept soundly on the shore.

When the fish had cooked through, I placed each one on a dry leaf. But my mind wasn't focused on the meal. I wanted to get in the water. For once, I could swim when I had plenty of energy, not at night after my day's labor. I could swim without my master finding me and whipping me.

Chowing down my breakfast, I watched the oncoming tide. Here I was, with no chores, no floggings, no expectations. I had to take in this moment.

Tossing aside the fishbones, I ran out into the sea, letting the tide roll over my ankles, my knees, and then my hips. The cold water felt exhilarating. I imagined I was with Tyra, enjoying a wade in the ocean on one of our rare breaks. I dove in the sea and swam like a fish, flapping my arms in broad, sweeping motions. This wide, open space was the closest to freedom I'd ever got.

I shot out into the air like a dolphin and gasped for breath before letting the waves carry me to shore. I crawled onto the sand, my hands and knees covered in mud, but my heart singing in tune with the ocean waves.

By this time Lars and Erik were awake and eating by the fire.

"Going for another swim?" Lars jested.

The humor in his eyes reminded me of my unkempt appearance. I glanced down, noting the outline of my chest could be clearly seen through my drenched tunic. I flushed, crept around them, and grabbed the cloak I had slept in last night. Behind the sacks, I knelt and tied my sword and satchel around my waist.

Then I sat down beside them, pulling the dry cloak over my shivering shoulders and hiding the sword at my side.

Erik regarded me. "You must be cold—"

"It felt great." My voice was stiff as I dusted the sand off my hands. If only they would stop staring at me!

"These fish taste delicious," Erik said. "How did ye cook 'em, eh?"

"Same as me, boy." Lars shoved him good-humoredly.

"I know." Erik laughed. "But 'tis a new day, ye know, and here we are—"

"Free," I finished for him.

He smiled.

"Not to mention we have a woman with us." Lars winked at me. "We're better off than I thought we'd be, eh?"

I fingered the hilt of my sword underneath the cloak. What was that supposed to mean?

Erik only smiled. "Aye, indeed. Maybe that lass will listen to my torturous sermons."

I stared at him as if I hadn't heard their argument last night.

"Don't listen to my good friend. We may be saving the Irish, but that doesn't mean we have to become like them." Lars rolled his eyes.

Erik bit down on his bottom lip.

I shrugged, my hand sliding away from the hilt. "I'm just glad I have some good companions during the beginning of my freedom."

After breakfast, we set off on our journey. Each man carried a large sack, while I carried the hidden sword and satchel underneath my cloak.

Lars ran along the shoreline, the tide rushing over his feet. "We're off to save the Irish!"

I glanced at Erik then ran after him.

The ocean roared, the tide flowed in, and my feet padded on the sand. I had never been able to escape chores and the bite of the whip until today. I had never been free to run on a beach without fear of getting caught for slacking.

But even as I ran, I could not fully take in the moment. I felt numb to the sand, numb to the sound of the ocean, and numb to the warmth of the sun on my skin. I was running free, but my heart was bound, unable to enjoy the things that used to make me feel alive.

I ran blindly, letting the wind caress my hair, letting my legs carry me across the wide shore. I had to forget.

We ran over rocks, over sand, through the cool, flowing tide, until we panted and ached and collapsed. Lars and Erik laughed loudly, but

I wanted to cry. I couldn't run away from the pain. I couldn't escape it. It was still there, throbbing like a wound from a sword that cut deep.

"We're actually free," Erik said.

Lars laughed and pushed himself back to his feet. "Free as we'll ever be—eh?"

Erik wiped the sand off his forehead. "I've never been adventuring before, except when I was on my trip from Ireland to here and that was a terrifying adventure." His eyes went from dark to bright in an instant. "But this one has a noble cause—to save a whole village. What could be more gallant, proper, and—"

"All right, we get the idea." Lars smirked. "Now, if we're going to reach Ireland before Ragnar, we'd better get going."

So, we were off again, now trudging down the beach instead of running to conserve our energy.

"Do you have family back home?" Lars asked me.

I quickened my pace past him. "Do you?"

"I asked you first."

Erik frowned at Lars. "Ye needn't ask. We all have our stories." He glanced at me. "Lars and I are pretty much on our own—besides havin' each other. My family died in Ireland, his died in various battles. We understand if yer the same."

"My mother . . ." I dropped my chin to my chest. I shouldn't think of her. Yet memories of her poured over me, and I longed to talk of her. I couldn't bring myself to mention her death, but the memory of her clung to me, and I knew she was the center of my story.

"She is the most selfless person I've ever known." I squeezed my eyes shut to ward off the tears and to imagine her, to remember. When I was tired, she did my chores for me. When I was sick, she cared for me. When I was troubled, she sang me to sleep. She told me to be free. She told me to be proud. Even as a slave. I took a deep breath. I wasn't a slave anymore, but I wasn't free either. Keeping my mother's pride was the only thing that would set me free.

Erik pressed his hand on my shoulder for a moment, but I turned from his touch, a shudder running through me. He bit his lip, then rushed to catch up with Lars.

A cold breeze cut through my cloak, and I wrapped my arms around my chest. I didn't want any man to touch me ever again. I stood still for a moment, biting my lip, feet planted in the sandy shore as the men kept walking.

My throat was thick with grief. I wanted to be like Mum—selfless, loving, gentle—and I wanted to be proud for her. I would keep my head up, like that doll as long as I was working for the pride of Mum. Wherever her soul rested, she would be proud when she saw that I had murdered Ragnar, as he had murdered her.

The excitement I felt that morning in the water had already vanished. I clutched the satchel that held the doll Mum had given me. I had shown her gratitude when she gave it to me, but I had silently scorned the gift, thinking it was a gift for a child. The doll was all I had left of her now.

"Sigrid?" Lars called. "Do you need a rest?"

Swallowing my tears, I cleared my mind as best I could and hastened to catch up with my new friends.

EIGHT

KAUPANG LAY BEHIND US, DIAGONAL toward the rising sun, while the path to Bergen wound northwest toward cooler lands. Because of my love of the ocean, I insisted we stay as close to it as possible, until we really had to head more west.

Lars readily agreed. He seemed to be intent on pleasing me, since I was still considered a "guest" on this journey of ours.

The wind curled my white-blonde hair behind me. Sea birds cawed and flapped their wings above us. Some dove down and scooped up a fish or another sea creature then flew toward the mountains.

Soon the ocean turned into a large inlet, but we continued to hike along it. The ground steepened, and we had to work to avoid the rocks hidden in the deep green grass. The still, clear waters reflected the grand mountains on either side.

As we plodded onward, I relished the taste of the salty sea on my tongue. The time passed quickly with the two men sharing stories. Lars rattled off the familiar Norse saga about Loki stealing Freyja's necklace and all the trouble she went through to get it back. Soon after, Erik shared a puzzling story about a man who got swallowed by a great fish. When the man had humbled himself and prayed to his God, the fish spit him out onto the shore.

I could relate to that man. I felt like I was trapped deep inside a great fish, crying out to escape. If only one of the gods could command it to spit me out.

"Why don't you tell us some story, girl?" Lars broke into my thoughts, giving me a start. "You've been as silent as mouse over there."

"Oh, I don't remember much." Sand sifted into my leather shoes as I tread along. Old childhood tales were the last thing on my mind.

Erik spoke. "What about something about your life? Your family, maybe?"

I couldn't tell them anymore of Mum, but maybe a bit about my father would do. "My father was a good man. He showed a kindness which I haven't found in most Norsemen. But I didn't get to know him long enough."

It pained my heart that I struggled to remember much of him.

"Sounds like an all right fellow," Lars said. "I'd invite him to come with us if he were still, well, you know."

I grimaced, but I knew he was only trying to be supportive. These men did seem to have similar gentle manners as my pa. I marveled at their patience in listening to me—nothing like the Norsemen who had taken advantage of me.

Lars cleared his throat and asked, "So tell us, Sigrid, what is it like to be the chosen thrall girl?"

My shoulders drooped. Though I knew he meant no harm, his words grated on me. Did he really think I wanted to talk about this?

A fire burned in my belly, raw and fierce. "I cannot speak of such things."

"Oh, come, I've always wondered, you know—"

"Be quiet, fool!" I spat at him.

He gave me a sheepish expression. "I'm sorry, lass. I don't know what I'm saying sometimes."

I held my breath for a moment then said, "Don't mention it again, understand?"

"Never again," Lars said. "I promise."

At dinner that night by the fire, I felt obliged to smooth things out between Lars and myself. I asked him, "Were you always a thrall?"

He paused for a moment, sighed, then scratched the back of his neck. "After a bloody raid in Ireland, I realized that pillaging wouldn't bring me happiness anymore, so I stayed in Kaupang looking for a way to make a living."

I stared at him, wondering how a Viking had changed to have such fierce devotion to the Irish people. "You fought the Irish?"

Lars nodded slowly. "Couldn't find a job, so I sold myself as a thrall in order to survive. Joar bought me. Once I met Erik, we became friends, and I realized how good the Irish are if you get a close look at them."

I understood him well. Working alongside Tyra had made me see we were all the same. I turned to Erik. "You were born in Ireland?"

He nodded and said, "The Norse captured me years ago. I became the head servant for Ragnar."

I gritted my teeth and feigned indifference. "Oh?"

"I told him stories at night for some time. I also aided him with tasks he couldn't carry out because he could hardly see past his own nose. I served him till he sold me to his brother Joar after tellin' him too many stories about Iosa. I heard he got another feller to take my place soon enough. Niels, I think. Ragnar's eyesight worsened about the same time I left, so I imagine he needed Niels to take him everywhere." He sighed and pulled his blanket more tightly over his shoulders. When he gazed off at the ocean, his mouth trembled. "I haven't been home in a long time. God seems so far off."

I squinted at the horizon as if trying to spot Erik's God. I agreed with Lars. If this God made Erik feel so guilty, he wasn't a God I wanted to deal with.

"Why do you believe in this God, anyway, if He's so eager to shame you?"

"Because his family made him believe ever since he was born," Lars grumbled.

Erik shook his head. "I believe in Him by my own choice. If I knew He wasn't a pint real, I'd have rebelled against my family's beliefs by now."

I stared at him. I had always doubted the Norse gods were real, but Erik seemed utterly convinced that his was the true God. Who was right? Were any of us right?

"Let's not talk about our differences," I said firmly, finding strength to my voice. "Let's save the Irish." It didn't matter what we believed; the truth would reveal itself in time.

Erik looked from Lars to me. "Perhaps tomorrow ye'll feel kindly toward God. Goodnight, Sigrid. Goodnight, Lars."

Glaring at Erik, Lars rolled up in a blanket. "See you in the morning, Sigrid."

ᚷᚷᚷ

I sat on the shore washing the fellows' dirty garments, though I myself had nothing to wear but the clothes on my back. I scrubbed them on a tray with a bar of lye, all of which Lars had brought for the journey. Men were the same everywhere, in that regard—using women to do the work for them. I clenched my teeth and scrubbed harder at the thought. The fools!

But truthfully, I appreciated the work because I couldn't sleep. The sun sank low, and the tide ran up and over my feet, ankles, and clothes as I scrubbed spots on the garments that were already as clean as I could get them.

"Mum," I whispered up at the bright sky, wondering if her spirit was somewhere up there in a better place. I sighed. For the first time that day, I could think about her without anything hindering me from tears. "Remember, I promised you I would kill Jarl Ragnar? Well, here I am, with a good Norseman and a strange Irish boy."

I cupped my hands in the tide and scooped up some water. Tears slipped down my cheeks. I raised the water over my head and poured the sea over myself. The saltwater was icy cold, but I didn't mind.

"We're going to warn the Irish about Ragnar then help them fight against him and his men. But I'm going to kill Jarl Ragnar, that beast." I gritted my teeth. "I'm going to kill him for you, then I'm going to join you amongst the dead."

I placed the tray of garments onto the dry sand, then I gripped the sword strapped on the belt at my side and drew the weapon out of its sheath.

I stood up. Seawater gushed over my feet and ankles. I stood still while it ground my feet into the sand. I extended the sword out, gripping the hilt and pointing the foible upwards. The blade's golden hue radiated in the sunlight.

"Someday soon I will come to you, Mum, wherever you are."

I slid the sword back in its sheath. Then, I drew out the small doll from the satchel around my waist and held her closely to my chest. Mum had believed in me. She had believed I could find something good and beautiful, find a purpose to strengthen me.

Keep your head up.

NINE

TRUDGING BEHIND THE MEN ALONGSIDE a river, I pulled my cloak more tightly around me. As we ascended the mountain, the air grew colder and colder until the cold sank into my bones.

It had been a week since these fishermen had rescued me. We'd left the inlet to travel northwestward through hills and small mountains. Now a large mountain loomed before us, and Bergen was somewhere on the other side. As I trudged behind them, I preoccupied myself with gazing up at the lush green mountains. White snow speckled the peaks.

"Hey, it looks like we will have to cross this river," Lars hollered back to Erik and me. "Too many boulders up ahead on this side."

We arrived at the large boulders Lars had described. He was right. The boulders were too much of an obstacle, but the wide, flowing river we had been following was about three feet deep. The current was steady and strong but did not look overwhelming.

Lars began stomping across effortlessly. I made my way forward into the water after him. The water swirled up to my knees then to my hips. I pushed forward, straining against the frigid waters so it wouldn't numb my legs.

"W—wait a second," Erik called after us. He still stood on the shore, his skinny legs shaking.

Lars turned back to him and smirked. "I knew you'd have trouble with this. Just thought I'd see how you would handle it with a girl around."

Erik's face turned pale, and his legs trembled. "Really, Lars, I can't do this. Is there some other way?"

I frowned. "You're stronger than I am—what's the matter?"

"He's deathly afraid of the water." Lars stomped back to his friend, water splashing in the wake of his rough strides. When he arrived at the shore, he bent down and spoke gruffly. "Climb on, boy."

Erik climbed on awkwardly, his eyes wet with shame, and Lars piggybacked his friend across that river. I watched with wide eyes. Why did mere water terrify this Irishman so much? I had never seen a greater coward in my life.

"About a week or so of hard traveling till we arrive in Bergen," Lars declared when we stopped and made camp for the night.

We sat down on the hard ground and warmed ourselves around the fire. Lars tossed the rabbit meat he'd hunted into a pan over the flames. "I still can't believe you don't have a knack for hunting, Erik. Did you ever give it a try? My grandpa always talked of hunting like it was *the* thing to know—a rite of passage, wouldn't you say?" Lars chatted on freely, without giving us much of a chance to respond. Erik and I both remained still and silent, staring into the hypnotizing flames.

I listened to the steady *whoosh* of the river and closed my eyes for a moment. I wanted dinner, but Lars wouldn't stop talking.

Taking a deep breath, I slipped off my woolen stockings and grimaced. Bruises from the pricks of pine needles swelled my feet, and holes marred the heels of my stockings. Mum had woven them when I was sixteen summers old. How they had lasted for two long years, I did not know.

"Did I hear someone say they needed these?" Lars asked playfully, handing me a needle and some rolled up thread.

I couldn't help but let a smile creep through my lips.

It was too hard to hide, the more they pried at me. Perhaps it was all right to relax, just a little. Perhaps they weren't like other men.

I took what he offered, then I began sewing up my socks in the intricate stitches I had learned as a thrall.

"You sew well," Erik said.

I shrugged. I didn't know how to respond to that. Must be a *wonder* to him, considering his own lack of skills. The man didn't even know how to hunt, for Odin's sake! Not only that, but Lars had to piggyback him through that river.

Erik cleared his throat and said, "Back in Ireland, my aunt would sew my clothes just like that. So exact. She was wonderful. And my uncle, he was like a father to me. I hope I can find them when we get there. I love my homeland. 'Tis all I hope for lately."

"It will be a pleasure to help the Irish people," Lars said. "Say, doesn't that smell good? Those herbs really do something to a slab of meat." He passed out sticks of rabbit meat and began telling a story.

My thoughts drifted off as I bit into the meat and watched Erik staring into the fire.

All my life I had been used to strong, hardy Norse boys who could throw a spear at an elk as naturally as if they were born that way. The boys back home would jump from sea cliffs into the ocean, dare each other to swim through a fjord without stopping, and fight each other with oars. Erik didn't do anything like that. He was muscular in appearance, but on the inside, he was too afraid to use his strength.

"And then, I snuck toward a few men fighting and raised my sword above a Scottish man!" Lars's voice was full of passion and nostalgia as he described a successful pillaging escapade.

His stories were beginning to weary me. It made no sense to me why he would talk on and on about his old raids, when he claimed no desire to go a-viking ever again. Men loved their battles, I supposed, regardless of which side they were on.

I tuned out Lars's voice as I secured the last knot. Barely examining the finished product, I tugged my stockings onto my cold bare feet then drew on my leather boots. I relaxed as the wool warmed my feet and ankles.

"I had never seen a greater victory in my life!" Lars declared, extending his hands out through the fog.

"I have witnessed greater victories than what ye describe," Erik said.

Lars tossed his head back and laughed. "Ha! What victory? The one about your God dying on a cross that those priests read about in their filthy scrolls? How is death any kind of victory?" He spread his hands out again then fumbled and dropped his stick of rabbit's meat into the fire.

I covered my mouth with my hand. The flames licked the meat, but Erik came to the rescue, prodding the burned meat out of the fire with a branch, impaling it through a new stick, and handing it back to Lars.

Lars grinned in short-lived gratitude and began devouring the burned meat. Thralls didn't waste anything. He paused between mouthfuls, as if he were about to continue his passionate outbursts, but Erik spoke first.

"Aye, Lars. The greatest battle of all was when God won over my selfish pride. That day I let Iosa live in me, and my heart was set free like a horse runnin' over a mighty mountain." His eyes glowed with an inner light.

Lars snorted. "How could a little thought in your head be the most honorable and bloodiest of fights?"

I stuffed the last of the rabbit meat in my mouth, too exhausted and annoyed to savor the taste. How many times had they talked about this this week? The men were kind to each other in everything but the subject of religion. If only they would keep their mouths shut about it altogether.

"But, Lars," Erik said, his voice breaking, "ye have to believe in Him no matter if it's logical—it's called faith. If ye don't, God must put ye where ye belong. 'Tis why it was the greatest fight for me. Now I won't suffer for eternity, but instead will praise my God forever."

"Put me where I belong?" Lars's face turned as red as Erik's hair. "Are you saying that if I don't believe in this being, my soul will descend to the underworld?"

"Well, I—"

"I've had enough of this, I tell you." Lars jumped to his feet. "If you really think I'm destined for that dreadful place, then kill me, boy. Do you hear me? Kill me!"

I jumped to my feet, my eyes widening.

Erik's hands folded tightly in his lap. "'Tis not my place to judge."

"Oh, *right*, I nearly forgot." He narrowed his brows. "Get up and fight me."

"Lars? I thought we were comrades."

"This girl opened my eyes when she asked me why I even came on this journey. I'm a Norseman, for Odin's sake! Maybe I'll still save the pathetic Irish village—but you?" Gritting his teeth, he clenched his hands into fists. "I can't stand you."

I glanced at them. "If this has something to do with me—"

"It has nothing to do with you," Lars snapped.

I backed away. What was going on?

Erik rose to his feet. Lars punched his face, sending him staggering backwards into the bushes. He swung his rabbit stick down at him. "You stupid boy!"

Lars dragged Erik toward the fire, then he drew out his knife. Erik screamed.

I bounded forward. "Stop it!"

Lars thrust the knife at Erik. Erik fell backward into the fire, narrowly missing the knife's point.

For a moment I stood frozen, rooted to the ground. My heart pounded. The flames burst up around Erik. He screamed again.

I raced forward and heaved him out of the fire. The flames licked my hands, but the adrenaline pumping through me kept me going. I grabbed a blanket and beat out the fire on him with my already-burned hands until the little flames settled down. I stared at the young Irishman. Ashes blacked his face, and torment filled his eyes.

My hands shook. They were brown, scorched, and bleeding. *I* was being punished for something I had nothing to do with.

I stepped between the men and faced Lars. I lifted my chin, like a proud Finnsdatter—daughter of Finn, my good pa. "I thought you two were friends." My voice was sharp like poison. "Are we going to save the Irish or what?"

Lars sat down and put his head into his hands. "Of course we are, Sigrid."

Erik wrapped the cloak around himself. "It is the only thing that binds us together."

TEN

I AWOKE EARLY THE NEXT morning. Lars was snoring loudly with his nose to the trees, but Erik was missing from his pallet. I knew where to find him. It was the same place he went every morning, and I wanted to talk to him, to see how he was doing.

Strangely, I wasn't afraid of meeting him alone. He seemed unlike any of the Norsemen I had known all my life. He was humble and gentle. He reminded me of my pa yet was even less intimidating than him. I would just make sure to keep some space between us.

Following the sound of the babbling brook, I crossed through the trees and fog to the stream and the mop of red hair. He sat on his knees on a dry rock, bowing down toward the river. His lips moved and his hands were clasped tightly together. He chanted or prayed something in great sincerity. No doubt to the God he so feared.

Beside him on the rock lay an open scroll, tiny letters etched into the parchment. I remembered it from the first night on the shore. Paper was rare, expensive. I had only glimpsed scrolls every now and then when wealthy merchants sold them in the streets, and I had never learned to read them.

I stepped toward him. I couldn't help but wonder what sort of God he implored to with such fervency. I took another step toward him, beginning to decipher his words.

"Oh, God," he whispered, "I am such a pint of a coward. No wonder Thou never speak to me! Thou mock me, Iosa, I know Thee do. Thou mock me for tryin' to save these poor souls. Aye, perhaps I'm selfishly tryin' to assure my own eternity—so help me God. But Thou art so good to me. Almighty Father, Thou art wonderful, and I thank Thee for keepin' me here alive."

All at once he stopped, lifting his head toward the clouds. "I'm speakin' to no one, aren't I? Tell me I'm a lunatic." He picked up a stone and hurled it into the water. His fury seemed to permeate the atmosphere. He raised his face again and extended his hands, as if struggling to grasp for something out of his reach.

What was wrong with him? He seemed conflicted between loving his God and fearing Him like a thrall feared his cruel master.

Then Erik spoke, so softly I almost couldn't hear, "If Thou art real, God, if all I believe is true, give me a sign. Please. If Thou love me, show Thyself to me, let me behold Thy glory so I may worship Thee from the depths of my heart."

I lifted my brows. I didn't know what to make of all this. Either he was a lunatic or perhaps he was just a young man struggling with his beliefs.

I tried to speak up, but the words caught in my throat. I walked toward him and leaned over to look at the scroll beside him. He was so absorbed in prayer and didn't notice my closeness. The pages of the scroll were yellow and torn in some places, and the letters weren't anything I'd ever seen before—Irish, no doubt. They were more rounded, horizontal, and intricate than the tall, vertical, rough Norse runes I had seen.

I glanced at Erik. I should make the most of his ignorance of my presence.

I squeezed his shoulders and shouted, "Got you!"

Erik jumped forward and flopped into the water.

I laughed. "You didn't even see me, so I—"

A high-pitched scream cut me off. Alarm flooded Erik's face as he flailed about in the water. The current was stronger than I had expected and pulled him along with it.

Panic flooded me. I grabbed a long branch and held it out for him. He reached for it, his hands missing by inches.

I leaned forward. "Grab it!"

The current swept him further along. I jumped off the rock and rushed after him. His hands flailed about, trying to grasp for something sturdy but stones slipped from his fingers. The jagged rocks tore at his clothing, and he cried out.

Not far ahead of him the water dropped down into a three-foot waterfall. I stretched the branch out to him. "Erik!" I yelped, my arm shaking.

But before he could grasp it, the current heaved him off down the waterfall.

His body flopped into a pool of deep, fast waters. He flailed his arms out as his head began to sink under. The current carried him swiftly onward.

What had I done?

My heart raced. I rushed alongside the land to keep up with him. The water whipped him about over jagged rocks, and he went under.

I started into the water. The cold liquid swirling around my ankles. "Erik!"

He surfaced, his red hair plastered to his face, and he gasped for breath, even as he struggled to stay above the surface.

I reached the branch out to him, and he caught hold of it. "Kick your legs," I shouted and pulled him toward land.

He obeyed my instructions, and soon he was close enough to reach out and take hold of the dirt ground. He pushed his body upwards and scrambled onto the shore.

"I'm sorry, I didn't think—"

"What are ye doin' here?" he shouted, shaking his mane of crimson hair. "How long have ye been here?" He looked behind me, around the forest and brook, then back at me. Fear glowed in his eyes.

"I came to see how you were doing. I'm sorry for scaring you. I don't know what got into me."

I was truly surprised at myself. After all that had happened to me, I hadn't managed to smile hardly at all anymore, let alone laugh. I used to hide beetles in my father's boots or dump a bucket of seawater on Tyra, and today that part of me had come out again, around Erik, of all people.

"I forgive ye." He gave me a pained expression. "I need to get back to my scrolls."

I followed him back to the spot where the scrolls sat on a flat rock. "I really am sorry."

He narrowed his brows. "Please, lass, leave me be."

I ignored his request and sat in front of the scrolls. There had to be something I could do to make amends. "Can you read me some of the scrolls?"

He sat down. His fingers curled around the paper. "Ye wouldn't like it. 'Tis about my God. No one likes my God." His voice cracked.

I looked down and studied the scrolls for a moment. If I was going to kill a man, I had better make sure no god would send me to the underworld for it. For all I knew, this God supported the virtues of revenge and might be able to help me. And if the Norse gods weren't real and this Iosa supported me, I wouldn't be guilty of running away or of murdering Ragnar for Mum's sake.

"Please, tell me about your God."

"What do ye wish to know?" he conceded.

"Tell me what your God thinks about killing."

Erik shrugged. "His law says, 'Ye shall not murder.'" He rolled out the crackled scroll. "Ragnar gave me these scrolls he had stolen from the Irish, so I could read from them for his entertainment. The Bible contains God's laws, stories of His people, and a bounty of writings about our Creator and His beloved Son." His tone was softer now, and a shy smile played on his lips.

"So, it says not to kill." This wasn't the sort of god I wanted or could ever believe to be real. True gods understood the need for revenge.

"Aye. And Iosa says that even hating a person in your heart is the same as murder. After all, we don't have any reason to kill anyone."

I furrowed my brow. "What about, say, revenge?"

His lips formed a grim line. "Revenge may seem well and proper, but God warns us against it." He found a place in the scroll. "Here it says, 'Do not take revenge, my dear friends, but leave room for God's wrath, for it is written: "It is mine to avenge; I will repay," says the Lord.' You see, the Lord will take care of all the evil in the end. Murder doesn't solve the hunger in our hearts for justice. Only trusting in God does. What do ye think of that?"

I touched the firm handle of Ragnar's sword underneath my cloak. As I massaged the glittering jewels, I imagined the day when revenge was mine. Whatever his God thought, Erik had no idea how satisfying that day would be for me.

"Are we going to kill Ragnar and his men when we defend the Irish?" I asked him. Thoughts spun inside me at what I'd do when I had the chance. Ragnar before me, distracted in the chaos of battle, right when I'd plunge a stab from behind him.

He looked at me thoughtfully. "They'd kill most the Irish if we didn't warn 'em and help defend 'em. Sometimes ye got to choose a side. It's not pure murder; it is defense."

It sounded off to me. One moment he said killing was wrong, the next moment he said it was all right. Nevertheless, I couldn't blame him for wanting to take a stand for his own people.

His lip curled. "Which side are ye on?"

For the first time, I realized what defending the Irish meant. I would not only stand against Ragnar, but against the Norsemen, my own people, my own heritage. I would stand against my mother, whose faithful devotion to the gods had many a time kept her all night in prayer. Would I still secure her honor in my stand against my own people?

"Sigrid?" he asked. "Ye are wanting to help us, aren't ye?"

I paused. I was trapped on this journey with these men. I couldn't survive on my own. I couldn't get to Ragnar on my own. I wasn't *that* much of a lunatic. "Yes, Erik."

He closed his eyes for a moment. "Good."

I examined a green shoot in the ground of pine needles. "We need to start our day's walking soon."

As I turned to stride away, he caught my hand. "Ye heard all I said to my God, didn't ye?"

My heart raced. I yanked my hand out of his. "Well—"

"—so ye know I'm not very strong. Ye know I'm weak."

I backed away, then paused. "I already knew that, fool, from the moment I met you."

ELEVEN

I STRODE AWAY FROM ERIK and the babbling stream. I made my way through the forest back to camp. Lars was roasting salmon on a spit, turning it round with one brawny arm.

I sat down beside him. Although I despised what he had done to Erik the other day, I couldn't blame him for hating the boy for his torturous sermons. I was weary of them, too.

"Erik's a fool," I said quietly.

"Of course, he is. He's been praying before the sun rose. If he doesn't stop soon, I swear I'm gonna beat him up again."

I studied him. "You hate him."

"I sure do." He sneered, then his face relaxed, and he looked at me, tenderly, in a way I'd never seen him look at me before. "Does that bother you?"

I pulled my knees to my chest in response to his too-affectionate gaze. "No."

Lars eyed my dripping hands, feet, and tunic. "You were by the brook with him."

"We talked," I admitted then frowned. "What's wrong with that?"

"Don't give in to his foolery. He's dangerous."

"Dangerous?" I broke a smile at his apparent joke.

He grinned for a moment, then narrowed his brow. "Did you know that if you believe in his God, you have to help the sick and the poor, and you have to love all people, even your enemies?"

"He told me that last part." I folded my hands in my lap and looked away from Lars's penetrating scrutiny.

His nearness sent shivers down my spine. I scooted a few feet away from him. I wanted to leave, but curiosity restrained me. It didn't make sense for a former Norse raider to suddenly forget his prejudice against the much-hated Irish. Did Erik really have anything to do with it, or was there something more? "Why do you want to save the Irish?"

He stared at the salmon, its pink color searing into a dark brown. Finally, he spoke through gritted teeth, "It is for Erik, Sigrid. Please, let that be my answer, and don't ask me about it again."

I paused then asked, "So Erik's still your friend?"

"I don't want him to die, at least." His mouth curved into a wry grin. "You needn't worry about me." He pulled the salmon out of the fire and let it cool off on a dry leaf. "Everything's all right between us. He just needs to say goodbye to his wretched God, and everything'll be perfect."

"He'll never do that." I remembered Erik's utter fear and guilt in facing his God. Despite how cruel he believed his God to be, he was persuaded of this Deity's existence, and nothing could ever set his mind aright.

Lars opened his mouth, but then Erik strode out from the trees, his face alight with a glow that reminded me of Tyra. "Are ye ready?" he asked us, fixing his gaze on me and not Lars.

Lars tossed stream water from a small bucket into the fire. As he picked up his sack, he pushed Erik aside. "Had a fine morning?"

"Aye. I prayed for you."

Lars scowled. "You wasted your time, and now we're starting late. Get your breakfast and let's go."

"I also prayed we wouldn't get caught in sour weather, or get hurt, or catch a fever. Wouldn't that be worse than gettin' a late start?"

I raised my eyebrows. Erik hadn't spoken about his God so confidently before.

Erik heaved his bundle over his shoulder. "Thank ye for speakin' with me this morning, Sigrid. Ye reminded me of a truth I have long forgotten."

My mind blurred for a moment as I tried to understand, but I shrugged it off. He'd never make sense to me or to Lars or to anyone else who had a mind of their own.

The next day, we reached the top of the mountain just as it began to rain. The deep green of valleys, hills, and smaller mountains stretched out below us.

We stared in silence for a while. Tension still drawn taut between us, making it difficult to enjoy the view. The rain trickled down our faces.

Lightning struck the sky as brilliant as the sun. Thunder followed, roaring through the atmosphere, shaking my very bones. Then it rained harder, drenching me through my cloak.

Lars jerked his head toward the forest below us. We raced to the shelter of a large pine tree. But the rain showered through. Another flash of lightning lit the sky. I shivered and pulled my cloak tighter around me in a vain attempt to ward off the icy bite of rain and air.

Erik clenched his teeth. "We need to find a shelter."

"It's your fault this is happening. Your God hates you and is mocking your prayers for good weather." He scanned the forest. "I'm gonna find a shelter. Stay here." Turning to me, he studied me from my head to my feet, making my stomach squirm. "Be safe, Sigrid. I'll return as soon as I can."

Erik murmured, "He hates me." His red hair was darker from the rain and clung to his scalp and the sides of his face.

"No, he doesn't," I assured him. Yet, Lars did tell me he hated the boy. It was merely talk though—he couldn't really mean it. Deep inside, they were like brothers. Weren't they?

Erik shook his head. "He didn't even look at me."

"He told me he'd never think of killing you," I said.

"He told ye that?"

"He tells me lots of things."

His face turned ashen. "What else has he told you?"

I cleared my throat. "Just that he wouldn't get out of control again, that's all. Nothing else that he hasn't already told you."

I set down the basket of berries I had picked along our journey and sank against the tree. I pulled my fur cloak more tightly around me. I was shaking, but I held my head high. Pride is what's on the outside, after all.

Erik sat down beside me. "Do ye think he's right about this rain? Do ye think it's my fault?"

"Your God has no power." I focused on the forest in front of us. "No doubt the true gods are punishing you for not believing in them."

His hands trembled in his lap, but he didn't reply.

I blew warm air into my hands and rubbed them together. It had been a long time since we had cold weather such as this.

Erik blew into his hands as well. "That feller best come back to us fast."

"Oh, he will." My own certainty surprised me. But it was true. He wanted me safe. I cringed at the next thought. Sometimes it felt like he wanted *me*.

The rain poured harder.

Erik moaned and pressed his palms to his face. "Have mercy on us, God!"

"It's just a little rain," I snapped. "Lars will come soon."

But my shaking only increased, and inside I was in as much pain as he. As thunder rumbled through the mountains, I remembered another stormy night similar to this one. Ragnar had been visiting his father's longhouse. He had been infuriated with the state of the chamber pot, so he had sent me out in the storm to clean it. I'd scrubbed the pot in the ocean, the thrashing rain blinding me.

At the memory, I covered my face with my hands. Along with Ragnar's stony image came the memory of Mum's soft, tender face, smiling as she mended Jarl Valdemar's tunic, the rain pattering outside on the turf roof of the longhouse. How could Ragnar have the malice to destroy her?

Ragnar and the rain—I hated them both. The ocean was my dream, but the rain my nightmare. The ocean was free, open waters stretching out across the earth. The rain was liquid arrows shot down by the wrathful gods. The ocean was my mother, gentle, embracing me, loving me, allowing me freedom. Ragnar was the rain, his wrath pouring out on me, enslaving me.

I held my knees to my chest to keep them from trembling. Mum was gone, and I might never see her again if I went to the wrong afterlife. I knew I hadn't much of a chance of seeing Tyra again either. While there was a possibility she could be with Ragnar at his father's residence in Bergen, I doubted I would get a chance to see her.

"Have mercy on us, God!" Erik cried aloud once more.

I clenched my jaw. Here I was with a reason for pain, and here was this boy with a strange distortion of Tyra's religion calling out to his God as if he was in greater pain than I? Who did he think he was?

I glared at him. Ten days of hearing his pitiful prayers and sermons had been far more than enough. His loud cries in the rain did it for me. I couldn't stand him anymore.

I stood up. "Erik, look at me."

As soon as he lifted his face, I punched him. He gasped in pain, but I only stepped closer to where he sat at the foot of the tree and struck him again. He crawled out into the rain, holding his bleeding nose.

"Aren't you going to fight me back? What happened to defense?"

"I don't fight my friends." He gathered himself to his feet and faced me.

I kicked him hard in the shins. He recoiled backward.

"But you'd fight your enemy?" I taunted. "Aren't you supposed to love your enemy?"

Erik paused for a moment, his gaze flickering to the side. A frown drew together his eyebrows, and he asked, "What is that?" He pointed down the hill into a thicket of fern trees. I didn't see anything.

"A fine excuse to not answer me!" I yelled, kicking him again in the shins.

Erik winced but did not seem particularly bothered by me now. "No, really, look, Sigrid."

Sighing, I squinted harder. A tall, shadowy figure was approaching us.

"It must be Lars," I noted and looked back at Erik. I grimaced at his bloody face. My stomach turned into a tight knot. He had deserved something, but perhaps I had gone too far.

"Sigrid," Erik said solemnly. "Looks like a bear or somethin'."

Shrugging off Erik's imagination, I ran toward the shadow. I was determined to find out what shelter Lars had found.

"Don't mock your friend's bulky figure," I hollered back to him, as I strode ahead. "Always love, remember?"

The freezing rainwater soaked my tunic, and I tried to cover my face from the relentless pellets. Lightning flashed through the cloudy sky and illuminated the thicket. Lars's chest was not this hairy. Erik had been right. I screamed.

"Step backward, bit by bit," Erik whispered, coming up behind me.

I didn't move. The bear stared right back at me then pushed aside branches and ambled toward me. Its sleek hair was drenched by the rain.

My heartbeat hammered in my ears.

The bear groaned, its huge body swaying toward me.

Slowly, I backed away. The bear rumbled.

I unsheathed the sword and thrust it forward madly, but I only stabbed the air.

The bear growled, loud and thundering, shaking the earth beneath my feet.

I didn't realize my eyes were shut until I opened them. The beast stood in front of me. I dropped the sword, and it thumped in the tall grass. Terror coursed through my veins.

A claw struck my abdomen, and pain sliced through me. I shrieked in agony. The bear's claws snagged on my cloak. I wriggled, struggling to free myself. The rain pounded on my open wounds, stinging my skin. I flailed my arm out to reach for Ragnar's sword, but it was far off on the ground, and I couldn't grasp it.

"Oh, God!" Erik cried from somewhere out of my line of vision. "God, save her. Don't let her die!"

I hated him for such weakness. How could he stand around and be too much of a coward to try to rescue me?

The bear growled and released me, peering down on me. With a monstrous roar, it lifted its sharp claws above me. I screamed and covered my head.

Metal flashed above me. "Sigrid!"

A sword sliced the bear's chest, narrowly missing my head, but it didn't stop the claws from striking me again. Blood seeped from my abdomen through my tattered tunic. My whole body ached.

A voice yelled something, but the words faded from my consciousness, and the only thing I understood was the chill of rain and the smell of blood.

TWELVE

I OPENED MY EYES TO the light of a curling fire. I tried to push myself into a sitting position, but a sharp pain shot through my body. Cloth rubbed against my wounds. I lay on a straw pallet with a thick, woolen blanket providing me warmth. Unable to turn my body elsewhere, I stared up at the light and shadows wavering on the ceiling of the rocky cave. Rain drizzled outside, its monotonous rhythm resounding inside me, taunting me.

A firm hand rested on my shoulder, and I looked up into the face of Lars. "Are you all right?" he asked.

"The bear?" I whispered, finding it hard to speak.

"He is dead."

He had saved me. I inhaled, long and deep. The slave girl was, somehow, still alive. "Is this the shelter?"

Lars nodded. "As soon as I found this cave, I went back out to find you and Erik and bring you here."

"Where's Erik?"

He smiled down at me. "I'm sure he's fine. But what about you?"

Fear prickled through my body at his casual remark. Did he not know where Erik was? I gritted my teeth, preparing to pull the truth from him.

A large, wrinkly man stepped out of the shadows.

I clutched the blanket close to my chest, but Lars only chuckled. "This is Gunnar. Don't be afraid of him. He is the owner of this fine lot of treasure and has been guarding it for twenty-seven years. He wishes to give us a few sacks to help us purchase a boat and crew to sail us to Ireland."

Wincing at the aching in my belly, I propped myself up with my elbows and took in my surroundings. Silver amulets, gold bracelets, bronze swords, coins, and crowns overflowed burlap sacks. My mouth hung open. Nearby, a simple dinner rested on a modest oak table. Gunnar handed Lars a wooden bowl, and Lars lifted a spoonful of the hot soup of fish and herbs to my mouth.

I opened my mouth and swallowed. The savory warmth entered my ice-cold body, relaxing my sore muscles. "That is very kind of him."

"Indeed. Tell her, my sir, why it is you offer us such generosity?"

The tall, hunch-backed man spoke stiffly. "Didn't really, well, I mean . . . " He cleared his throat, staring directly at Lars instead of me. "I did it to appease my guilt of killing the Irish and stealing this treasure from them long ago."

He said it so methodically that it was hard to believe he truly was filled with regret. Yet perhaps he was a timid man.

"We thank you," I said as sweetly as I could muster.

Gunnar shrugged. The man before me seemed so subdued, as if he would rather not be talking at all. Such a quiet fellow. Was he hiding something?

"When I filled Gunnar in with the details of our mission, he not only decided to give us a good portion of this treasure, but he decided to come with us and give the rest of this treasure to Ragnar." Lars grinned at Gunnar, his brow raised mischievously. His confidence in the old man reassured me. "But really, Gunnar will lead Ragnar to the cave to delay him from going to Ireland. That way we can journey to Ireland before he does and warn the Irish of the oncoming pillage."

I couldn't help but smile. A solid plan. If Ragnar and his men had not sailed to Ireland already, anyway. At the reminder of our journey, I thought of the Irishman again.

"Is Erik all right?" I asked, then gulped down another bite of the soup. The heated stew warmed me, but now my stomach felt sick with nausea. Lars didn't care about Erik, so who knew what had happened to the boy I had beaten up?

He examined me thoughtfully. "You're alive, Sigrid, and that's all that matters. That bear could have killed you, you know. Forget about that redhead for now, okay?"

I wasn't foolish enough to express any more concern for Erik. He was my friend, yet he was also my enemy. I despised his weakness, but I didn't want to destroy him—only beat the fear out of him.

My eyelids drooped from weariness.

"And this is all Erik's fault!" Rage entered Lars's voice. "He did nothing to help you, the fool. He simply stood there, frightened by it all, calling out to his God."

"What else would you expect of him?" I closed my eyelids and set the bowl aside, yet I couldn't stop wondering why Erik wasn't here.

Lars grabbed my shoulder and shook me. "Stay awake, Sigrid. I have something for you."

My body tensed quickly at his touch, but I swallowed the feelings down. He had saved my life. He was only trying his best to take care of me.

Lars reached down, and he raised a silver amulet above me. It was in the shape of a cross. "I want you to have this. Hopefully, it will eradicate all of Erik's cursed prayers and give us good luck on our travels."

I reached for the gleaming amulet. I had never owned anything so beautiful. I placed it around my neck, the metal cold against my chest. "Thank you, Lars."

Lars looked pleased. "Of course, Sigrid. You're worth it." A lanky body with a soaked mop of red hair body tumbled through the opening of the cave and collapsed at Lars's feet.

Lars snorted. "You sure had a fine time."

Startled at his laugh, I frowned. Maybe Lars had beaten Erik up again, or blindfolded him, or done something to him so he wouldn't be able to find this cave until now. It angered me that Lars had left Erik out in the storm. Had he only gone out of the cave to find me? How could Lars treat Erik so, while promising to help the Irish? I gritted my teeth. It didn't make sense why he would continue this journey if he despised his Irish friend. Did he come to save the Irish only because he hated the Norse for enslaving him? Or was he now continuing this journey simply for *my* sake?

I sat up, gasping softly at the pain in my abdomen. "Don't worry, Erik. You're safe here."

Gunnar eyed me. "You know him?"

I blinked a few times. "He's Erik, and he's an Irishman. He's a big reason we're saving the Irish people."

Gunnar lifted a bushy brow at Lars. "You know him, too?"

Lars pressed his lips in a thin line. "Yes, I suppose I do."

I caught my breath. He *supposed* he did? The two men used to love each other. Making jokes together. Formulating a brilliant plan to save the Irish together.

Did my presence on this journey somehow awaken Lars to Erik's faults? *By the gods, what have I done.*

Gunnar plopped a mat on the ground and nodded to Lars. "Take care of your friend as you did with the girl."

A sharpness edged his voice. Did he resent Lars for disturbing his twenty-seven years of silence? And yet why would he then be so willing to give us his treasure?

Forcing a smile, Lars heaved the slender young man over his shoulder and laid him on the mat a few inches from mine. He began tending to the Irishman's wounds. He rinsed his bloody head with water, then wrapped clean cloth around it.

When Erik awakened, Lars kneeled beside him. "Your nose is bleeding. That rain did more harm to you than the bear did to Sigrid."

Heat flooded my cheeks. It wasn't only the rain that had harmed him. But I didn't want to mention that I had beat him in a fit of anger.

Erik lay on his back against some pillows that belonged to Gunnar. "No, the bloody nose is from . . . " He swallowed, shifting his gaze toward me for the slightest moment.

Lars tilted his head, grinning at me. "You beat him up, didn't you?"

A flush creeped across my cheeks. I pulled warm covers over my body. My torso ached. "I got a little angry."

Lars stifled a laugh then looked down at Erik and sighed. "I am sorry, my friend. Now, both of you, get some rest. Goodnight, my friends. Thank you again for your generosity, Gunnar."

The old man remained silent. He shuffled about and laid out some blankets for Lars near Erik. Then he ambled over to a dark corner of the cave and laid down on his own pallet.

Before too long, the old man and Erik were snoring. The rain pattered outside. Only a faint gleam of fire flickered in the cave.

Lars knelt beside me. "Sleep knocked him out pretty fast."

I could hear the grin in his voice.

It was probably my fault, not the bear's, that the Irishman fell asleep so fast. "I shouldn't have beaten him."

"Why not?"

I raised my head to examine Erik's sturdy back. "Maybe we're being too hard on him, Lars."

Lars bent down and searched my face, as if to keep my attention away from the redhead. His brilliant blue eyes terrified me. I froze, unable to speak.

"You and me—we'll survive him, then?" His deep, clear voice made me quiver inside. It reminded me of the Norsemen who'd claimed they took advantage of me for the honor of Jarl Valdemar.

Lars traced my cheek and tucked a tendril of my hair behind my ear. The touch of his finger brought back the flood of memories.

Adrenaline shot through me; I pushed his hand away. Something about him made me want to shrink to the size of a berry, or a pine nut, or something so small you can't even see it. I wanted to disappear.

I looked him straight in the eyes. "I think you'll survive Erik very well, friend," I said in the amiable manner he often spoke in. But the words were painful to usher out of me. "He doesn't endanger my life, though, that I'd have any reason to survive him."

He said no more, but as he sat there in the darkness, watching me with those terrifying eyes, I felt a deep need to sob. I was small to him. Just as I was to those filthy Norsemen at the funeral.

THIRTEEN

THE NEXT MORNING GUNNAR SERVED us all a breakfast of porridge. I sat up against the cave's stone wall with some blankets laid over me as he handed me a clay bowl. Lars hunched over the fire eating silently, for once, while Gunnar moved about the room tidying up the cave to keep busy. Erik rested against the wall a few feet away from me.

I sipped the hot gruel, wondering what we would do today. Erik and I were much too weak to travel anywhere, thanks to that bear and my own temper.

"Sigrid, here."

I turned to Erik. He slowly reached out and handed me the sword that I had left out in the rain, his hand trembling.

"Thanks." I set it beside my pallet on the dirt ground, hoping he wouldn't think much of it. When I had more strength to carry its weight, I would return the sword to its sheath that was still strapped to my side.

I licked another spoonful of porridge.

"Are you goin' to tell us where a thrall like you got a sword like that?" Erik asked.

Lars rose from the fireplace. "Yeah, we've been wondering. We've seen it on you before."

"I just, I—" I fumbled for words and set down my spoon. "It was my father's."

Lars studied me. "You're a thrall. And a Norse thrall for that matter, which means your father was nothing but a thrall, too." He paused for a moment. "You can speak freely, my friend."

Though Lars and Erik already knew I had escaped my fate in the afterlife, if they knew I had stolen Jarl Valdemar's sword, they would question me further. I could not risk them finding out about my quest to avenge my mother. Maybe Lars wouldn't mind, but Erik would be ashamed of me. And for some uncomfortable reason, I cared about that.

"I can't say right now." Or ever.

"The rain has died down. I'll take you outside, where you may speak freely to me." To my chagrin, Lars pulled me to my feet and wrapped an arm around me.

Erik stared at us as we exited the cave. I stared back as his friend led me away. Why did Lars have to make such a scene?

When we came outside, Lars smiled down at me. I rested on a fallen log, holding my stomach in a vain effort to ward off the pain.

"How's your injury?"

I grimaced. I was less than eager to talk about the vicious ache in my belly. Talking only made it worse. "It's fine."

Lars paused for a moment, then broke out, "I know you're lying. Tell me why you have Jarl Ragnar's sword. I've seen it in his hand many a time."

I bit my lip, heat flaming my cheeks. He knew. I couldn't tell him my plan to use the jarl's sword against its previous master. But neither was I strong enough to stand up and leave.

"I know you are the chosen thrall girl," he said. "So Valhalla wasn't much of a promise to you?"

I hesitated. He was asking so much of me. And yet his voice was soothing. Maybe he deserved to know some of the truth as my fellow traveler. Only some.

"Ragnar, well, he laid his sword in his father's longship, and—"

I cut myself off, swearing at myself for saying too much. I ought to have refused to answer him entirely.

"You *stole* Ragnar's gift to his father?" Lars jerked his head back. "By the gods, why would you do a thing like that?"

I cleared my throat. "Don't speak a word about it ever again. Please."

"I will keep your secret," he murmured. "The gods are insane to demand a girl die to serve her master, anyway."

I peered down at my slim, aching body wrapped in cloths and back up into his hardy complexion. "Do you think they did this to me? To punish me?"

He sighed. "Erik has angered the gods much more than you have. It's his fault."

I furrowed my brows. "You left him in the cold. He could have died."

"I'm done with him, Sigrid." Lars grimaced. "I don't want to follow his God. Ever. But I want to the warn the Irish and help them and—" His voice faltered. "I want you."

He pressed his lips against my forehead. I gasped, and my heart jumped unsteadily in my chest. I couldn't tell him about the rapes during that funeral night, about the fact that he wanted the exact thing I abhorred. Even without considering what had happened to me,

I knew I couldn't trust Lars. His erratic behavior, his mistreatment of Erik, and now, this.

"What about Erik," I murmured, not even knowing why I said it.

"Erik, the boy you beat up. What about him?" He drew his arms around me and pulled me close to his face.

Desperation gripped me. My mind was chaos. "I don't know," I tried to wriggle out of his arms. "Please, Lars, let go of me!"

He loosened his grasp and frowned down at me. "What's wrong, my dear?"

I clawed at him, trying to escape. "Let me go, please. I cannot marry you."

"And why is that?"

"I don't love you that way."

He stared at me, without blinking, a yearning in his gaze. "I'll do anything, Sigrid."

"Never!" I yelped.

He gritted his teeth. "You love Erik, the fool! I knew it was odd that you kept questioning after him."

"He's a lunatic." I strained against his powerful hold. "I could never love him."

Lars shook his head. "Talk all you want, but I know what's going on between you two."

"We're just friends!" I shoved my body against him so he would loosen his hold. "Please," I let out a sob, "let me go. You don't know what's happened to me."

If I couldn't win by force, perhaps I could by pity.

Lars grasped me from under my arms and held me out in front of him like a little child. "What has happened to you, Sigrid?"

I swallowed back my tears and clenched my jaw. "You know. You know what they do to the chosen thrall girl at their ceremonies."

I gave him one more shove then staggered back to the dry shelter of the cave, clutching onto my abdomen. The throbbing pain in my belly was nothing compared to the pain inside.

FOURTEEN

"HAVE ANY IDEA IF RAGNAR would be in Bergen by now?" Lars asked the old man.

I tramped through the trees, grasping onto a fern or pine now and then to support me and keep me from tumbling down the slope. After a few days of resting in the cave from our wounds, we had set out to traveling again, this time with Gunnar. Erik was feeling much more capable of walking, and the wound in my abdomen was much less poignant, though it still ached and at times seared with pain. I never wanted to see a bear again.

The old man scratched his disheveled gray and brown beard. "If he left a little over a week ago right after the funeral, he's sure to be in Bergen now. Traveling by longship is much faster."

My abdomen burned, so I paused to hold onto it. The men halted as well for another break. I hated that I was the one to slow down their travels. If only I hadn't been stupid enough to run to a hungry bear!

"At least we'll have a smaller crew than Jarl Ragnar, and we can travel faster," Erik remarked.

"Yes," Lars said. "That's something in our favor."

That night, we made camp near a wide, glistening lake. The air smelled sweet and cool, caught with the scent of the lake nearby. Lars and Erik brought out their nets from the sacks and went off fishing, as if they were brothers again. I turned to Gunnar. "I'm going to wash my face."

At his slight nod, I dashed through the trees till I reached the lake, purposely choosing a spot some ways from where Lars and Erik fished. I put my hands on my knees and panted for air after my short sprint. My wound ached again, and I breathed in and out until my breathing returned to normal.

Finally, to be alone.

I dipped my feet in the stream, the crisp, fresh water tickling up my ankles. Scooping some water into my hands, I washed my face, enamored by the refreshment I hadn't felt in days. I wasn't thirsty. We had plenty of water in flasks back at the camp. I was hungry. Hungry for the feel of water washing over me.

The full moon shone on the water, revealing my own reflection. Tendrils of my hair pasted themselves above my ears. My white-blonde locks appeared as a mop of tangles and dirt, and my bland gray eyes studied me with hard indifference. Even near the calmness of water, I no longer felt at peace. A scabbed scar crossed my cheek from the bear's roughness that rainy night—the cursed animal.

I removed the satchel tied around my waist and drew out the small doll. Siri. The doll's gentle face and joyous complexion drawn carefully in thin, dark lines dumbfounded me. Could I ever be that happy? Could I even find such peace in the afterlife? I stuffed the doll back in my satchel then retied the small bag around my waist.

Throwing off my cloak and setting my sword aside, I plunged into a three-foot portion of the pond. I washed my face and hair. The stream water seeped through my cloth bandage, stinging my abdomen. Ignoring the twinge of pain, I scrubbed until I could scrub no more, then I sat in the shallows and closed my eyes. I dreamed of Mum and listened to the rhythmic sound of free waters.

She had been beautiful. Kind, too. Why couldn't I be like her? But she was dead because of me. Couldn't I have done something to stop her?

I wept and sank deeper into the delicious water till it rose to my chin. How could she care so little of herself and so much for me? She knew full well what Ragnar was capable of.

I gripped the sword from beside the creek and clambered out onto the dry land. Rising to my feet on the forest floor, I faced a shady oak, my ragged tunic dripping wet. My abdomen throbbed with pain, but I was too angry to care.

First, I imagined that the bear was watching me from the shadows—tall, dark, and fearsome. I let the sharp, piercing, blackness of his eyes take form within two niches of the tree trunk. His arms were easy enough to imagine—the wide, long limbs of the tree. His dark fur transformed into a black cloak, and his claws turned into an agile hand clasping a slender sword. After that, I couldn't see anything else but Jarl Ragnar. My enemy.

I cringed as I recalled his hideous scowl, his obvious disdain for me. He was the exact opposite of Mum—consumed with himself instead of others. Since Mum had blocked his way, he simply removed her. Her life hadn't mattered to him, as little as the life of a flea mattered to me. Ragnar was a monster, a horrid, ruthless creature that wanted nothing but power over helpless people.

Ragnar's sword shimmered in the moonlight. Small round crystallized stones of red, yellow, white, and green hues at the hilt, so precious, so lovely, yet fashioned into a weapon of destruction.

With as much effort as I could, I gored the tree until I made a deep scar into its trunk. I still was not satisfied.

"If you could see," I paused to catch my breath then continued, "oh, Ragnar, if you could see what you've done to me, you would be glad of my torment. I will strike you down quickly like you killed my father, with the mercy you will never deserve!"

I poured my wrath on the oak, every ounce of my energy gathered for the one purpose of defeating the man who had taken everything from me.

"Sigrid?" came a voice, shaky, but strong enough to break through my thunderous whacks and shouts.

Heart racing, I left the sword in the trunk and dove back into the pond.

A shadow loomed over the moonlit stream. "It's only me," Erik whispered. "I heard something, and I came here because I thought—"

"I'm bathing." My tone was sharp. I sank deeper into the water, which soaked my burning abdomen.

He slapped his hand over his face. "I'm so sorry," he murmured, then hastened back to camp.

FOURTEEN

"HOW LONG TILL WE REACH Bergen?" I asked Lars as we ate breakfast two days later.

He poured water into a clay mug and handed it to me. His gaze wavered over me, studying me. "I saw it from the hilltop yonder," he murmured. "Should be there in a day or two."

Discomfort spread through me at his open perusal. He studied me too often, too freely. I would never again be able to enjoy the admiration of a man. The wound of that funeral day pierced far deeper than the bear's claws.

I shifted my attention to Gunnar. "You think so, too?"

The old man nodded. "We'll be there by nightfall, lass."

Erik rose from his blankets and shuffled toward the fire, his face groggy from lack of sleep. He dished out a scoop of fish stew into a small bowl from the pot over the fire.

"Your hair's a mighty mess this fine morning," Lars said.

Erik smoothed back his rumpled locks. "I couldn't sleep." His voice carried an honest weariness, and I pitied him.

"You know something, lad?" Lars smiled ruefully. "When your face gets all red, like your hair, you look like a blazing wildberry."

Erik swallowed some of the broth and glared at him. "Will people stop remarkin' on my hair?"

We stared at him. His voice hadn't been soft or gentle or quiet at all. The poor fellow was in a mood, I supposed.

He glanced at us, then back down at his stew.

"Maybe we should start, so we can make it to Bergen before dark." Lars thrust his pack over his shoulders.

It wouldn't get dark till much, much later during a short period of the night, but we had many miles to travel. After Erik finished his broth, we were off, scaling down the valley. Thankfully, my abdomen ached less today, and we didn't have to stop as many times.

After traveling for a few hours, a gust of sea air swept over me and filled my lungs. I could taste the ocean. My white-blonde hair flew back at the gentle caress of wind. I raised my hands in awe. All around me I could feel it—the overwhelming sensation of waves and sand and a little bit of freedom.

I am coming back to you, my old friend. We're almost there.

Almost in the same town as Ragnar. I was eager and terrified all at once. I plodded downward into the valley, Lars and Erik in front of me and Gunnar behind me. The ferns and pines towered above us, their branches hiding much of the great blue sky.

The brown wooden tops of longhouses came into view. As we neared them, pleasant sounds filled the air. Bouts of hearty laughter. And music—oh the music! Pipes, horns, and lyres, ringing out into the valley and echoing through the mountains.

I sniffed the air, and my stomach growled. The delicious aroma of meat sizzling over a fire. A cow, perhaps?

Gunnar paused, his mouth curving wistfully. "I haven't heard this sound or smelled food this good since my fellows and I rejoiced over a plunder. Either someone has returned from a-viking or will soon set sail for a raid." He lowered his voice so only I, who stood the nearest to him, could hear him. "May the gods bless them." He then hurried to catch up to the others.

I regarded the old man. He seemed to be in a good mood today. But didn't the old man regret his former plunders and wish to give the treasure to the Irish as recompense? Why, then, would he wish for the gods to bless such Norse raiders?

Lars halted, interrupting my train of thought. He looked back at me. "Sigrid, you and Erik should stay here for your safety."

I nodded. If Ragnar saw and recognized us, we'd be dead or else put to good use under the cruel master's supervision.

Erik stared at Lars, no doubt noting the irony of Lars mentioning his safety, when he'd left him out in the storm a few days back. Then he said, "Aye, you may be right. Sigrid and I can't be seen by him."

Lars and Gunnar bade farewell to Erik and me. The men lifted the sacks of treasure they would use to lure Ragnar to the cave, then headed off. Erik and I watched them depart from us into the thick trees.

Avoiding eye contact with Erik, I explored the area surrounding the brook we had been following for a place to sit. I found a flat rock, sat down, and dipped my feet in the cool stream. Erik sat down beside me, crossing his legs so his feet did not touch the water.

The two of us didn't speak for a while. I stared at the unending rush of water, the sound of the rippling stream relaxing me. Erik shifted next to me but still didn't say anything. Suddenly, it occurred to me that he had reason for feeling uncomfortable around me, and it was entirely my fault.

The silence grated on my nerves. "Forget about the other night. I had clothes on."

He raised a brow but said nothing. The silence continued. My cheeks burned. Of all the things I could have said, I had chosen the worst. Apparently, I didn't know how to make normal conversation. What was it about the Irishman that made me care about how I spoke or what I did around him?

I hated that I desired to please him, and, if I were even more honest, sitting here with him made me feel not so alone. It wasn't anything like what those Norsemen made me feel. Or what Lars made me feel. Here I was safe. Safer than I had been in a long, long time. Perhaps he felt uncomfortable around me, but in some strange way, his gentle presence put me at ease.

I drew out Ragnar's sword from its sheath. It shrieked as metal slid against metal. "This isn't my sword. It's Jarl Ragnar's."

I didn't look at him but stared at the sword I held out over the brook.

"Could I . . ." He cleared his throat. "Would ye mind if I held it?"

I was relieved at his answer. I had expected him to ask why Jarl Ragnar would give me such a weapon.

"You don't need be so shy, you know." I handed the hilt to him.

He grasped it, then rose without a word and turned away from the stream and me. Never once had he touched the water.

Holding the sword up to the light, he studied it for a long, quiet moment. "I've never laid eyes on a weapon so beautiful. May I ask where ye—"

"I heard something," I exclaimed in a hushed whisper.

More rustling in the trees followed. I squinted toward a thicket. Erik followed my gaze.

"Look!" I pointed to a doe behind some branches.

But he put a finger to his lips. Setting the sword down on the rock, he took a slow step toward the doe who nipped at some shrubbery.

I narrowed my eyes. "I thought you couldn't hunt."

He took another step, so silent that the doe hadn't a clue of his presence. He hid behind an oak and drew out his knife, watching the doe's every move.

Then he threw the knife, striking down the deer with one fatal blow.

SIXTEEN

I HASTENED TOWARD WHERE HE knelt on the ground. "How?"

His gaze darted about the creature in deep concentration. "This will last the three of us a week. Fetch the sack while I cut it up. Can't have any fleas—"

"Erik, for Odin's sake!" I raised my voice, unable to contain my bewilderment. "I thought you couldn't hunt."

"Lars fancies huntin' and takin' control of things, so I let him take control of the huntin'."

I smirked. "How very thoughtful of you."

Erik sighed. "Hurry and get me a sack, please."

His command caught me off guard. He'd never told me to do anything before. But I turned to fetch it for him anyway. The boy was stupid, having deceived me and Lars for no sensible reason. Why did he act so oddly about a thing like hunting?

At camp, I found the empty sack and slung it over my shoulder. Then I made my way back to him, balancing on a fallen log with one arm stretched out and the other clutching the sack. I began humming an old Norse song.

"What are ye doin', lass?" Erik smiled up at me as I approached.

I lost my balance. I tumbled off the log and down a small hill covered in pine needles. At the bottom of the hill, I held onto my ankle, wincing at the sharp twinge of pain. I cursed myself. Why was I such a fool at times?

Erik hurried toward me then offered his hand. I took it, begrudgingly, and he pulled me to my feet.

"You all right?"

My ankle hurt, but I only gave a half shrug. I fetched the sack and tossed it to him. "So, can you sword fight? Like, with people?"

Erik laughed, stuffing some of the deer meat into the sack. "I haven't in years, but I remember a wee bit from what my father taught me." He threw the sack over his shoulder then grabbed the legs of the carcass and heaved it over his shoulders as well. "We best get on back to camp so Lars won't worry about ye if he returns."

Erik bore his prize, and I limped after him. He glanced back at me then slowed down to walk beside me at my own pace. Gratitude filled my heart, but I kept my gaze ahead so Erik wouldn't notice.

We arrived at our smoldering firepit. He brought the deer back out and resumed the long process of skinning it. I watched him work quickly. He must have learned a great deal from his father, for he could hunt and skin an animal more easily and naturally than any Norseman I had ever met. If he was so skilled with a knife, he had to have some skill with a sword as well. I certainly could use some lessons, if I was going to kill a man.

After he finished skinning the deer, we roasted enough meat for dinner. We salted the meat and wrapped it in cloth to save for Lars and Gunnar, then we ate our portion of the delicious meal quietly, as the sun began its slow descent in the sky. When we finished, Erik sprawled across the ground on his stomach.

"Erik?" My voice lowered. Maybe I shouldn't ask, but this might be my only chance.

He rolled over. "Yer not goin' to sleep, lass?"

"We can't just sleep—Ragnar's around, and who knows when Lars will come back."

"What do ye want, Sigrid?" Erik looked at me, bemused, seeming to sense my hidden motive.

"Could you teach me how to fight with a sword? I know I couldn't learn it all in one night, but maybe you could show me what you remember." I paused and studied the grin that spread across his face. I hadn't seen that particular face in a while. It rather suited him.

Erik propped himself up with his elbow. Then he spoke before I could press him further. "What would a girl like ye do with sword-fightin' skills?"

I hesitated, knowing I could never reveal my dark motive, then I faked a smile. He thought it was funny, so I'd play along. "There are plenty of female Norse warriors."

His raised an eyebrow. "But ye? With a sword? We are defendin' the Irish, Lars and I. I didn't think ye'd want to fight, too."

I slid my sword out of its sheath and raised it in the air. "That's all I've ever wanted to do—defend people, that is." The lie slipped easily from my mouth. I had never imagined myself in a battle, but if a battle were to happen—by the gods, I wasn't going to hide away while the men did all the work!

Erik rose to his feet. "Ye cannot fight, lass. I will not let ye."

"But what if a Norseman came against me?" I challenged him, my hands gripping the sword in front of me. "I wouldn't be able to defend myself, simply because I was never taught how. I need to be a part of this, Erik." My voice quieted as I searched his face. "Please teach me."

I couldn't believe I was entreating this fool to teach me to fight. Maybe he was lying again, and the only thing he could kill was a deer. Whatever the case, I needed to learn to handle a sword for the day I faced Ragnar.

Erik shook his head.

"Well, I'm not going to let myself die, even if you will." I lifted my chin and began to limp away. My ankle stung, but no matter. I'd go and teach myself.

But Erik touched my arm, making me jump. "Ye will be safe with the other women and children in hiding, we men will protect ye."

I jerked my body away from him. "But I am strong enough!" I directed my sword at his chin. "I'll prove it to you."

Erik raised his palms and smiled, a hint of mirth behind his calm eyes. "Ye don't need to prove yer strength with yer sword—what's that got to do with being strong anyway?" He pulled a blanket over his shoulders and sat down again by the fire. "Sigrid, ye don't have to wholly understand me, but I beg ye not to fight."

My sword still wavered in my hand. Ragnar's sword. How I hated my old master! If Erik understood such hate, he would surely know why I had to complete this task for Mum's honor—wouldn't he?

"Why didn't you tell me you could throw a knife like that?" I glowered at the deer bones burning in the fire.

Sweat glimmered on his pale skin, no doubt from the fire, though the air was wrapped around us like ice. "I try not to be proud."

"Proud?" I scoffed. "Don't tell me, your God doesn't allow pride? Honor?"

"Those are mighty different things. Pride is for yer own sake; honor is for Iosa's."

"Whatever the difference, they are what I live for," I declared. "They are what I plan on dying for." I glanced over at Erik. I didn't know why I'd told him that.

"I don't care about such things," he said gently.

"How can anyone not care about pride?" I asked, then spat out, "I mean, that sounds humiliating."

Erik quavered, that familiar, sickly fear concealing his handsome face. "I'm not tryin' to humiliate myself, ye see, I am tryin' to humble myself. I am tryin' to humble myself because God deserves all the praise, and I don't deserve any of it. It's a good thing, ye see?"

I scowled. "I will never live for a God who beats all the pride out of His thralls."

"It's by God's grace I am choosin' to beat the pride out, while He's here loving and helping me be the person He's set me out to be." His face brightened, his own words comforting him in some mysterious way.

"Why do you believe that?" I directed the sword at his neck, in mock display.

For a moment he sat silently in the dirt, his eyes moist. Then he pulled out the small scroll from his belt and held it out to me. "He's strengthened me to believe in my heart, with the Holy Spirt and His life-giving Word. I thank Him that I still believe, though I haven't seen another believer in ages."

Who is this Holy Spirit? And what is this "life-giving Word"? Did they help Tyra to believe Iosa, too? A coldness seeped inside my bones. She had tried to take my place in going to Valhalla. Did it have something to do with this Christ? She and Erik were both fools for this Christ.

"I don't believe you. Lars is right—I know it. Lars is going to kill you one day, and then what will you say to that?" My words were bitter, and I instantly regretted them. I cared about the fellow sometimes, didn't I? But shouldn't he know the truth?

"'To live is Christ; to die is gain'—'tis what Paul said." His tone was plain and simple, as if the mysterious words he had spoken bore much clarity. "If I live, I live for Christ, and if I die, I gain the reward of entering heaven's gates to worship my God forever."

I locked my gaze on his and clamped my mouth shut.

Erik stood up with a wrinkled brow, directing my attention back to the sword I was gripping tightly in my hand. "I think we've done enough fightin' for tonight, lass." He raised his scroll, the slightest smile curving on his lips. "Would ye like me to teach ye to write Latin letters?"

"Latin?"

"Aye, Latin is the language we Irish use to record Scripture. A monk taught me the secrets of the written word."

I almost asked him why I would ever need to write Latin words, but then I came to my senses. I had always wanted to unravel the mysteries of markings, a skill so few people possessed, let alone mastered. I often wished thrall girls could learn to read, but the boys in the higher classes, if even they had the chance, were the only ones allowed. Erik was offering me a chance of a lifetime. Mum would hate it if I passed it by.

"Well, do ye want to?" Erik asked again.

I drew out the silence between us as long as I could, debating what to do. Finally, I surrendered and said, "Oh, all right." I slid the sword into its sheath.

At my agreement, he unraveled the crisp, precious paper. Markings scattered across the scroll.

"Why don't I give ye a word at a time, instead of teachin' ye the sounds of the letters? What word would ye like to learn first?"

I sat down cross-legged beside him near the fire's warmth. "Ocean. Sea. Or whatever you call it in Ireland."

"The Latin word I learned is *oceanus*." He smiled thoughtfully. "Yer favorite word?"

"Yes."

Picking charcoal from the fireplace, he wrote the letters down on a blank space in his scroll. "*Oceanus*," he said. "Now you try."

The markings were strange and meticulous, so it took me a while to copy what he'd written down. But once I had, a joy surged through me.

I grabbed a stick and copied the letters again, this time in the dirt. When I'd copied them a third time, I smiled up at Erik. Now, whenever I saw those letters, I'd know exactly what they meant.

"Well done," he said.

I had written a word! Soon, I'd written the large letters in the dirt twenty times around the fire. I grinned. "Now look what I've done! The fire is surrounded by an ocean. How is it ever to escape?"

He broke into a great laughter which caused his green-gray eyes to sparkle. My heart leapt, and for some reason I felt glad, so glad that I had made the fellow laugh.

SEVENTEEN

"PSSST. SIGRID." A SOFT YET insistent voice whispered. "Wake up."

My eyes fluttered open. Above me, the sky glowed with the faint light of dawn.

Lars peered down at me. "Hide under here." He covered me with the sack before I could say a word. I groaned at the heavy bag weighing me down, but soon quieted myself at the sound of a familiar voice.

"Where is he?"

My blood ran cold. Ragnar. Was my chance to kill him right in front of me?

"He's right here, sir," Lars said.

What was Lars thinking? He knows Erik used to be Ragnar's head servant. I lay still and quiet, hugging myself underneath the heavy sack.

"Look at me, boy."

"Greetings, Master." Erik didn't sound scared, but he had to be.

"Is this that redhead I sent away?" Ragnar's voice sounded so bewildered that I stifled a laugh.

"'Tis I, sir."

There was a friendly pat. "I thought I'd never see your beautiful Irish face again. Though I can't see much of you with these eyes of mine—ha!" There was a pause, then Ragnar roared, "What in the name of Thor are you doing in Bergen?"

"After you sent me away, I was your brother's thrall for a mighty long time," Erik replied. "I am now returning to my home in Ireland."

I was shocked at his openness with the man.

"Then you will go," Ragnar said solemnly, "but first, take me to the gold your friend here told me about."

The Irishman said nothing. My ears rang at the hush that followed.

"Well?" Ragnar boomed. "Do as I say, or the grave will be your new friend, ever waiting as it is."

"Is that all right, Lars?" Erik asked. "Will ye wait—"

"Of course, he will wait for you, boy," Ragnar growled. A loud whip resounded. "Get to it!"

I almost jumped up to intervene, but the fear of Ragnar was like a great weight holding me down. Their voices faded away, as did the flurry of footfalls of those who had accompanied the jarl. Another whip rang out in the distance.

I flung the bag off me, now fully awake. I started to run after them.

"No!" Lars shouted. He grabbed my arms.

I tried to escape him, but the pain in my ankle from yesterday's embarrassing incident sliced through me. I could not run. Not to save Erik nor to slay Ragnar.

"Erik's fine," he said.

"No, he's not." My voice was stiff. "Why did you do that?"

He gave a half shrug and released me. "Do what?"

"You know what I'm talking about! Why did you let Erik go off like that?"

Lars paced beside the fire. "Well, I didn't mean for it to happen—honestly. But when Ragnar saw Gunnar, he . . . " He bit his lip. "Well, he was carrying the treasure and all, and since . . . "

Lars didn't speak for a long time.

I stared back at him. "Lars?"

"Will you promise to tell no one what I'm about to tell you? Not even—especially not—Erik?"

"What—"

"Do you promise?"

I looked down at my hands, biting the bottom of my lip. How could I promise such a thing? But if it was the only way to find out what was going on, I'd have to do it. "I promise."

Lars took a deep breath. "Gunnar didn't feel bad about his youthful days of pillaging. In fact, the treasure didn't even belong to him."

My thoughts jumbled to a halt. "What?"

"It belonged to Jarl Valdemar, and now, it belongs to Jarl Ragnar." Lars watched the water babbling through the stream. "I made a deal with Gunnar to keep it a secret from you and Erik—mainly Erik, since his God hates stealing."

I groaned. "His God hates everything. But seriously, Lars, you mean to tell me we stole treasure from Jarl Ragnar? Do you have any idea what this means?"

"Now I do." Lars paced back and forth beside the stream. "As soon as Jarl Ragnar realized that the stash was buried in a cave in the mountains, he knew it was his father's plunder. He drew out his sword and killed Gunnar. The servants held me back, and the old man had nothing to defend himself with."

Lars strode away, his head down.

"You are a fool, Lars! It's all your fault that the old man's dead!" I yelled after him.

Lars quickened his pace.

I hunched my shoulders and dropped my head in defeat. He had lied to us. And now he had let Erik lead Ragnar to the cave in place of Gunnar.

But I was trapped here with Lars. I drew a heavy sigh. I am so sorry, Gunnar. You didn't deserve this.

"We have to go," Lars's voice called out.

I lifted my head and stared at the shadowy figure across the fire. "Without Erik?"

Erik was the reason Lars wanted to go in the first place. Lars had fought against the Irish before, pillaging and ransacking villages like any other Norseman. Why would he want to save his enemy from his own people, especially now that Erik wasn't with us?

He raised his face to the sky. "Now is the time to head to Ireland and attempt to reach the land before Ragnar. I really do believe this is the only way, Sigrid."

The flames illuminated his expression full of tenderness, yet I could find nothing within myself that desired to trust him.

I tightened a fist, but my hand was sweating, and I felt that no matter how hard I tried, everything was slipping away from me. "But Erik is your friend." *And mine.*

Lars shifted his feet, discomforted. "I really don't believe that anymore."

"You always say exactly what you think. But you don't mean it this time—you love him! We can't leave him." My voice choked. How would Erik fend for himself? He claimed to be able to swordfight, but I knew Ragnar was an excellent swordfighter.

"You're being irrational. We have to go, Sigrid. Now or never."

I fought the hurt and desperation stirring inside me. I remembered Tyra, who could very well be serving in Ragnar's residence right now in Bergen. Would any of the thralls there recognize me? Possibly. But they were thralls, like me, and they could be persuaded into secrecy. I simply couldn't go with Lars on this "noble quest," not when he'd done so much to betray us. I couldn't leave Erik behind, the poor boy who didn't deserve any of this. And Tyra was the only one in this world I could trust. It was worth the risk. "Erik's still going to Ireland, eventually," I reasoned. "So will I."

"You don't mean with Ragnar—"

"I have a friend, and she's a concubine of Ragnar's. I might be able to see her again."

The color drained from his face. "Are you suggesting that I should do this alone?"

"You said you loved the Irish because of Erik." I looked up at him, doubt trickling into the cracks of my broken heart; doubt that had always been there, distrusting him. What did Lars have to gain in warning and defending a meager Irish village? Even if he still loved Erik deep down inside, I had never entirely understood how friendship could make him so determined to help his previous enemies. "At least, you said so when I first met you." I searched his face, fighting back tears.

Lars clenched his teeth. "I don't believe he is my friend anymore."

"But deep inside, you know he is." I managed a half smile. "Right, Lars? Why else would you do this?"

The question burned within me, aching to be answered. I didn't understand why Lars was treating me like this, like I wasn't worth knowing the truth. I deserved to know it. Maybe I could trust him again if he would only tell me.

Hurt penetrated through his gaze. "You're my friend, Sigrid. Do you know that?"

"Yes." I lowered my head, doubting it was true that he was *my* friend. "Despite your mistakes, I know that you are a good man, Lars, or you would have hurt me by now. You saved me from the bear. And I'm thankful for that."

"But you love Erik more, in ways you don't admit to even yourself."

"No! He is as much a fool now as he was weeks ago, as much a fool as when I beat him up. He is so weak he makes me sick to the very pit of my stomach." I turned away from him, hoping this fight would not turn physical. I was all too familiar with the strength of Norsemen.

"Then why do you want to stay here, Sigrid?"

I steadied the tone of my voice. "I'm going to try to find my friend to see how she's doing, and after that I'll come with you. Wait for me, please. And wait for Erik."

"We need to leave *now*," Lars murmured. "So, if that's what you want, then fine. I don't need you."

His comment plunged like a needle inside my heart, but I quickly brushed it aside. "This was Erik's idea. He deserves more than to be left with Ragnar. He deserves so much more than anyone's ever acknowledged him for."

He raised his hands to the sky and uttered a curse, a curse in a language that I couldn't understand. I had never heard him speak it, but his voice was as fluent as if it was his first language. Was this the answer? Was this what he had been keeping a secret for so long?

Before I could say anything, he snatched his bow and turned to the forest. "Breakfast," he said hoarsely.

"Erik killed a deer last night," I informed him, though hardly able to contain my excitement about my new discovery. Norse wasn't the only language he knew, that was certain.

Lars glared at me. "He said he couldn't hunt."

"Long story," I said hurriedly. "Now let's go back to camp and eat. Tell me about *your* secrets."

I was practically jumping with anticipation. I pulled Lars by the hand, and he followed with reluctant steps. I began roasting pieces of venison in a pot over the fire, even as he stood there in silence.

After a long pause, he gave a bark of laughter. "Sigrid, I'm not telling you anything."

"Don't worry, it all makes sense now. You're Irish!" I rolled my eyes. "Why hide that?"

"You're a girl," Lars said. "You can't understand men and their honor."

I gestured for him to sit beside me on a rock. "I happen to know a lot about it, actually."

He refused to play the game and remained standing. "I'm going to go for a walk by the stream."

"I'm coming with you."

"You can't leave the venison."

"I don't care."

Lars skirted the stream, and I waded in it.

"All I want to know is why you're ashamed of being Irish."

He paused, letting the silence fall, long and painful. Then he spoke up again. "I fought them, Sigrid," he choked. "Now will you leave me alone?"

I was shocked by the tears I saw forming in his eyes. So, it wasn't Gunnar who had regretted plundering the Irish, it was Lars.

I sorted out the truth as I spoke. "But now you want to go back to them. You're sorry you betrayed them, and now you want to go home."

"Yes," he murmured. "That's something of the truth. I'm half Irish, half Norse. Now please, go."

"Thank you for telling me." I locked my eyes with his. "I will leave you alone now, Lars."

His bulky frame seemed to crumple at my gaze. "Thanks."

EIGHTEEN

AFTER BREAKFAST, I SET OUT to find Tyra. I figured the old residence of Jarl Valdemar would be the best place to search for her. As I wandered through the forest, I found myself hoping the Irish might be able to be spared from Ragnar's crew. If Lars could hire them first.

Still, I wished he had waited for Erik and me. What was to become of the redhead?

The fresh morning air gushed into my lungs with each determined stride. The thought of Erik leading Ragnar back to the cave where we'd come from jumped into my mind, but I laid aside my annoying worry about him and turned my thoughts to Tyra, my dear friend whom I had thought I'd never see again. Though I hated to watch her be the object of the cruel man's affections, for the sake of seeing her again, I hoped Ragnar still had a liking for her enough to bring her along to Bergen.

In the village, merchants on the sides of the streets called out their wares. Travelers lined the streets, eyeing the barrels of wheat, displays of silver, and high stacks of lumber.

A short, broad-shouldered man was selling a dozen thralls, calling out their prices in a strange accent. I walked past the chained captives, giving a slight nod of acknowledgment to one of the women. My heart was heavy. Thralls seemed to be the only ones to realize the injustice of what was being done to them.

A merchant hollered out the cost of the furs he was selling. With that price, they must've been from France.

"Hey, there, shabby girl over there! I've got somethin' to make you look fine! Wanna come see?"

I turned to him. "I am not interested—but could you direct me to where Jarl Ragnar has been staying?"

He raised his bushy brows. "Jarl Ragnar, ay? What could a girl like you be doing having business with him? He's got enough pretty girls waiting on him already."

I cringed. "No, it's not like that. I just—I'm looking for an old friend."

The man chortled. "Ah, well, I don't know how kindly Ragnar would be in letting you see a friend. But—" He directed me to a nearby longhouse. Then he put his hand to his lips and lowered his voice, "I heard he left for some treasure last night."

"Indeed, he did. Do you know by any chance if he brought a woman with him here named Tyra?"

He gave a half shrug. "No one knows how many women Ragnar keeps, let alone what their names are."

"Of course. Well, thank you."

He gave a tight-lipped smile, and I left him. I followed his directions through the outdoor market then veered to the left into a wooded area. I found the trail the merchant had spoken of and went along it. Soon, I arrived at the door of a great pine longhouse. I knocked. She had to be here. She had to.

A few seconds later, the door creaked open. A slender, blue-eyed girl with dark lines drawn on her eyelids appeared. She wore a frown on her red-tinted lips, and dangly bracelets and necklaces around her neck and wrists. The make-up hid her face so well that at first I was shocked at what had become of Tyra, but then I saw the long, wavy brown hair. Tyra had black hair.

"Who are you?" she muttered.

"I'm here to see Tyra."

I let out a breath of relief. She did not resemble anyone else in Jarl Valdemar's longhouse back in Kaupang. She and the others living here must be the thralls from Ragnar's longhouse, not Valdemar's old house. These thralls had never seen me up close before.

"Tyra, Tyra . . ." The girl rolled her eyes. "If you're one of those helpless widows coming here for charity, Tyra's not here. She's at that Stellan's house, the fool—they're both fools, if you ask me. All they talk about is the poor, helpless people of Bergen. They look at each other for fleeting moments, but never touch each other. What kind of romance is that?"

My throat closed with unease. "Where's Stellan's house?"

"Stellan's house? Ha! Why would ya want to go there, lass?"

I grimaced. "Tyra's the closest friend I have in this world. Please, tell me."

The girl sighed. "Two longhouses that way on the right-hand side." She pointed in the direction of the wharf. "Keep her there all night, and I'll give you one of my bracelets. Never lets me have the jarl to myself, you know." She winked at me.

Gasping out my thanks, I hastened down the street to the door of Stellan's longhouse. I knocked loudly, scarcely able to contain the excitement that bottled up within me.

A bearded fellow appeared. His eyes lit up at the sight of me. "Welcome. Whom do I have the pleasure of meeting?" He reached his hand out.

"Sigrid." I hesitated then shook his hand. I did not know what to make of his strange hospitality. "You are Stellan?"

He nodded. "We have plenty to offer here, Sigrid—blankets, clothing, shelter, food. All in the name of God's mercy."

"I'm looking for Tyra, sir."

His mouth curved into a bright smile. "Come on in, Sigrid, she's right in here."

I followed him into the warm, homey longhouse. A fire lit up the room where many women worked at their looms and children played. Straw mats and wool blankets lined the outer edges of the narrow room.

Stellan strode ahead of me. Tyra sat at a loom, weaving a multicolored blanket much like the one she had been working on in Kaupang. My heart leapt at the sight of her. Stellan leaned over and whispered something to her.

She narrowed her eyes at him. "Sigrid? Who's Sigrid?"

Stellan motioned me to come.

Tyra blinked dumbly. "Sigrid?" Her mouth fell open, and she cried out in disbelief. "Sigrid, but ye were dead—but ye are—oh, Siri. Oh, Siri, ye aren't dead—ye didn't—" She threw her arms around me and wept. "Ye are alive, my dear friend. Ye swam, didn't ye? You're the greatest swimmer alive."

"Tyra, I love you," I choked, trying not to let the tears slip. "I love you."

As I embraced her, I realized her abdomen was large and round. She shook my shoulders, stirring me from my thoughts. "What have you been doing this whole time, all these weeks? I thought you were dead, Siri, after all the horrid things they did to you, and your poor, dear mother—I'm so, so sorry."

My friend's expression was full of sorrow. I knew her sympathy was about both the cruel funeral rituals and for my mother, but I couldn't accept it, not when the pain was still so fresh and raw. I had tried to ignore it most of the journey over the mountain, and I would keep trying until the day I put myself to death.

I lowered my head. "Don't mention her, or any of the funeral rituals, please. And please, don't call me Siri."

Tyra was quiet for a while. She folded her hands in her lap, underneath her large round belly. At last she spoke in a somber voice. "Ye've changed, Sigrid."

"How?" My voice was wobbly. I knew I wasn't the same girl, but how did she sense this? Would she still want to be my friend if she knew I wanted to take revenge on Ragnar?

"I don't know, it's just that ye look—Never mind, my friend." She forced a smile. "Tell me how ye got here. I'd like that."

I described how I'd escaped Jarl Valdemar's longship, how I'd met Erik and Lars, our grand adventure, and the strange old man guarding the cave. She took in every word with full acceptance and love toward me. I had forgotten the pure delight of being listened to by Tyra. At last, I explained to her that Lars would be traveling to Ireland alone now, because I had wanted to see her and he was unwilling to wait.

"And that's about it." I ended with a sigh, hoping she wouldn't realize it was one of disappointment. "Erik is leading Ragnar to the treasure, so Lars can get a head start."

She touched my shoulder. "I am so glad ye found these good people and have sought after a noble cause. And I am so, so glad to see your face again, my dear friend."

I sensed a sorrow in her tone. "Oh Tyra, how have you been doing all this time? Has Ragnar been awful to you?"

Tyra lowered her face into her hand. "Oh, Sigrid, I can't explain."

"Do you hate him?" Every fiber of my being had been both longing and fearing to know the truth.

Letting her hand fall to her side, Tyra shook her head wearily. "Oh, no, Sigrid. I love him, but not in the way he wants me to. I love him as God loves him, as God loves us all. I am only one of his many women, and only a week ago I hated him to my very bones. But God graciously brought me to the place of loving him as I ought."

"You sound like Erik." I laughed silently to myself. Far too much like him.

"Does he follow Iosa?" Her higher tone revealed her sudden interest.

"I believe you love the same God but in different ways. I think Erik's downright scared of your God, but you're downright in love with Him."

She rubbed her chin. "Why is Erik afeard of Him?"

"Because Erik's the weakest man I know, if he even *is* a man." My words were harsh like a slap in the face, but I didn't care.

Tyra's face looked grave. "In our weaknesses, God's power can shine through. In our brokenness, light comes pouring through the cracks."

I stood up and regarded my surroundings. "These people are all Irish, aren't they?"

"No, not all of them. Stellan takes in widows and children who need a home. Most of them are Norse, but so is Stellan. I told him about Iosa a week ago, and he believed. Then the Holy Spirit, who is God living and guiding us in our hearts, put it on his heart to care for those in need. Now he is tellin' these women about Iosa."

"Why do you come here?" I asked her. "You already have a home."

Her face lit up with joy. "I help him care for these people and pour the truth into their lives. This blanket I am weavin' is for that elderly woman over in that corner. Winter's beginning, ye know, and she hasn't enough bedding to warm her at night."

I looked over at the old woman snoring in the corner. Her skin was very wrinkly, and her body trembled as she slept. She'd be dead if no one cared for her.

"Does Ragnar notice you're gone?"

"He doesn't care. He only wants me at night." She flipped her long hair behind her, so it wouldn't become entangled in the threads of the loom and returned to weaving the blanket.

I watched her skillful hands weave the yarn through the taut threads. The monotony and delicate work reminded me of my mother.

My dear mother must have been a gift from Frigg, the goddess of motherhood. As a child, Mum would tell me how Frigg gifted special yarn to mortal women whom she favored. Frigg must have favored Mum. Her yarn looked no different from the rest, but whenever I held a blanket she'd made, I'd feel my mother's presence. And now, as I watched Tyra, I felt it again. Oh, how I missed Mum. How I wanted to disappear from this life and see her again! Perhaps Tyra could soothe my weary spirit for now.

"Are you going to Ireland with Ragnar?" I asked her.

Grimacing, she slid her fingers through her hair. "He wouldn't leave without me."

"I want to go, too. I don't know how it will work now, now that Lars has gone already."

Tyra hushed me and closed her eyes. She put her thumb to her chin, her mouth slowly curving into a grin. "I have an idea."

I raised my eyebrows.

"Why don't we ask Gerd if she wouldn't mind you switching places with her? She looks a lot like you. Ragnar won't notice the difference with his poor eyesight and all. He never sleeps with Gerd anyhow. He just has her do the cooking, washing, and clothe-making with the rest of us."

I gave her a playful swat on the arm. "That's brilliant!" I hugged her. "Oh, thank you, Tyra. We shall journey to Ireland together."

Tyra gave a sad sort of face again, then stopped weaving. "I still cannot believe ye are here, Siri—I mean, Sigrid. You are here, and there's something I must tell you."

"Yes?"

She stood up, grabbed my wrist, and led me to the corner near the snoring old woman.

"What is it?" I gave a watery smile, concerned at her sharp movements.

She looked at me, looked back at the room, then looked me square in the eyes again. "I'm pregnant."

I broke into laughter. "You scared me, Tyra, I thought someone died or something! I figured that out by now. That's wonderful news!"

Tyra lowered her voice, so I almost couldn't hear. "Ragnar hates children."

"He doesn't have to take care of the child."

"You don't understand—he *killed* the last children his women birthed him." Tears streamed down her cheeks in little droplets. Tyra covered her face with her hands. "Oh, what am I to do? Iosa, help me!"

I wrapped my arms around her. "Please, don't cry, Tyra. You'll get through this."

"I—I hope so. It's been five moons since I conceived."

I remembered how she had held her abdomen in Kaupang, and how I had thought she was ill, however much she had cast aside my concern for her. Why hadn't I realized the truth before?

Stellan came toward us. I backed away, and he knelt before Tyra. "All will be well, dear one. Trust in God with all your heart. He loves you and your child." He stood. "Aine and the others are arriving."

She took a deep breath. "I'll be fine." She brushed away tears and turned to greet the Irish.

ᛉᛉᛉ

The widows gathered in a circle, chatting amiably amongst themselves. A few children sat by their mothers, while the rest played with one another nearby. One by one, a few thralls entered the longhouse and seated themselves among the women. Some Norsemen and women appeared as well and sat down among the rest of them. They wore finer clothing which marked them as freemen. Widows, thralls, and free people alike greeted one another with warm regard. I had never seen such a sight before. Classes amongst the Norse rarely associated with one another as if on equal footing. Had Iosa changed their hearts toward one another?

Tyra and Stellan joined them, but I stood in the corner, watching the crowd. My stomach felt sick. Each person in this room must follow Iosa, this strange half-god-half-man figure.

"Dear Heavenly Father," Stellan prayed, "thank You for this day You have created for us to enjoy. Please help us to honor You today. Remind us of the hope we have in You. Encourage our hearts. Thank You for sending Iosa to die for our sins. Let us rejoice in Your salvation today. We pray in Iosa's name, amen."

Murmurs of "amens" followed. I was clueless as to what the word meant, so I remained silent. Tyra motioned for me to join her, so I walked over and settled beside her on the earthen floor.

Stellan continued. "Before we begin, I would like to announce that Tyra will be leaving us all for some time, around a month or so. Please pray for her as she serves Ragnar on his pillaging voyage to Ireland and shows God's love to him."

Several of the women came over. I moved away from Tyra as they surrounded her and embraced her. For a while they prayed with her and spoke encouraging words to her. Each man and each woman had that same unmistakable glow in their eyes as Erik and Tyra. I could tell they loved her.

"And now I'd like to introduce you all to Sigrid." Stellan pointed me out. "Sigrid is her dear friend whom she had thought died—remember Tyra's stories about her?"

Many of them nodded. Men and women approached me and greeted me.

"Welcome, dear," a woman said in the most tender-hearted voice I'd ever heard.

Swallowing hard, I drew away from them until everyone sat down again. Then I seated myself down behind a tall man to avoid all the glances. Even as their love kindled something in my heart toward them, I began to feel an awful sensation in my gut that made me want to leave. Lars would have felt it, too. This was all so strange to me. There had to be some ulterior motive to their open affection toward me. What did they *really* want?

"Who needs prayer today?" Tyra asked.

A young boy with tousled blond hair spoke up by his mother's side. Most of the children were playing with toys at the end of the longhouse, but this child had stayed by his mother the whole time. He rested a hand on his mother's shoulder. "Broder wants to sell Mum and me."

Tyra gasped, "I am so sorry, Colm."

Several people expressed their sympathy to the mother and son, their voices sympathetic and soothing. I had to admit it—none of this seemed to be a façade.

An idea came to me, a way I could help the mother and son as well. I stood up, rising above the tall Irishman seated in front of me. "I know someone who is purchasing thralls so he can have help rowing to Ireland. His name is Lars. This man hopes to warn the Irish people about Ragnar's attack. I bet if you asked him, he'd let you come along and stay in Ireland once you get there. He isn't too bad of a fellow when it comes to women. Tell him Sigrid sent you."

"Truly?" Colm's mother asked, her face flushed with joy. "That would be a mighty blessing if I could take my boy home, to our real home, and be free."

A few other Irish thralls spoke up. "We'd like to go too."

Once again, men and women surrounded Colm's mother, Colm, and the other thralls who had decided to go. They prayed fervently for them. I had never heard such prayers or seen such compassion before. These prayers didn't feel monotonous or recited. They felt real and powerful. They trusted this God was hearing their requests, and they believed He was going to do something on their behalf.

"Why don't I go and tell my friend about you?" I suggested. "He is leaving as soon as he can."

Stellan shook his head. "It is too dangerous for a young woman at night. I will go. Where will I find him?"

I paused to think about it. "My guess is he has found an inn for the night. Ask around for the name Lars. Knowing him, he's probably gotten to know half the village by now."

Stellan nodded. "I will go to the local inn and find him."

For the rest of the meeting, the Iosa-followers prayed for sick ones, for guidance, and for all who did not believe in Iosa to be drawn to Him. Then the tall man rolled out scrolls and read from them. He spoke of the Spirit and the flesh, but they made no sense to me. However, the people around me murmured and discussed the Scripture with deep interest and understanding. At last, the man rolled up the scrolls and set them aside.

Then, the people raised their voices in song. Their loud, soaring notes filled the longhouse with passion as they filled my heart with wonder. Tyra's voice rose above everyone else's, high and strong.

"The Lord is my light and my salvation—whom shall I fear? The Lord is the stronghold of my life—of whom shall I be afraid? When the wicked advance against me to devour me, it is my enemies and my foes who will stumble and fall. Though an army besiege me, my heart will not fear; though war break out against me, even then will I be confident."

Fear, I thought. Confidence. Erik loathed himself, but Tyra had a confidence in her God that shone bright and clear in her smile, her laugh, her song. If Tyra's God and Erik's God were the same, why did Erik act so afraid?

He ought not to be such a coward all the time with the kind of God he has. I wondered if talking to Tyra would give Erik an ounce of confidence and make him stop acting like such a fool. Perhaps they would meet each other on the voyage, should Ragnar drag the Irishman along.

When the thralls and free people left, Tyra and I bade our goodbyes to the widows and children then returned to Ragnar's longhouse. Ragnar's other thralls were already fast asleep on either side of the longhouse, and Ragnar was still chasing after treasure. I didn't need to worry about him finding me out.

But I did.

"He's going to find me; he's going to kill me," I repeated in a panicked whisper, pacing about the room.

Tyra laid down a blanket over a mat for my bed. "Go to sleep, Sigrid. He's not goin' to recognize ye." She stopped me from pacing and tugged me over to my mat. I pulled the blanket over me, weariness seeping through me. Tyra curled up beside me. "It's going to be okay. You're going to be all right, Sigrid. God's going to protect ye. I prayed for it. The Irish did, each one of them."

My pulse quickened. "You told them about how I was the chosen slave girl?"

Turning on her side to face me, she smiled. "I told them to pray that God would protect ye. That's all they needed to know. God knows the rest."

I squeezed my eyes shut, willing myself to sleep so I wouldn't have to listen to her any longer. I loved her, but I couldn't bear her words. I couldn't bear to hear about a God who hated killing.

"We also prayed ye'd find what you're looking for."

My eyes flitted open. The idea struck me. It reminded me of the doll in my satchel lying beside my pillow. The doll with her head straight up. The doll with her pride.

"What am I looking for?" I whispered.

Tyra pulled her blanket up to her chin and stared up at the thatched roof above us. "Sometimes I feel like there's this huge space inside me, wider and emptier than a starless night. Nothin' I do can fill it up. Nothin' but God, nothin' but the grace He has given us through Iosa. That may not be what you're looking for, but it's what we all *need*, Sigrid. If it weren't for God bursting inside of me, I wouldn't be able to stand Ragnar. I'd run. He'd catch me and whip me. I'd run again. But with God, I've learned to have compassion on Ragnar. I've learned to fill this void with Iosa's love and His strength."

Tyra gave a gentle, rippling laugh. "God is good, Siri. He is so good. He gives me strength. He gave me the strength to tell Ragnar about Him. Ragnar hasn't changed, but I have. And I pray someday he will change—and ye will, too."

I said nothing.

"Good night, dear friend. I love ye. Iosa loves ye."

I moved my tongue around my mouth, but I couldn't speak. I couldn't tell her she was wrong about her God, about everything.

She had felt something, but it was only a feeling; she had thought something, but it was only a thought. Iosa didn't love me. Iosa didn't even know me! Tyra's experience with Ragnar was awful, so she had to deal with it the only way she knew how.

Yet my heart was touched by her love and her strength. It couldn't have come from a fake god, but it was beautiful. It was a pity her beautiful soul was wasted pouring into the life of that wretched man. Would she ever realize her efforts to love him could never thaw his icy heart?

NINETEEN

THE FOLLOWING MORNING AT BREAKFAST, Tyra asked me to accompany her to Stellan's since Ragnar had not returned yet.

While I wasn't excited about the thought of hearing about Iosa all day, I agreed. I would do anything for Tyra. I just wanted to stay by her side.

When we had arrived at Stellan's longhouse, Stellan greeted us warmly. "The Irish thralls have set out with your good friend Lars, along with a few other thralls he bought."

Lars. He was completing our mission, all alone. Would he succeed in warning the Irish before Ragnar got there on his swift longships? I sighed inwardly. I didn't need to fret about Lars. He was being sensible, doing as he ought to. It was Erik who troubled me. Ragnar was a pitiless man. If Erik couldn't find the cave with the treasure, who knew what could happen to him? It irked me to admit it, but I worried about that fellow.

Tyra spoke to me, drawing me out of my thoughts. "Sigrid, many of the mothers need help with the children's clothes. I could use yer sewing skills."

I surveyed the room at the sorry lot of families without husbands or fathers. As she had told me, they were mostly Norse, but a few were Irish. It was a marvel that all could be living together in such harmony.

"Of course, I'll help you," I said.

I followed Tyra's orders, not because I was forced to, but because I wished to please her. After all, these poor women needed all the help they could get. It was an unusual feeling—extraordinary, really—of working to be of some use, instead of doing it for fear of a lashing.

A few hours went by, as I sewed the children's clothing. Tyra sat beside me sewing some fabric as well while she chatted with the women. When I had finished my work, a middle-aged woman approached me.

She jerked her head toward her loom. "Would you mind working at it for me? I have other business to attend to in the market."

I agreed and sat at her stool before the half-finished blanket. An hour passed. I labored with the wool, weaving it through the loom, over and over. For the first time in my life, I found pleasure in the simple chore. I watched as the colors came together in a beautiful pattern of alternating blue and yellow.

Then a pale girl with many freckles approached me and spoke to me in a soft voice, "Will you come play with us?"

I eyed the group of children behind her, who were watching me curiously. Perhaps I looked like a pleasant addition to their game.

"We are going to play 'Run away'!"

I remembered the simple game of chase from my childhood. I set the yarn down and stood up. Soon I was caught up playing with the children. Their laughter soothed me. Tyra and the other women laughed at the sight of us chasing each other about. There was abundant joy in the place, so much more than I had ever experienced. If only Mum were here.

"You really love these people, don't you?" I stopped before Tyra, breathless.

"I do," she answered, a blissful look in her eyes. "They are my family."

"It must be comforting to be with some of your own people." I regarded the other Irish women and children.

"Yes," she replied. "But I am just as much doin' it for the Norse. We are all the same in the end, Sigrid. We all need Iosa to truly live."

I stared at her, disagreeing but admiring her confidence. "Tyra, I love you." Then I hugged her tightly, and she returned my embrace.

In the early evening, Tyra assigned me to a pot of stew to watch over. As I stirred the meat and herbs, I watched Tyra hold a partially made dress beneath a small girl's chin to gauge the length.

"Ah, Mita, you've grown so much!" She tickled the child under her chin. The girl giggled and ran off with the unfinished dress, looking playfully back at Tyra. Tyra laughed. "Go get 'er," she told a little boy.

Soon all the children were laughing and dashing back and forth through the narrow room once again. Their never-ending energy amazed me. Tyra watched the children as if they were her own.

But they were not. They were children of unknown mothers, and yet Tyra loved them as if she had borne them herself. Even if I tried, I knew I could not muster up that kind of love, except for Mum. But I loved Mum because she loved me. These children loved Tyra because she loved them, and she loved them for some unknown reason! Tyra's love made no sense. She gained nothing from loving these impish children.

I jabbed a piece of meat with the wooden spoon, easing it back and forth till it tore in half.

"Oh, Tyra, take the children outside, will you?" raged the old woman in the corner I had pitied the other day. "It's about time I had a bath!"

Tyra ushered the children out the door, assigning the oldest one to keep watch over them. "All right, Noomi." Tyra hastened over to the other side of the room again.

"I don't get enough baths around here," Noomi muttered.

Tyra helped the old woman undress, and she supported her into a large bucket of water that had been warmed by the fire. Then she scrubbed the old woman's hair and skin with lye. The whole time, she talked softly to the elderly woman, to ease her temper. Soon Noomi was dressed and drying by the fire with a toothy smile on her face.

Tyra let the children back in. They scampered about the room to find places to play around. Tyra watched them, a quiet smile building on her face. She seemed to oversee everything while Stellan was gone. When Tyra left, how would Stellan care for these people?

By evening, my body was weak and tired, yet it was the most invigorating exhaustion I'd ever felt. I had done something that had meant so much to these women. Their grateful looks and smiles were all I needed to feel like it had been worth it. When Stellan arrived home, he and all the women and children ate up the lamb stew around the fire.

"Would ye like to come with Stellan and me?" Tyra asked me when we had finished. "We're off to make some deliveries to the poor."

I looked at her through bleary eyes. In truth, I wanted to lie on a warm mat and sleep the night away. Yet another part of me longed to please my sweet friend and to be around her.

"Of course," I answered, though exhaustion drained me, seeping the energy out of me. Being with her was too lovely a thing to miss.

"Ye really don't have to, Sigrid," she said. "I know ye must be tired from the day's work."

I shook my head. "I want to spend more time with you. It's been too long."

Her face lit up. "It certainly has."

We set out to bring food and warm blankets to poor people around Bergen.

I trudged behind Tyra and Stellan through the town. Longhouses lined the street on either side of us. I held a bag of dried meat and fresh herbs and vegetables. I had never seen anyone treat people like this before, like they mattered despite their place in life.

"Why do you do this?" I asked.

"We are loving them because God loves them," Stellan said. We approached the slave quarters of a nearby longhouse. It was a small thatched-roof hut where thralls crammed inside.

"But if your God loves them so much, shouldn't He be the one giving?"

Tyra smiled, her face radiant with peace. "He is givin'. He is givin' us the love so we can learn to give it away." She paused before the door. Then she knocked a steady, memorized rhythm.

A young man opened it, dirty and tattered clothing marking him as a thrall. His eyes widened as soon as he saw the supplies we carried in our arms. "Do come in."

We entered the straw-thatched hut. Stellan and Tyra greeted each one of the thralls with warmth. "It is so good to see you all again," Tyra said.

Tears fell from a thrall woman's face as she grasped Tyra's hands. "I don't know what we'd do without you all."

I watched in wonder as Tyra and Stellan prayed for the thralls. They prayed for good health, food to fill their stomachs, and favor from their master. They even prayed for their master, that he would come to believe in Iosa. The way they prayed for him wasn't hard or bitter. Their words were full of compassion. How could they care for their master despite his obvious neglect toward them?

When Tyra and Stellan had finished, the thralls expressed their deep gratitude for the supplies.

I tried to hide behind Tyra, but a woman asked, "What's your name?"

"Sigrid," I answered her shortly.

"You have good friends, Sigrid," she told me.

She embraced me when I left. Everyone said goodbye to not only Tyra and Stellan, but to me as well, as if I were a part of them. Yet I had done nothing but involve myself in their good deeds.

When we left, the young man who had opened the door for us bowed his head in respect. "I thank you, Tyra." He raised his head, searching her face tenderly.

Tyra lowered her head, blushing.

"God bless you, sir," Stellan shook the man's hand earnestly.

And we turned from them and left the hut. We began the trail back to Stellan's house. The wind was sharp, like a blade, but my mind was flooded with questions as I pulled my cloak around me more securely to fend off the chilly air.

"What do you think of every man looking at you like that?" I asked my friend.

Tyra chuckled, glancing warily at Stellan. "Oh, I don't know, Sigrid. Maybe I should shave my hair."

"No, it's beautiful."

"It is!" Stellan responded, too quickly, in my opinion.

Tyra rolled her eyes. "That's why I should shave it off."

We laughed, a good healing laugh that cleansed my soul. I forgot all about my weariness. When I was with Tyra, I could breathe again.

The days swept by like waves, over and over, the same thing—helping, caring, serving. But most of all loving. Loving in a deep, tender way I had never seen before in such magnitude. A love as deep as the ocean.

I wasn't sure if I had any of that in me. I mirrored Tyra, did what she did, faked a smile as hard as I could, worked as hard as I could. I did my best, however little it may have been compared to Tyra's work.

While we cared for people, I waited in anticipation for Ragnar to return. A feeling like that of the rising sun coursed through me whenever I thought of his death—my victory.

But did I have that in me? Could I slay him, slay myself, then leave Tyra and these needy people behind?

At night, I escaped Ragnar's crowded longhouse. I ran through the forest as far away as I could without getting lost. I found a nearby fern tree and stood before it, letting my imagination take over. I slashed the tree, over and over. If it didn't teach me how to handle a sword, it at least released the anger bottled up inside me. At the end of seven days, I was sure I would chop it down if I gave it one more blow, so I switched to another, larger fern.

The nighttime reminded me of who I was and what I had come to do. I forced myself to think of only two human beings: Ragnar and Mum. I was alive to slay Ragnar so I could meet Mum again.

That was all.

One morning, after serving the poor for eight days straight and tree-fighting for seven nights, someone knocked on the door of Stellan's longhouse.

Stellan opened it. Standing on the threshold was the girl I had first met at Ragnar's longhouse. The one who had mocked Tyra.

"Is Tyra here?" she asked, a hand on her hip. Her gaze flashed to Stellan, then at the women and children behind him, and then at us. "Jarl Ragnar demands to see her."

"He returned from treasure hunting, Freyja?" Stellan asked, his voice calm and composed.

"Last night," Freyja nodded. "And he wants to spend time with Tyra before he leaves. Come on now, girl!"

I stood frozen at Tyra's side.

Tyra sat still, her eyes clouded as she seemed to be looking but not seeing.

"Jarl Ragnar *demands* it."

Tyra stirred from her stationary stance and headed to the door. I followed close behind.

When Tyra came to Stellan, she stopped and stared up at him. Stellan looked back at her, the muscle in his jaw working. He held out his hand, and Tyra trembled as she took it.

"Stellan," she choked. "If it weren't for Ragnar I'd—"

I wept inwardly at the pained look on her face.

"I know." Stellan's hand tightened around Tyra's. "May the Lord be with you on your journey."

Freyja clenched her teeth. "Jarl Ragnar will be with *you* if you don't come this minute."

Tyra didn't glance at the girl as she walked past. I paused before exiting and turned to the man, Tyra's love.

"Thank you, Stellan, for all your kind hospitality."

"Come on!" Freyja commanded.

I couldn't bear it. I slapped her cheek. "You aren't going to even let us say goodbye?"

Freyja screeched, touching her cheek. "You think I'm doing this because I want to?"

"Sigrid," Stellan said.

I ignored him and stared at her, my jaw set. I knew the feeling of doing what you didn't want to do. But I turned away.

"Sigrid," Tyra's voice was soft.

"She deserved it."

I paused, then looked up at my friend. She appeared on the verge of crying.

Freyja came up beside us. "Hurry up! I've never seen more impudent thralls in my life."

TWENTY

WE ENTERED THE LONGHOUSE, MY sweaty hand clasping Tyra's. Every widow and wife was busy either weaving or sewing. At the sight of us, their fingers paused at their work and they stared at us. A strange silence fell about the room. I recognized the meaning in their looks at once. Tyra was in trouble.

Freyja turned to me. "You stay here and put yourself to some use. And you," she turned to Tyra, "Ragnar wants you." She tugged on her arm and took her behind the curtain, where Ragnar's room must have been.

I stood still and listened.

"Where have you been?" Ragnar growled.

My limbs shook at the familiar voice.

"It took you forever to come," he thundered.

"I have been at Stellan's, Master."

"Who do you think you are to run off to that man's house, girl?"

"Ye never said I couldn't, sir. And I always come back at night. Ye haven't seemed to mind, Master."

Ragnar made a low, guttural sound, and a whip resounded. Tyra screamed. I clapped my hand over my mouth to keep myself from crying out. Freyja had apparently seen enough, for she slipped back into the main room to rejoin the working women.

I reached for the curtain, but Freyja pulled me back. "He'll kill you!" she snapped.

I struggled out of her grasp, straining my body forward, but Freyja held me tightly. She was too strong for me to push aside. I finally gave up and stood there for a long time, Freyja holding my wrists firmly, until the noise of the lashing stopped.

At the sound of voices talking, I looked up at Freyja. "Who else is back there?" I whispered.

She shrugged and strode past me. No doubt she hadn't forgotten how I'd slapped her not long ago. "The new head servant who led Jarl Ragnar to his treasure since the jarl freed Niels and gave him a position as captain."

So, Erik had secured that vital position and Niels was free. Certainly Erik would be coming along to Ireland as well. I was glad for myself but terrified for him. I liked having him around—but, by the gods, Ragnar better not kill him in a rage before he reached his homeland.

"He never found the treasure?" a woman asked.

Freyja was not interested in giving details. Instead, she leaned toward a nearby woman and spoke in a quiet, yet distinct voice, "I caught a few more glances at the young man—he sure is a sight to see."

"In a good way or a bad way?" the young woman asked.

Freyja laughed, a deep, low laughter. "Oh, better than you've ever laid eyes on." She spoke in a wistful way that, no doubt, made each woman picture him in their minds. She muttered something more, but I could hear only the last part: "So very thin but strong, and the most charming red hair."

The women murmured their approval and Freyja's friend gave a long sigh. I rolled my eyes.

"What is wrong with you foolish women?" I asked. "He might have a wife and children of his own." I couldn't stand having a bunch of girls sighing over him. He'd feel uncomfortable, I knew, and he was too weak to defend himself. "Who do you think you are to let your minds run over such childish things?"

"We're only amusing ourselves, darling," replied Freyja, a lilt in her voice.

I glared at her. "You ought to be ashamed of yourself."

She scowled and tried to shoo me away. "Get to work now. Clean the master's chamber pot."

With practiced obedience, I grabbed the chamber pot and a dirty cloth and headed to the door.

I made my way toward the dock. I could have used the well water, but I always found that saltwater cleansed chamber pots more thoroughly. Of course, Ragnar would ruin its luster in a short amount of time, but what better place to perform the lowliest chore than the ocean?

I arrived at the wharf, the sea before me, glistening in the noon sunlight. Hundreds of longships made their home in the bay, tied and fastened to the land. A rush of joy surged through my chest. I leaned out on the railing overhanging the ocean, my white-blonde braid falling over my shoulder. The creaking of the longships and the wailing cries of the seabirds were delightful.

A mountain, lush and green, rose ahead of me, and the sea swept in the bay on either side of me. If I squinted hard enough, I could see where the fjord ran free into the open ocean.

I stood there for a while, breathing in the briny sea air, so familiar and strong, like a whiff from home. I pulled out my doll from her satchel, dear Siri the thrall girl, with the beautiful green dress and the straw hair. She evoked memories of Mum. *Tonight*, I thought. On our first night at sea, I would do it.

I prayed the gods would give me the strength to defeat him. I would have to be strong and alert against this sword-fighting warrior. I shuddered as I imagined him raising his sword above Mum as she cried out to me, flailing her arms out toward me. My lungs were on fire as the ropes tightened around my neck. My voice squeaked out to her, but Jarl Ragnar's sword shot downward, stabbing my mother in the chest.

I squeezed my eyes shut. There's no reason to remember such things. I'll be with Mum again in no time.

A hand rested on my shoulder. I jumped and whirled around.

"Greetings, lass," Erik said, a grim smile on his face.

I shook myself. "By the gods, you scared the life out of me."

"I hope not."

So very thin but strong, and the most charming red hair. Now that I thought about it, Freyja had described him exactly as he was. Lowering my head quickly, I stuffed the doll in its satchel and fastened the small bag around my waist. "How did you know I was here?" I grabbed the chamber pot and hunkered down. The foul odor turned my stomach.

"A lass told me ye were cleanin' the chamber pot, and I assumed since ye fancy the ocean so well."

I raised the loaded pot and tossed the contents into the harbor. We both backed off.

"How clever of you," I muttered.

"Why didn't ye go with Lars?" he asked, his voice sad. He seemed to still respect the man who had hated him enough to kill him. Or maybe he wanted to believe that Lars was the same man he had known before this whole adventure. I wanted to think well of Lars, too, but I simply couldn't anymore. I could only hope he completed our mission honorably.

"I stayed because of Tyra," I explained. "She's my friend, and I wanted to be with her."

I sank the clay pot into the water, letting the remaining particles loosen, so I could rub off the scum with the dirty cloth. I didn't know how true it was that I'd stayed only for Tyra.

"So, Lars went alone." He broke the silence.

"He set off a week ago, with plenty of Irish thralls, just as we planned." I scrubbed the circumference of the pot. "He's still trying; I can't believe it, but he's still trying."

"May God be with him."

It made me uncomfortable that he'd wish good things for the fellow who hated him. I changed the subject. "How was it, taking Ragnar to the treasure? Did you remember the way?"

"Aye, I did," Erik replied. "I wrote down the directions in the scrolls. I write down everything, ye know, when I have the time."

I scrubbed then rinsed the clay pot out again. After I emptied the water, I placed it on the ground. It gleamed from the light of the noonday sun. "I heard Ragnar never got the treasure."

Erik sighed. "Aye, that's what I came here to talk to ye about. Do ye know where Gunnar is?"

My mouth opened for a moment before I spoke. "He's dead. Ragnar killed him. That's why you had to show him the way."

I had promised Lars, so I dared not say more.

"Oh." He looked up at the green mountains and whispered, "I'm mighty sorry."

"Why didn't Ragnar get his treasure?" I put my hands on my hips, asking the long-awaited question.

His forehead wrinkled. "He and Joar fought over it. Jarl Ragnar won."

"He killed his brother?"

"Aye," Erik grimaced. "And when Ragnar realized what he had done, he burned the whole lot of treasure. Now Ragnar has doubled his regrets: killin' his brother and burnin' up the treasure."

My nails bit into my palms. I glanced at the ocean, then at the town packed with people, and finally up at Erik. "By the gods, what's he going to do next? Slaughter the whole village?"

Erik shook his head. "He regrets it, Sigrid. He regretted it enough to burn up mounds of treasure. Maybe that's the next step toward him asking Iosa for forgiveness."

"Forgiveness?" I was dumbfounded. "How could anyone forgive *him*?"

"The Ruler of heaven and earth can," replied Erik weakly, hurt edged in his voice. "But ye wouldn't believe that. Ye don't care."

"Then why do you even tell me?" My blood ran like fire through my veins.

He turned away and whispered, "Because I care, lass, even if it's all hopeless. I care even if there's no point at all."

My fingers tightened around the chamber pot. I hated his foolish ways. Did he care, or did he merely say what his guilt-causing God told him to say?

Raising the pot to my shoulder, I glanced at his tall, gentle figure. "Let's go back. They're preparing to leave, you know."

ᛉᛉᛉ

Over the course of two days, Jarl Ragnar selected men from Bergen and Kaupang to plunder with him on four large longships. Then they began to pack all the goods they needed for the journey.

On the second day, Tyra drew Gerd outside of the longhouse away from the other women, while Ragnar was out on some business. "Could you do us a favor, Gerd?"

She blinked three times.

"Don't worry, it won't be of any cost to you." Tyra smiled, then gestured to me. "You see, Sigrid here is wanting to go to Ireland. She looks a mighty lot like you, and so we thought perhaps you could switch places."

Gerd's eyes bore into me. The same plain gray color. Her white-blonde hair curled down her shoulders like mine did. She was slenderly-built, like me. Did she have this terrible feeling always weighing her down like I did?

Gerd finally spoke. "So you're telling me, she's goin' off with the men plunderin' for riches and I'm stayin' here?"

I twisted a tendril of hair around my finger. Putting it like that sure didn't make it sound all that wonderful.

"If you don't mind," Tyra replied. "It's your choice, of course."

My friend was too kind. If this had been my plan, I'd threaten her with my sword.

I watched Gerd pull her brows down in deep concentration. "That don't seem fair. That don't seem fair at all! I've never gotten to go plunderin' before—not in my life."

Tyra forced a smile. "But you see, Gerd, you won't be in any danger of getting taken advantage of if you stay here."

"And you know how awful those men can be," I added. "I've heard they especially get antsy for women on the high seas."

I swallowed hard at the words that came out of my mouth. How would I survive them?

Gerd crossed her arms and huffed. Then she scratched her chin for a full minute before she responded. "So those men will take all they want from her at night, and I'll stay here safe and sound?"

I sucked in my breath.

Tyra hesitated. "I am praying to Iosa against that happening to Sigrid, but you certainly won't be bothered in this longhouse full of women. What do you say, Gerd?"

"Well." She twisted her mouth and looked at me. "You sure ya don't mind those men gettin' their hands all over ya?"

Her words hit me like a boulder, and I wanted to flee the room. I stood frozen, her question echoing inside me, haunting me. She had no idea that was the last thing I desired.

Tyra glanced at me and bit her lip.

I nodded at her in response. "Of course, we women must risk many terrible situations in life in order to get what we want."

While rape was the last thing I desired, there was one thing I desired more that made the risk worth it all: slaying that awful man.

"All right, if you say so," Gerd relented with big sigh. "Just stay away from Niels, ladies. He seduced Freyja one time to sleep with him against her will."

My shoulders tightened. Niels. The former head servant of Ragnar had been as cruel as the jarl at times, being eager to do whatever his master asked of him.

After Gerd went back inside, Tyra clasped my hand. "I am praying hard, Sigrid. That's all I can say."

"We'll avoid him," I said. "We'll try to get onto another ship or something. He is the only one besides Ragnar who knows who I am, the only one who'd remember."

"Yes, Gerd, we'll do what we can."

I had to think twice at her use of my new name. I was Gerd now. I drank in the morning air deeply, realizing for the first time how crisp it was today. I would have an identity on this voyage, and it wouldn't be me. Niels had better not find me out, and those men had better not even think of touching me.

When the time had almost come to depart, I ran to the wharf. As a child I'd often liked to watch the men prepare for the raids, packing things up, ecstatic for their upcoming plunders. Now, I wanted to experience it again, the watching and the anticipation, as I had so often done with my mother.

Yet as I drew closer, I observed a large crowd of people wailing and mourning and some men pushing a longship out to sea. I watched as the slave girl clutched the side of the ship, staring back at the land, seeming to even stare back at me.

"Oh, dearly beloved Joar!" the people called out. "May Valhalla greet you warmly!"

The men ignited their arrows on fire and began shooting them at the ship. Soon flames consumed the vessel. I had not thought quickly enough. I couldn't rescue this thrall girl, as Tyra and Mum had tried to rescue me.

The men were rattling shields loudly. Longship funerals were not common, but the wealthy Jarl Valdemar had requested on his deathbed that each one of his seven sons ought to have one. I searched the front, of the crowd, the honored place where Ragnar belonged. Ragnar didn't even bother coming to his brother's funeral, the wretch!

I spotted Erik at the edge of the sea, staring out at the longship they were preparing to burn. I made my way over to him. He dipped his head in acknowledgment of me as I approached him.

Dark clouds hung about, looking eager to empty themselves. Wind flung my hair in my face.

Men and women wailed according to proper custom, just as they had for Jarl Valdemar. The memory of that funeral made me sick to my stomach. I missed Mum more than ever.

I hugged my arms to my chest in the freezing rain.

"You know a lot about that girl." His voice was quiet and even.

"Yes." I hadn't talked about this with him before, but he knew as well as Lars what I had been chosen for.

His lips formed a grim line. "What do ye know of her?"

A lump formed in my throat. "She is scared, so scared to die, so scared that the fire will hurt, and the afterlife will be worse than real life."

We watched as the men shot more and more flaming arrows, and the fiery longship plunged into the sea along with all its possessions. The memories tore at me. The life bleeding out of Mum. The pure, unrestrained fear that gripped me, as the rope tightened around my neck, bit by bit. The burning, burning fire, and the sting of the saltwater. The panic. The horror. The going down, down, down into the depths of the sea.

"The fire is awful." My voice shook. Suddenly, I grew conscious of myself. Why was I talking like this? I didn't know why I was telling him about my horrible past.

Erik pinched his lips together. "I'm sorry ye had to go through that. The rituals, too. No one should have to go through such things."

I swallowed the words that threatened to come out. He would never understand what I'd gone through. I searched for something else to say. "I—I swung the sword at a tree the nights you were gone."

"Ye did?" Distress shone in his eyes, as if sword handling was the most awful thing I could teach myself, the mere woman that I was.

My cheeks flushed. I realized I had hinted at the violence in my heart. I assessed the turmoil of the sea, determined to avoid his gaze.

I thought he would say something about his God not liking swords, but he was silent.

Though I was trying to be proud of my tree-whacking abilities, the crashing waves were nothing compared to the gnawing fear inside me. I didn't know how to kill a man. I feared for the future. I feared I would never regain the honor that was stripped away from me on that night of Jarl Valdemar's funeral.

TWENTY-ONE

I HELD MY SMALL BAG of belongings close to my chest, as the men packed supplies onto each longship. Tyra stood beside me. The men sang in low, merry voices in anticipation of their great victory and the heaps of stolen goods they'd have to share with their families.

Though I used to enjoy watching them as a child, my stomach was churning, dampening the joy of this moment. I tried to keep my head up, to act normal, like I was supposed to be here, but inside, I could hardly keep myself together. Someone was going to find me out.

One man grazed his eyes over me as he gripped a barrel in his brawny arm.

My legs trembled, and I nodded vaguely toward him in acknowledgment.

He snarled before throwing the barrel into a ship. Did he know who I was?

Tyra tugged at my arm. "You're just beautiful. They're not thinking anything else."

I pressed my lips together. I sure hoped she was right. As far as we knew, none of the men besides Ragnar knew Gerd, so I'd rely on his poor eyesight to keep me from being exposed.

Soon a man shouted at us, "Wenches, this one's your ship, right oe'r here, with Cap'n Niels!" He directed us to a longship, where Niels stood upright on the deck.

A sour taste filled my mouth. Niels knew me. Niels knew me too well. He would surely tell Ragnar exactly who I was. And, at the remembrance of Gerd's warning, he probably wouldn't mind taking me to bed with him while he was at it.

I glanced at Tyra anxiously.

She clutched my arm and whispered into my ear. "You are welcome to back out if you think it's too dangerous."

I pushed my shoulders back and lifted my chin. "I'll risk it, Tyra. I'll risk it all."

If it came down to it, I would find a way to kill myself rather than let Niels take advantage of me. But I couldn't miss this chance to kill the man who deserved death more than anyone.

Tyra and I settled in the hull with Freyja. Men filled the longship—brawny, reeking, unshaven Norse raiders. *Vikings*, as the Irish called them. I was no fool; I knew the danger these men could cause a young woman like me. Thank the gods I had a weapon, yet I would be killed if Ragnar caught me with it—his renowned bronze sword. I had to keep it safe and close to my side, hidden under my cloak.

After the longship was filled, men from the land pushed the longships out into the waters, and the fleet set off. The rowers maneuvered the ships out into the open sea. Clear sky came into fuller view, and the waves lapped gently against the sides of the ships. Cool salty air gust past my face, making me tremble under my cloak.

"Get to work, girls." Freyja threw some clothing into our laps along with spools of thread with needles sticking out of them.

I picked up the clothing and a needle and thread and glanced around. There was no tent set up to obscure our view of the deck. Niels marched back and forth through the hull and to the other ends of the ship, and I quivered each time he passed. At least he was focused on captaining his ship, and not on us women. I relaxed a little as I saw Erik rowing the ship near us.

He met my gaze and smiled. I slipped a needle through a cloak then motioned to the redhead. "Tyra, this is Erik."

Tyra smiled at him and said, "Good evenin', Erik. I've seen you around, but never got the chance to talk with ye."

"Good evenin', Tyra."

Silence fell. Erik kept rowing. His arms strained against the waves, pushing us forward.

Niels strode past us and yelled, "Left oars only!"

I lowered my head and sewed the fabric quickly.

Tyra cleared her throat and attempted conversation with Erik again. "I heard ye read to Jarl Ragnar out of the scrolls last night during dinner. It's rare to meet someone who can unravel the mysteries of the scrolls."

The boy paused at his oar. "Ye believe, too?"

"Pa taught me as a young child all about Iosa back in Ireland. I will never forget that pure, unselfish love he showed me and everyone he met. So beyond human love. Ye don't know it until ye see it, you know?"

"I know precisely." I'd never seen his expression so full of delight.

"You're Irish, too, aren't you?" Tyra asked, her needlework sitting untouched in her lap.

"Aye, I am."

She spoke to him in Irish. Erik's eyes lit up as he replied. The thick tongue confused me, but their low, gentle voices were beautiful. I sewed the coat, listening for a long while, trying to understand something of what they were saying. Finally, I'd had enough. "Can you speak in a language I can understand?"

Tyra smiled and shifted effortlessly back to Norse. "My Irish name is Ciara, but ye can call me Tyra. That was the name they gave me as a thrall."

I remembered Tyra telling me this before, but I hadn't given it much thought at the time. It must be strange to have two names.

"Do ye have an Irish name, too?" Tyra asked Erik.

"Eamon." Sadness filled his gaze. "But that's a different life. This life is a new life, a new adventure in the realm of Norway. I just have people call me Erik now."

Tyra gave a little head bow. "'Tis a pleasure meetin' ye, Erik."

"Will you change your name back once we get to Ireland?" I asked him.

"My family won't be there, so, no." Erik lowered his chin. "I s'pose the true meaning of my old name is that my family gave it to me and called me by it. I don't want anyone to say it anymore, for their sake."

At my nod of understanding, Tyra and Erik conversed further in the Irish tongue, eagerly spouting off the strange flurry of words.

I watched them uncertainly. What had happened to Erik's family? How did he know so certainly that they were gone?

Tyra embraced Erik. "My dear brother."

"He's your *brother*?" I exclaimed.

"No, not in that way." Tyra shook her head and laughed. "But we are children of God. He is a Christian, like me."

I knew that. They worshipped the same God. The only difference was how they reacted to their God; how they saw Him. Did Tyra believe Iosa hated killing, too?

"Erik, you told me that your God does not like murder." At his nod, I turned to Tyra. "Is it true?"

"It is indeed," she whispered. "Why would ye even need to ask that?"

I was grieved that I had offended her by my question, but I had to get some answers. "I want to know about your God."

I threaded the needle in and out in slow movements, waiting for her reply. If this God were real—if there was any chance He could be—well, I had to consider what He could do to me.

Tyra reached out and rested her hand on my shoulder, searching my face. "What is it ye need to know?"

"You know Ragnar is an awful man. Is he going to a good place?"

"Ye care about him?" She squeezed my hand, her voice tremulous.

Erik shook his head. "She doesn't care for him."

Overhearing us from a few feet away, Freyja snorted from a few feet away. "Ragnar's going to Valhalla—all the honorable jarls go there."

"Only if they die in battle," I reminded her, ignoring Erik's brutal honesty.

"Oh, please," Freyja said. "Why do you care about him?"

Tyra squeezed my hand again, comforting me.

"She doesn't care for him," Erik repeated.

"I care!" I threw my hands in the air, flustered. Why was he so certain of that? So certain of the very thing that was most true about me.

Erik's lips parted as if to speak, but then Tyra broke in. "It's right that Gerd should wonder about the afterlife. "Unfortunately, if ye fail to accept God's grace through His Son Iosa, ye will not go to a good place, whether ye've committed murder or not." She turned to me. She squeezed my hand. "All have sinned, Gerd. Without Iosa, I'd burn in hell, too. But with him, I have life, and I have it to the full."

The thought of going to hell sent fear pulsing in my veins. But it sounded too horrible to be true. And a full life? It sounded too *wonderful* to be true. It couldn't be possible. Whoever Iosa was, He belonged to the Irish—to Tyra and Erik. I belonged to the Norse gods, who, if they disregarded my sin of escaping my fate, would bless me for my resolve to honor my dead mother. Wouldn't they?

I returned my attention to my work pulling the needle back and forth through the cloak.

Perhaps this would be the night I would see Mum's face again. That was what mattered. The question was, where was she? She had not been a valiant warrior, so she couldn't have gone to Valhalla. I had a chance of going there for the fight I'd go through against Ragnar, but Mum had died in the sea.

Odin, I pleaded to the god of life, *see the honor Mum had, that she would love me so. Please bring her to your place if she is not already there. And, somehow, see my act against this evil man as honorable, too.*

My prayer seemed futile as soon as I ushered it out. I felt no power in it, as I had felt in the prayers of the people in Stellan's house. My belief in the Norse gods was so dry, while Tyra's faith in Iosa was living and active like a growing flame, ready to capture anyone in sight.

Anyone but me.

As the longships caught the westward current, a few men secured long, thick ropes to connect each longship to one another, then the rowers lay down to sleep. Freyja, Tyra, and I put away our half-finished garments and curled up with thin blankets in the hull. I took note as Freyja slipped her shawl into her bag by her feet. I would need that for later.

Erik placed a sack between himself and us women. Fierce determination filled his eyes. "Please, don't hesitate to wake me if there's a problem. I would not on my life let anyone hurt you."

Something stirred inside me. I felt like I wasn't just a thrall, but I was a woman. I wasn't a piece of gravel, I was precious gold. What gave Erik such deep concern for us?

Tyra clasped his forearm. "Thank ye, Erik. It means much to all of us."

I could only stare at him as he lay down on the other side of the sack. I didn't know if it was real, or if it was all a scheme for him to take advantage of one of us. But he, I had to admit, seemed entirely different from any man I'd ever met.

I pulled the thin blanket over me. I lay still and awake till all I could think of was my glorious task before me.

One man began to snore loudly. Beside me, Tyra's eyelids drooped close. One by one each man or woman fell into deep slumber, weary from the day's travels.

When darkness came late in the night, only one man was awake—Niels, keeping watch until the current changed.

I found Freyja's bag near her feet and drew out her shawl. I pulled it around my head and got on my knees. I crawled toward the side of the ship, alert for any slight noise I made. Ragnar's ship floated nearby. In that ship there was a tent set up in the hull, where Ragnar slept inside. I had to find the plank they used to cross over to the other ships. And I had to cross without a sound.

Niels caught my gaze, but I wasted no time at the task before me.

"Niels," I whispered. I crawled toward him, so I was a few feet away. I made sure to cover my head with the shawl, so he could barely see my face in the darkness.

He sat straight up.

"Gerd? What are you doin' here?"

My chin trembled at his lilting tone. I was not here to gratify his desires. I gathered myself to my feet, clutching the ends of my shawl tightly. My heart clambered in my chest. I spat the words out quickly, "Ragnar wants me. Can you help me find the plank to cross?"

Niels eyed me from my head to my feet. He found the plank and laid it across the two ships. Then he stepped startlingly close to me, eyes gleaming.

I backed away and clenched my hands into fists to keep them from trembling.

He chuckled quietly. "Your jarl is waiting. You ought to go to him." He turned away and sat down again in the stern. He fixed his gaze on the water.

I pressed my hand to my heart. He had not recognized me. By the gods, he had not recognized me! Eagerness rose through me. Clinging to the shawl with one hand and holding out the other to keep balance, I stood up on the plank. I took a deep, courageous breath of air. *I can do this.*

Taking one step in front of the other, I wobbled slowly to the other side. I kept my focus on the ship in front of me and gulped down breaths to stay quiet.

"You can do this, Sigrid," Niels called from behind me.

I started and lost my balance, the shawl slipping out of my hands. The water rose toward me, ready to swallow me. The shawl had already vanished into the sea. I reached out and caught hold of the plank. My feet splashed lightly into the water.

I heaved my body upward. My mind raced. He knew who I was. He knew what I'd done.

My body dropped back into a dangling position. "Niels," I gasped. "Help me."

"I can't." He shrugged. "You'll have to do it by your own strength. You made it this far, escaping Valhalla itself, Sigrid. You can get yourself out of this one, too."

"You can't tell anyone who I am."

"Did I ever say I would?"

I cringed at the playful tone of his voice. I had always been suspicious of Niels. As the head servant, he had always acted like second-in-command to Ragnar. Now he wasn't even a thrall. Ragnar had set him free, so he could do as he pleased. My stomach tightened at the thought.

"Hard to cross planks in the dark, eh?"

My feet and hands still held me secure, dangling below the plank. I thought of Mum. I thought of Ragnar. I gritted my teeth and dragged myself up, so I lay on my stomach, gasping on the plank. I edged myself forward till I made it to Ragnar's longship.

"Well done," Niels said from the other ship. His mildness surprised me. He had always been cruel and merciless in whipping the thralls back in Kaupang. Had he changed? Would he keep my secret?

"Sigrid," he said.

I raised myself up, so I could see him.

A strange grin spread across his face, and I knew immediately what it meant. It was the same grin he had given me that funeral night when it was his turn to have me. "I can make a deal with you, my dear."

My blood boiled. "I will not make any deal with you!"

He stared at me from the other longship. "Either that or you're dead, pretty wench. Sleep with me every night, and I'll never tell the man."

"I'm not a wench," I whispered sharply between clenched teeth. "I'm just a regular thrall woman. I weave and sew and cook. That's it! Understand?"

Niels leaned over the edge of the longship and smirked. "Seemed to do pretty well at pleasing all those men at the funeral."

"You awful, awful man!" I hissed.

"I'll go tell him right now, in fact," Niels said, stepping onto the plank. "He won't mind."

The memory of what Gerd had told Tyra and I flashed through my mind. "Don't you dare or I'll tell him what *you* did."

He jolted to a stop and looked at me. "What are you talking about?"

"You know what you did to Freyja," I spat out, enjoying how my comment seized him like a claw around his throat.

His face turned pale. "

I smirked and lifted my chin. "Believe me, Niels, you won't want Ragnar finding out. You'll be dead before you know it."

He sat down in the stern. "Fine. Have your fill of lust. The jarl's more handsome than I, after all."

"What are you two talkin' about?"

We both turned. Erik stood up on Niels's ship, gripping his knife in his hand.

Niels smirked. "None of your business, boy. Go to sleep."

A few other men were already waking up at the sound of our voices. I had lost my chance to slay Ragnar for tonight.

TWENTY-TWO

THAT EVENING, A SUPPER OF the raw cod fish was served. The men on Niels's longship gathered around and chatted as they ate. Warm fish satisfied my stomach after the long day's work. Wind rippled the sails lightly, so peaceful like the gentle flap of a seabird's wings. I chewed the fish slowly.

As we ate, I pondered last night's escapades. I had failed. The way I reasoned it, I couldn't murder him until we arrived in Ireland, until the battle cry arose, until everyone scrambled about killing one another and seizing the possessions of the Irish. I'd have to wait, with the jarl insufferably near to me.

"My good thrall, won't you tell us one of your fascinating tales?" Ragnar asked Erik.

The Irishman grinned and rose to his feet. "I'd be glad to, Master."

He brought out his scrolls from his sack in the hull. I knew well what kind of stories he'd tell before he even began—stories about his God.

Erik read about a man named Moses who received ten rules from his God on a mountaintop. When he reached the sixth rule, "Ye shall not murder," my attention was rapt.

Questions flooded my mind. I had heard this before when I'd talked with him near the babbling stream. I could not help but wonder again why his God hated killing so much.

I leaned over to Tyra and whispered, "You said your God loves us, right?"

"He does," she said softly. "So much."

"That means obeying these commandments is optional, right?"

Tyra looked from me to Erik. "Did your mother let ye do whatever ye wanted?"

Mum had let me obtain everything I could have, which wasn't much, the thralls that we were. She had allowed me to learn to swim with the help of my father, and she had allowed me to have a mind of my own. As a thrall these allowances had been more than enough.

So, his God hated sin. No wonder Erik never seemed to consider taking advantage of me or the other women. No wonder I felt safe with him. Still, I could not feel safe with his God who forbade me from killing the man I loathed.

When the Irishman had finished another story about a fiery furnace, we settled down to sleep. Ragnar nodded to Tyra, so she bowed her head and followed him to the other longship. I lay down near Freyja, with Erik lying a few feet away from us, blocking us at least partly from the other men. He gripped his knife in his hand, even as he slept. It comforted me to know he was ready to awake any moment to protect us from the insatiable Norsemen.

My eyelids drooped as I wrapped a thin blanket around me. I released a long, deep sigh. Darkness rocked me into sleep.

The fiery furnace Erik had spoken of entered my dreams. Iosa was not with me as he had been with the three men in the tale. Fire surrounded me. The flames pressed in closer to me until they covered me from head to foot.

And I had no escape.

Sharp cries awakened me from my dreams. I jolted up and looked where the sound was coming from. In the bow, Ragnar lifted a long, sharp whip and lashed Tyra with it.

My frame grew shaky when I saw the slash marks on Tyra's tunic that draped over her rounded abdomen. Could he be trying to kill the baby inside her?

"She doesn't deserve it," came a voice from beside me. I turned to Erik. Behind him, two men had just stood up, likely hearing Tyra's cries. But when they realized what was happening, they grunted and lay down without a word of protest or concern.

Tyra's sharp cries cut into me like I was the one being slashed by the whip. I scrambled past the resting men to the bow of the ship.

"Don't!" I screamed. "It's not her fault!"

He was the one who got her pregnant.

Ragnar raised the long whip and lashed Tyra across the back. She cried out again, holding her round abdomen.

"It's not your fault that you told me about your God?" he roared. "You couldn't help it?"

"I will not stop," Tyra said in between lashes. "I will not stop telling ye the truth, Master." *Crack.* "I will not stop, because the God of the universe sent His Son to die for your sins—" *Crack* "—including this very sin that is taking place." *Crack.* "God loves ye, Jarl Ragnar."

I flung my arms around her. The whip bit me, and I cried out as it scorched my already-wounded back.

It was the best thing, better than him hurting Tyra beyond what she could bear. Better than him whipping her till she gave birth too early. Better than killing my dear friend and her newborn infant. It was the best thing I could do.

"No!" Tyra pushed me off her. "What are ye doin', Gerd?"

I stumbled backward, surprised by the force she exerted on me.

Ragnar snarled. "Go away, fool. You weren't invited on this trip in the first place."

"Don't kill her," I yelled, grabbing a hold of his ankles.

He clutched my wrists and hurled me off him. "You little wench!"

I stumbled backward. Just as I got my bearings again and prepared a fist to whack at Ragnar, Tyra grasped my wrists fasts and held me down. Her grip was tight and painful on my skin. "I thank ye for your help. Now leave us be. You've already been hurt enough."

"No, Tyra!" I whispered, fear pulsing through me. "He's going to kill ye, and the little one inside ye."

"I know what I'm doing, Gerd," she said steadily. "He won't calm down until ye leave."

"But—"

"Tyra, you fool!" Ragnar's voice bellowed from above us. He struck my friend with the whip. She cried out and clung more tightly to me. I was unable to move, to do anything, with her fingers clasped around my wrists.

"Ragnar, let's have a talk," she said quietly. Blood trickled on the back of her worn tunic.

Ragnar lashed her again. "A talk? You fool!"

She stumbled forward and cried out. I stood up, my back searing with pain. Ragnar blocked my path from running to her.

Oh, Tyra. Oh, dear, dear Tyra.

"Please," Tyra beseeched him, her voice choked with tears.

He wrinkled his nose. "Not with that white-haired rat around."

She gave me a look, and so, with a sigh, I turned away. There was nothing else I could do.

I moved through the sleeping men back to the center of the ship. Peering back, I saw Tyra talking calmly to Ragnar as she massaged his shoulders. She handed him a jug of mead that he drank down quickly. Ragnar pulled a blanket over his chest, his face grim. What strange magic did my friend have?

Erik sat in the stern where I had left him. He had watched the whole incident without doing a thing—the coward! He reached out to me, but I shrank away from him and sank to the ground. My back burned.

"What were ye doin'? Are ye all right, lass?"

I pulled a blanket around me. "I'm fine." I lay down, trying to ignore the gnawing, aching wound on my back.

"It's unbelievable," Erik said after a while. "She has so much faith in Iosa."

The wind bit hard, and rain began to patter on the ship deck. I shook my head and drew the thin blanket tighter around me, nestling in the hull. *That Iosa.* He was the reason we got our backs whipped. I could feel Erik's gaze on me, so I tried not to shiver or chatter my teeth. I didn't dare to cry.

The sky was dark, the darkest it had been in a long time. Autumn had brought a longer period of darkness to the night. My eyelids closed.

"I don't know what makes her like that," Erik whispered, as if talking to himself. "She's just—she's strong."

I kept my eyes closed.

"Tyra doesn't care what people think of her; she sticks to what she believes and loves as hard as she can. She's never afeard."

"Unlike you," I muttered.

He gave a start. "What, lass?"

"You feel guilty about everything, and you're the most timid young man I've ever known. I don't know what it is about you, Erik. For Odin's sake, if you have the same God as Tyra—shouldn't you act at least somewhat like her?"

"I should." His voice was small and weak, like a child. He drew a heavy breath and bowed his head. Then he began singing softly. I listened to his song, wide awake and cold and aching.

"Trust in the Lord with all your heart and lean not on your own understanding; in all your ways submit to Him, and He will make your paths straight." He sang it over and over, with a melodic tenor voice, seeming to gain some inner strength through the song—some sort of dignity I had hardly heard in him before.

It's about time, I thought. *It's about time he learned a bit of pride.*

The sweet song of the redhead drifted into the night. I heard Tyra's voice too, faint and far off. And the longer I closed my eyes, the more I could hear Mum's voice, singing by the pot of stew over the fire, or as she braided my hair, or as she tucked me in for the night in the cold, dark hut I'd grown up in.

The songs eased the bitter cold around me as well as the soreness in my back. But it could not soothe the gnawing pain within me. Whatever happened, I had no idea where I was going after I died. My confusion left me bare and empty. Nothing could fill me up. Not even a God of freedom—because freedom meant letting go. And I could never let go of what Ragnar had done to me. I would forever cling to my hatred of him. The miserable feeling inside me expanded as the night dragged on.

TWENTY-THREE

"ABOUT EIGHT MORE DAYS TILL we reach Ireland," Niels informed us all the next day during breakfast. "And around two more days till we reach the small Pictish tribe."

The men raised their oars and cheered, greed for plunder rumbling in their brusque voices.

I set down my spoon into my morning gruel, remembering my own piece of plunder. I felt the silver cross amulet around my neck. It was a luxury I could trade for food or clothing if I needed to, but for now, as Lars had said, it was a symbol of good fortune, that would, hopefully, grant me Ragnar's blood. Indeed, it had already protected me from Ragnar's scrutiny, allowing me to board the ship and voyage so far in safety.

After we'd finished the gruel, Freyja tossed Tyra and me some fish to skin and some clothes and blankets to stitch. She kept herself near the bow of the ship, near Ragnar. The jarl's orders, although she didn't seem to mind. He seemed to be madly in love with her one day and smitten with Tyra the next.

The men sang as they rowed, the rhythm of their song matching that of the dip, pull, and lift of the paddles. We seemed to fly over the waters, and there was not a storm in sight for miles.

Niels glanced at me as we went along. "A fine sewer, you've always been."

I worked the needle up and over one of the men's stiff tunics, just as I had done for Jarl Valdemar's funeral garb.

"A fine paddler, you are." I returned the compliment through gritted teeth. Why was he talking with me? Hadn't things been set straight between us? He wasn't allowed to do anything to me.

Niels laughed, his face reddening. "Thank you, good thrall."

I kept my head down. "Talk to me all you like—just not when you're supposed to be paddling."

He laughed as if I had made the funniest joke in the world, then he raised his paddle blade and dipped it into the water.

That night, the sea whipped the ship back and forth in a soothing rhythm.

"Then Iosa covered the man's eyes with mud," Erik described, placing his hands over his eyes to put the picture in our minds.

The men had circled up tonight in the hull, listening to the Irishman's strange tales. I rested against a sack as I wove thick brown yarn through a small loom. While Eric's gentle voice carried over the water, Tyra poured mead for Ragnar or massaged his shoulders. He never seemed to tire of the feel of her hands. Two nights had passed since Ragnar had become enraged with Tyra and lashed her. He had forgotten about Freyja a few hours later, and he was just as in love with Tyra as he had ever been. My back had not forgotten his anger, though. It ached when I moved.

Ragnar's face turned red with fury. "Your God can't do such a thing! And you've told that story many times now. Don't you have a tale *not* about your wretched God?"

Erik stared intently out at the ocean for several seconds before he cleared his throat. "Once in a faraway country, there lived a young man whose father taught him proper sword-fightin' at age twelve. He practiced every day, determined to become a skilled swordsman so he could defend the people he loved and fight their enemy across the sea. By the time he turned fourteen, he was winnin' matches against his friends."

I wove the yarn in and out as I listened. If this story was about who I thought it was, it already explained everything. The knife, the look in his eyes, the inner strength I knew he had, should he let it out. This boy wasn't at all who I thought he was when I'd first begun to get to know him traveling through the mountains with him and Lars.

"One day," he continued, "the enemies of this young man's country attacked his land. He and his father valiantly protected his mother, two sisters, and baby brother. His father had a red beard and an axe and a tunic fringed with purple. But every feller in the battle, enemy or kinsman, had a beard of some color, a weapon of some kind, and a tunic of some fashion. So, when this young man, flustered with the frenzy of battle and concerned for his kinfolk, saw a man with a red beard, an axe, and a purple-fringed tunic come runnin', he thought for certain that this man was his enemy."

I paused at my loom.

Erik slid his hand over his forehead, his speech tight. "The young man clutched his sword and thrust it into the man's heart. The red-bearded man fell to the ground. But the face the young man saw was no enemy—t'was his own dear father." Erik's voice trailed off.

Ragnar grumbled. "So he killed his father, then what?"

Erik lifted his head, looking directly at Ragnar. Silent tears rolled down his cheeks, but his face was expressionless. "The young man almost killed himself, but he remembered his family was hiding in their house, so he returned to them. He was too late. While he had mourned, the rest of his kinfolk were killed." Erik's shoulders shook with emotion. "His enemy captured him, takin' him as a slave to serve him in a land far from his own."

I studied Ragnar and quivered at the thought that he might guess what I now understood very well—this tale was true. If he did, he would no doubt give Erik a good lashing for describing a tale where the Norse plunderers were the enemies.

Erik wore a pinched expression. A vein in his neck stuck out. Though he had remained strong throughout the story, it had taken great effort.

I was ashamed of my own ruthless people, and though I didn't wish to admit the connection I felt with him, I understood Eric's anguish over his father's death. Ragnar had killed my pa, too. Not to mention my mother. Maybe killing his father and failing to defend his family were the roots of his tremendous guilt.

Ragnar's nose twitched. "So, the young fellow survives the battle? What happens next?"

Erik swallowed hard, as if he hadn't intended to go this far. "Well, I—that is, the young man—sailed off to the enemy's country on a ship with pillage and other captives. Whenever the young man was so deep in despair that he could not row the ship, the cap'n would throw him into the water and laugh at him."

Erik's cheeks flushed. "The young man could not swim, so the cap'n would wait until he almost drowned before takin' him out of the water once more."

Ragnar grinned and sat back in his chair, arms behind his head. "Then?"

Erik paused and then cleared his throat. "For days, the young man wished to kill himself."

A muscle jerked in his jaw. He stared up at the sky, a pensive expression on his face. I eyed him in anticipation. What had changed the poor fellow's mind? Why hadn't he killed himself long ago?

"One day another captive reminded him of the God many in his country revered. The kind captive spoke of this God with earnestness, encouraging and praying with the young man each day. As the days passed, the young man grew to understand and know his God more than ever. He came to fear Him."

Before I knew what was happening, Erik was flailing in the water and Ragnar was laughing. Erik cried out and writhed about, splashing water into the boat.

"I was the one who captured you, boy." Ragnar laughed so hard, tears slid down his cheeks. "I cut your mum and sisters and little baby brother's throats."

Erik cried out to his God for mercy, but his head went under the surface.

I screamed.

Throwing aside my loom, I dove in after him. Erik struggled under the water's surface, and I caught hold of his arm. I fought to remain above the water, kicking my legs violently, but the weight of Erik's body pulled me under.

I kicked harder, straining against his weight. My head bobbed out of the water, and I gasped for a breath before dragging Erik to the surface, too.

Ragnar cackled.

The frigid waters splashed into my face. I clenched my teeth. The horrid man. "Help me!" I shouted to Erik.

He followed my lead and kicked hard.

I reached upward and grabbed the edge of the longship then pulled Erik over. He managed to take hold of the longship, too, and we hauled ourselves onto the ship.

I coughed and leaned forward, salty water spewing from my mouth.

Ragnar sneered. "I wasn't going to kill you, boy. Thralls make good money, after all—and excellent stories."

Erik coughed out seawater. "Ye killed my family?"

Hurt pierced his expression. Now he had even more of a reason to hate Ragnar. Was it reason enough to help me with my quest?

"I kill lots of people." Ragnar shook his head and crossed his arms over his chest. "Now get back to rowing. Storytime is over for tonight." He turned to Tyra. "Come with me, my love."

Tyra stood tall, her long black hair cascading down her shoulders. She glanced at me anxiously.

My heart ached.

Ragnar linked his arm with hers and led her to their end of the ship.

Erik returned to his oar nearby and began paddling.

I huddled up in a blanket near where Erik rowed, fatigue weighing me down.

"This is why you're afraid of water," I said.

He nodded, arms trembling.

"The ocean is a good place, if you embrace it."

His tired eyes fixed upon me. "I've tried, but I can't. Maybe some things God will never help you overcome." He dipped the oar in the water again.

"Tyra wouldn't agree." I could almost hear Tyra refuting him, telling him that God helps us overcome all things, in His timing.

Erik strained harder against the current and laughed. "She's probably right. If only I could have faith like hers. That confidence."

"You can, Erik," I told him, remembering his tale from tonight. He had been a valiant swordfighter once. He wasn't as weak as a lamb after all. "I think you are stronger than *you* think you are."

He powerfully swept the oar through the water. "Stronger than this?"

I let out a little laugh. "Yes. I have seen it in you before, Erik."

He paused at his oar. "Dear Sigrid, I almost could think you believed in Iosa yourself."

"Of course not." I grimaced. "Iosa isn't the kind of God I could ever believe in. But you're the only good man I know in the world right now, Erik, and I believe in you."

The Irishman took a deep breath of air, his chest expanding. "Thank ye, Sigrid. You have no idea how much that means to me."

TWENTY-FOUR

TWO NIGHTS LATER, NIELS GAVE a long, fervent shout: "Land hooooo!"

I yawned, wiped my eyes, and pushed myself to a seated position. My back tinged with pain, but I was easily able to ignore it now. "What's happening?" I whispered to Tyra who already sat awake nearby.

"We've reached the Pictish village."

I raised my head. Large mountains filled our view, with forests scattered near and far. The village was said to lie in the woods behind a gathering of trees and a precipice of rocks. Apparently, Ragnar had scouted it out on his last pillaging voyage in preparation for a later raid. "Rouse from your slumber," Ragnar bellowed. "Get your armor on and paddle to shore!"

The men rose from their sleeping mats and scrambled to obey the jarl's orders. Each man donned tough wolf skin and grabbed long, gleaming swords. All carried large round shields in their other hand with alternating red and blue colors and a small dome of iron in the center.

An energy surged through the men like lightning. They grabbed their oars and raised them up. "For the north lands!"

They maneuvered the ships quickly to shore. Before too long, the fleet landed, and the armed men hustled off the ships. They trudged through the sand then began to climb up the precipice to where the village lay still and calm. The Picts were doomed. If only we had known to warn them as well, then Lars would have been able to alert them of the upcoming attack.

Erik, a Norseman named Axel, and us three women stepped off the longship into the shallow water. The icy sea lapped up my ankles as I staggered with them to shore. Erik jumped toward the land, avoiding the water's touch as much as he could. When we reached the sandy shore, we watched the men climb.

Ragnar and Niels still stood at the bottom of the precipice, preparing to follow the last man up the hill. Niels held a large shield in one hand and led Ragnar with his other hand. Ragnar carried a long spear. They would work as one. Interesting how a free man was more eager than ever to obey his beloved master. Strangely, it sounded familiar to Tyra and Erik's God of freedom. Was that what they meant by following Iosa out of love?

Ragnar turned to us. "Guard the ships with your life," he growled.

And with that, he and Niels followed the rest of the men.

I watched as they disappeared into the woods. Every bone in my body cried out against them. I couldn't understand this thirst for innocent blood, nor would I ever care to try. Only a few men in the world were wicked enough to slay, and Ragnar of course was one of them.

Tyra was on her knees in the sand. She cried out to her God, tears streaming down her face. "Lord, help us. Oh, Lord, please come and do something!"

Erik wept beside her and prayed aloud. "Oh, please, Iosa, have mercy on these Norse raiders. Help them to see Thy light. Please, Iosa, make an end to this. Open their eyes so they may see Thy light."

I had never been so close to a raid in all my life. I had *heard* of them, oh so many times—but I had never *heard* them. The sounds were awful. Screams. Houses falling apart. Shouts. Fire.

I looked at Tyra and Erik. What good would praying to a nonexistent God do? I remembered how I'd cried out to the gods during the rituals, never receiving an answer. They didn't care. Just as my prayers had not brought me out of the pit of humiliation and misery neither could their prayers halt the swords of the Norse warriors.

"I can't wait to see what Ragnar brings back to me." A slow smile built across Freyja's face.

I gritted my teeth. That was all she could think about, while children screamed and houses caught on fire?

"You sure he'll bring you something?" I asked her.

Freyja laughed. "I'm his first wife. He will."

"His first wife? Weren't you born a thrall?"

Freyja's face went red. "I am the daughter of one of the richest families in Kaupang." She shook her head. "Ragnar loved me once; he loved me so much he had thralls serving me. And I deserved it. He told me I was the most beautiful of women. He told me he'd never get another woman." She stared fixedly at Tyra with hot tears in her eyes. After a moment, she brushed them quickly away.

"I'm sorry." I touched her shoulder. It amazed me that Ragnar could have ever loved so much, even if it was short-lived.

I turned toward the ocean, watching the soothing ripples of the constant ebb and flow of the tide.

"I lost everything once he got a new concubine," Freyja continued in a low voice. "I became his possession. I had to work, and I had to make all his women work, too." She spat the words out like venom.

"The only thing I didn't lose was my love for him. He treats me the same as the rest of them—and that wretched Tyra has caught him under her spell!"

"She doesn't mean to."

"Oh, I know. Poor, innocent Tyra doesn't mean a thing." Freyja shook her head. "It doesn't make the pain disappear, though."

I ached for her. Freyja had a reason for bitterness, for hatred. So had I.

I lifted the amulet from around my neck. "Here. In case he doesn't come back with anything. It's supposed to bring good fortune."

She stroked the silver cross with her thumb then slipped the amulet around her neck. "Thank ye, Sigrid. I will treasure it."

I had never seen her so serious and sad. I almost wanted to embrace her.

Green swirling lights illuminated the sky. A tingle rippled through me, and I shuddered. Those lights meant only one thing: the gods were angry. We would all be destroyed.

The shouts of conquest from the raiders turned to shouts of fear. Men burst through the trees, carrying sacks of plunder. Terror contorted their faces. No matter about the plunder they still had left behind. The gods were angry at us.

"Retreat!" Ragnar roared, leading the men back to the shore.

"Tyra, Erik!" I called, but they seemed ignorant of what was happening around them.

Green waves of light spread across the sky like mist above the sea's horizon, growing brighter with each passing second. Tyra and Erik were still on their knees on the sandy beach. I wondered at how quickly the lights had appeared, as if an immediate answer to Tyra and Erik's prayers.

The Norseman scrambled down the rocks, one by one, swords, shields, and bags of riches in tow. I turned toward the longships, ready to board and escape the gods' wrath.

"Fill the ship with the loot and be quick about it!" Ragnar shouted. Then he seized Tyra's arm and jerked her to her feet. "What do you think you're doing?"

Tyra looked shaken, but her voice was steady. "We were prayin', Master."

Ragnar scowled. "Prayin' for what? To send the north lights and cause destruction?"

Tyra only seemed to grow taller at his words. "Prayin' for this hateful battle to end and for God to show ye His great love, Master." A loud shout arose behind them as the surviving Picts scrambled down the rocks to the shore, weapons in hand.

The men chucked their heavy sacks onto the longships. Ragnar released Tyra and barked more commands out to his men.

I grabbed my friend and yanked her onboard the nearest longship. With all their might, the men pushed the longships into the water. An arrow flew past me, and I dove to the deck.

"Row!" Ragnar roared.

TWENTY-FIVE

I PRAYED TO THE GODS and Iosa, in case He was real, to keep the arrows away.

"Ragnar," Tyra screamed above the splashing of the oars, "remember our baby."

I lifted my head and looked around for my friend. In the hull, Ragnar stood over Tyra. He drew back his leg and kicked her in the abdomen.

"Tyra, no!" I rushed toward her, but Ragnar grabbed me and flung me backward into some barrels.

My head swirled, and my back throbbed. My vision blurred as I tried to stand. The world tipped sideways, and I lost my footing and fell. Pain shot through my side, sending a groan through my throat.

Tyra screamed, a deadly, hollow scream that filled the air. It seemed to fly out into the sea and up the Scottish cliffs for all creatures to hear far and wide, birds, fish, and human alike. She was in far more pain than I was.

"Can't handle a little overdue punishment? I've had enough of your prayers and talks about your God. And now you've brought the north lights upon us. Curse you," Ragnar roared, kicking her once more.

Tyra gasped in agony. "Ragnar, my jarl, the baby."

Freyja ran up to Ragnar. "She's giving birth to your child. Let me take over from here. Command your ship."

Ragnar slowly backed away, staring wide eyed at Tyra.

"Get some water!" Freyja yelled at me.

Adrenaline coursed through me. I grabbed a bucket and dunked it into the sea. A man's cry of pain broke out, and I looked to where the sound arose from.

An arrow had pierced a man's shoulder, blood tricking down from the wound. I sent another prayer to the gods for safety then shut off the panic which threatened to consume me.

I plopped the bucket of water down beside Freyja. She wet a cloth and dabbed Tyra's forehead. Freyja had evidently assisted with births before, but I had only watched them. We laid Tyra on a blanket. She gasped for air, her face shaken with panic, her body in the grip of an intense contraction.

I bent down to her, my knees trembling.

An arrow whizzed right past Tyra's head. She cried out all the louder.

I hunkered down and clutched her hand, gazing into her tortured eyes. "You're going to be okay, Tyra. You can do this."

Freyja dabbed Tyra's forehead, murmuring for my friend to breathe.

Tyra gasped for air. Her face was contorted into a mess of agony, and I had never seen her so afraid in my life.

"We're free," Ragnar declared.

The men cheered, but I only held tighter to Tyra's hand. I closed my eyes and willed myself to hold the tears in.

She was going to be okay. She could do this.

Four hours later, Freyja washed the tiny baby in seawater and wrapped her snugly in a blanket. The child was pale and sickly looking, much smaller than a regular newborn. The babe had been born months before she was supposed to. Would the child survive?

"A girl." Freyja handed the infant to Tyra.

Tears slid down her cheeks as she held the newborn close to her chest. The babe's cries pierced the air.

"Oh, Tyra." I hovered over her to peer down at the girl's miniature face. The infant had big blue eyes like Tyra and fine blonde hair like Ragnar. She was beautiful and perfect. "It's going to be okay."

Tyra smiled softly. "She has my eyes."

At her words, I knew she hadn't given up hope of this infant's survival. I smiled back.

My body yearned for sleep. Freyja had already lain down. I didn't blame her. She had helped so much, regardless of her underlying hatred for Tyra. She understood the pain of childbirth, I was sure of it. Though she had never told me of children, I could see the genuine empathy in her face.

Tyra kissed the baby's forehead, and the newborn's delicate hands flailed in the air. "Children are a heritage from the Lord, offspring a reward from Him."

She sang to her God and rocked her baby in her arms. "Thank Ye," she whispered, then kissed the infant's forehead again.

"Does he have a name?" Erik asked.

Tyra laughed then said, "'Tis a girl! And her name's—"

"Name him Stellan, after his father!" Ragnar bellowed.

My mouth fell open. He didn't believe the babe was his? Tyra had told him the babe was his!

Tyra ignored Ragnar and sighed delightedly down at her daughter. "Oh, Inge, oh, beautiful Inge." She then lifted the child toward me. "Would ye like to hold her?"

I reached for the child and tucked her snugly in my arms. Mum had taught me how to hold infants. Thrall mothers had always needed a moment of rest. I'd also held my baby brothers and sisters before they'd died, so many years ago.

Inge's big blue eyes stared up at me in wonder. An expanding, deep love for her burst within me. I had never felt this way before, but Tyra's extraordinary tenderness was contagious. The child looked so small and helpless. How could anyone dare hurt such a thing? *Freyja, goddess of fertility, don't let this baby die. Please.*

TWENTY-SIX

THE MEN CELEBRATED THEIR VICTORY over the Picts with food and drink, reveling in the loot they'd plundered. The longships swayed about fitfully from their drunken carousing. Tyra and her baby rested near me, their bodies moving in small, quiet breaths. Freyja snored a few feet away. I lay awake, tucking my body into a ball with my thin blanket wrapped around me. The festivities were too loud for me to sleep, so I consented to listen.

"Come on, boy." Ragnar taunted Erik from the stern of the longship, his slurred voice showing signs of drunkenness.

Niels drawled, "Just one little sip, you softie."

"No, sirs," Erik said with such a natural, unassuming tone that it was hard to tell he was outright disagreeing with them. "My God wants me to stay alert so I may discern what is right and what is wrong."

The men snickered. A loud splash came from the other side of the ship. Erik cried out, and the men laughed louder. I tensed and started to fling off my blanket, then I froze. If I ran up to them, they'd see me. Before I could decide to do anything, they pulled him aboard again, coughing and wet.

"What's with that girl o' yers?" a man teased. "Is she gonna give us a babe soon, too?"

"That's just Gerd," Ragnar huffed. "Never found her pleasing to my taste. She just does the dishes and all that sort of work."

"Just the dishes, eh?" Niels spoke slyly.

I bit my lip, remembering my lie to him the first night out at sea. I'd said I was going to sleep with Ragnar, when I'd really meant to kill him.

One man laughed. "Is she much for looks?"

Niels was quick to say, "Oh, no, sir."

He described my ugliness, even though he'd told me of my stunning beauty. Remembering the strange grin he'd given me on the first night at sea, I shuddered. He wanted me for only himself.

Another man roared, "By the gods, Niels, she's as stunning as that fine concubine of yours, Ragnar! Maybe even more so."

The men murmured in agreement.

"You mean more beautiful than Tyra?" Ragnar growled.

"Yes, sir. That's the one."

"Bah! All her stupid talks about her God wear my ears out! Anyone want her?"

I squeezed my eyes shut. Was this the effect of the mead or was it purely dishonorable? Norsemen strove for honor in all areas of life, including their relationships with women. Had he any pride at all? Tyra, for Odin's sake, was his possession! Did he now mean to freely hand her off to another man?

The raucous Norsemen laughed.

"Who'd want a wife with a child clinging to her all the time?" one man grumbled.

The men muttered amongst themselves, clearly seeing this as a problem.

"I can fix that," Ragnar snarled.

Niels slapped him on the back a few hardy times. "Good sir, you know how to fix anything!"

The men broke into hysterical cheers.

I gaped in horror. Tyra would go mad if Ragnar destroyed her little one's life. And Inge! Oh, Inge. She didn't deserve to die.

"Who will get her once the baby's gone?" another asked.

Ragnar perused his men. "The one who captures the most thralls in Ireland."

They murmured their uproarious agreement. My stomach lurched, and I felt like vomiting. How could he?

"What about your other wife? Freyja?"

"No," Ragnar said gruffly. "She's mine."

"And her friend, that Gerd?"

"By the gods, you can have Gerd," the jarl muttered. "I have Freyja."

The men argued over who would have me, one after the other, back and forth like children squabbling over the last bit of bacon. I pressed my fist against my mouth to keep from screaming in protest. They couldn't do this! Not again, not ever. By the gods, didn't anyone have a drop of mercy?

One of them piped up, "Why don't we *all* have a chance at her tonight?"

I sucked in my breath, feeling like a hundred pounds of seawater was sweeping over me, drowning me. I couldn't stand this happening to me again.

Then I heard Niels speak up. "Sirs, I beg you! She has never married nor been a concubine. Only one of us may have her. We must toss a coin."

My underarms went sweaty. I felt submerged in my body's stickiness, though it was so cold I could see my own breath.

I tossed off my blanket and crept closer to the men, crawling on my hands and knees. Lying low, I spied on them from behind a sack as Niels procured a coin and tossed it in the air. My heart pounded. The metal glinted in the moonlight. He tossed the coin several times, for each couple of men, gradually narrowing it down to fewer and fewer people.

Erik stood to the side of the crowd, doing nothing. The fool. He feared their mockery. He was too much of a coward to even consider saving me from their filthy hands.

I curled up behind the sack and gulped down air to stay quiet, though I was screaming for justice inside. Where was their sense of honor, for Odin's sake? Didn't things like this happen only at funerals?

I pulled a blanket over my head, shunning the thought of what loomed ahead of me. The thought of a man touching me—it was unbearable. It couldn't happen. It couldn't. I wouldn't allow it. I had to escape, the only way I knew how.

I crawled away from the men toward the bow. At one side of the ship, I stood up and reached out my arms, pointing my hands to prepare to dive.

"Stop!" Niels yelled.

Ignoring him, I dove into the chilly sea. Under the surface of the waters, I heard their dim shouting.

I raised my head out of the water to suck in a deep breath. They were still barking at me like a pack of dogs. I eyed the dark form of one of the other longships bobbing up and down in the murky waters. An oar hit my skull, sending my head throbbing. I groaned at the pain, clutching the back of my head. Then I swam downward. I paddled underneath the nearest longship till I reached the other side. The cold water pierced me, and my fingers and toes grew numb.

For Mum's sake, I had to stay alive long enough to complete my mission.

I shot my head out of the water, gasping for breath.

A man peered over the side of the longship at me. I dove back under and tried to swim forward, but my arms tangled in a heavy fish net.

The man dragged me back aboard the longship in the net. I screamed. I was caught like a fish, ready to be eaten. I panted under the net, the cold air stabbing my skin. I pulled my knees to my chest, shaking from the icy breeze. My whole body was drenched; my long hair dripping, heavy and wet.

The man hauled the net off me. I tried to lunge back into the water, but one of the men snatched my arms. Dragging me over his shoulder, he jostled me back across the two other longships till he reached Niels's ship. He deposited me at the feet of Niels.

"Do not do this." Erik stepped toward me.

Niels grasped my arm then gripped Erik's tunic with the other hand and shook him.

I struggled against his grasp, but he held me fast beside him.

Niels seized the poor fellow so close to him that they almost touched noses. "Do not mistake me, boy!" His voice dropped to a hoarse whisper. "I *love* her."

I gasped both at his words and at the tight grip he had on my arm. "Niels, if you love me, don't pretend I am not here! Speak to me face-to-face like a man."

He glanced ruefully at me. "But *you* are *not* a man." He bellowed out to the Norse fellows, "Give me some room, and get this redheaded fool out of my way!"

Erik drew a long, steel sword out of its sheath. Swallowing hard, he pointed the sword at Niels. "Sir, if ye wish to harm my friend, ye will have to harm me first."

"The luck of the matter is I've already got her." He squeezed me so hard my bones ached. His nails dug into my skin. Nasty, long, filthy nails. Niels jerked me in front of him, so Erik wouldn't dare to attempt a stab.

I clenched my fist in anger.

Erik lay down the sword and kneeled before Niels.

What was he doing now? How would this get me out of this mess? What good would it do to surrender to a cruel Norseman like Niels?

Niels rested his hand on the hilt of his sword. My anger melted into fear. Surely Niels would strike Erik at any moment.

"Niels, sir," Erik said in a soft, broken voice. "I have always fancied yer leadership and good humor. But now ye are tryin' to do somethin' awful, somethin' I have no power to stop. But please, sir, consider what ye are doing for this lady's sake, for my sake, for the sake of the one true God who has created ye! And, in the name of the God I serve, I tell ye, sir, do not harm this young woman. Let the lass alone!"

I stared at Erik, the speech echoing inside me as my wet dress clung to my skin.

Niels was silent for a moment, stiff and at a loss for words. I looked up at him right as he forced a grin in that mocking, boyish way of his. But he couldn't hold the grin for long. He shook his head, fear and remorse surfacing again in his vivid blue eyes.

He released me. "Be gone, before I change my mind!"

I almost dashed back to the hull at once, but then I glanced down at Erik. He still knelt on the wooden planks of the ship, his head bowed low, and soft murmurs escaping his lips. I knew he was praying to his God, and yet this time, for some reason, it did not disturb me. I was in awe of him, in a way I could not understand.

But I could not stay here, lest Niels change his mind. I scrambled to my spot near Tyra in the hull and laid down. I closed my weary eyelids, pulling my thin blanket over me. I was grateful that it offered some warmth to my drenched body. Soon after, I heard Erik lying down a few feet away from me, with a sack between us.

Tonight, I would sleep in safety.

TWENTY-SEVEN

ERIK HAD SAVED ME. WONDER filled me again at the thought. By no means did I believe his wretched God had done anything because of his prayers. He, Erik, had saved me by his own power, the power he was learning he had within him, as small as it may be.

"Erik?" I called to where he sat rowing.

He raised his eyebrows at me.

"I just wanted to say, it's a good thing you found the nerve in you to do what you did. I've been waiting for you to realize you had that in you."

"Aye?" His cheeks turned red.

"I mean, with the kind of God you believe in, seems as though you'd be moving mountains all the time or making seas part like in those stories you told Lars and me."

"I am thankful that God is patient with me. My faith is like a grain of sand, but day by day, God is growing it into a rock. In no time we won't have to travel by ship anymore, I'll just part the seas and let you walk straight back to the north lands."

I laughed, but I could not dismiss the thoughts running through my head about his God. "If your *God* is so good, why do you bow to your enemies? Hold your head high and face them boldly, and stop being such a . . . " I wrinkled my nose. "You know."

"I don't know what you're wantin' me to be." Erik shrugged. "All I know is what God wants me to be."

So, the boy wasn't supposed to care what I thought, only what his God thought. But would he care that I would kill myself before the fleet sailed back to the north lands?

The next morning, dark clouds concealed the sun with such a heaviness that I had a strange foreboding the sky knew something was wrong. Lightning struck the sea's horizon and thunder cracked. Rain pattered on the ships' hulls, forcing me to huddle with Tyra in a corner with blankets to keep warm.

The men bailed out water and tied down the barrels and chests of supplies with strong rope. They let the sails down and allowed the waves to whip us about. Men's paddles stood no chance against nature's storm.

Tyra held the crying Inge close, pulling a heavy wool blanket over her to protect her from the rain. Ragnar stepped toward us, his dark figure hovering over the mother and her child. He smiled down at Tyra, a smile that gave me an uncanny sensation.

"May I hold her?"

Did he know the child was his? Or was he mocking her?

Tyra studied him, her brow furrowing.

"Let me hold her, dear," he said in the gentlest voice I'd ever heard come out of his mouth. I didn't know it was possible for such an evil man to speak in such a way.

Tyra relaxed and her eyes twinkled. She seemed won over by his soft tone. She handed Inge to him, and he took her in his large burly arms.

The memory of last night struck me. Ragnar had assured his men that he'd do something about Tyra's child. I felt sick to my stomach.

"Tyra." I touched my friend with a trembling hand. "I don't think it's wise to—"

She hushed me and silently gestured up at Ragnar. He held the infant tight against his broad chest with one burly arm.

Inge sobbed in his chest, frightened by the rain. Or was she frightened by this wretched man? Did she sense something was terribly wrong as well?

"Tyra, please, I don't think—"

Ragnar tore Inge from his chest and hurled her far out into the sea. I heard a short wail then a dull, muffled splash.

I screamed and reached out my arms toward the ocean. I sprung, my legs ready to dive in after her, but someone held me back. Ragnar. As he grasped onto me tightly, I looked in the direction Ragnar had thrown the child.

Inge was gone.

Tyra screamed as she never had before. The rain pounded harder than ever, and my white-blonde hair flew in my face. Each longship tossed from side to side, the wind whipping us about.

Ragnar released me and turned away. "Most horrid of men!" I leapt onto his back and pounded his neck with my fists. But he only paused for a moment and then laughed.

Fury raged within me, like boiling water that was near to gushing out of its pot. In this moment I hated Ragnar as fiercely as I had the day he had slayed my mother. I wanted vengeance on him more than ever.

But Ragnar gripped my arms and threw me off his back.

"Niels, tame the beast!" he yelled.

I reached to grab the sword strapped to my side, but Niels grasped my wrist, holding me back. He drew out a whip and lashed my back, sending me to my knees. I cried out at the sharp pain stinging my back. He lashed me again, and I gasped.

He kicked my side, sending me onto the ground. I groaned, the misery inside me thicker than dense mud.

Somewhere nearby Tyra was sobbing in her hands. My body was on fire with pain. My throat ached. Tears blurred my vision, but I blinked them away and grit my teeth. Had her pain overwhelmed her? Had she hardened herself toward the man at last?

Did she hate him like I did?

All day, Tyra sobbed for the child she had barely known, as she tried to focus on her thrall duties with Freyja and me. The rain continued to pour, and it soon transformed into biting hail.

As night drew in, the storm began to die down. I huddled closer to my friend, crying for her silently. I wished I could hold her, but I knew she would not let me, for she had already refused the blankets and comfort I'd offered her.

Late into the night when the sky had reached its darkest, Tyra called to me, "Gerd." Her voice sounded parched. I crawled to her, longing to do anything I could to alleviate her pain.

She clutched my hand. Her own hands were freezing cold. "Oh, Sigrid," she whispered into my ear.

I wrapped my arm around her, my own body much warmer than her shivering frame.

"I know ye hate Ragnar."

I withdrew from the embrace and gazed at her, the emptiness inside me so vast that it threatened to consume me.

"I know ye want to kill him," she murmured. "That first night, at the sea, I saw ye going to him."

I caught my breath and looked at her in alarm before quickly looking away. My cheeks burned.

But I pushed away the shame that washed over me. "I must take revenge on him, Tyra. He has killed my mother and now your little girl. I'm not letting him get away with that!"

Silence fell, and I regretted the harsh tone of my words. I couldn't talk like this around my tender-hearted friend.

I stared at her, pleading with my eyes. "You don't like my hate, I know. But I must kill him, Tyra. I must bring honor to my mum and to Inge, if you will let me."

She stared back at me, her expression hard as stone. "Please." She clenched my hand so hard it turned white. "Please, get rid of that man!"

My limbs shook from the cold about me and from her cold words, a coldness that I'd never expected to come out of her mouth.

She let go of my hand, then she curled up into a ball at my feet, wrapped her arms around my legs, and began to cry. "I give up, Sigrid. I hate Ragnar. I've hated him since he was a child ruthlessly teasing his father's goats, and I was the young thrall girl who had to somehow continue on milking them, as upset as they were." She gritted her teeth. "Oh, yes, Sigrid, I *hate* him."

I was taken aback by her confession. What about the undying love she had professed for him before?

Tyra wept at my feet, the pieces of her broken heart laid bare before me, with no one to mend it.

I ran my hand over her back in a vain attempt to soothe her. Her words unsettled me deep in the core of my being. Shaking the feeling off, I squeezed her hand. "Don't cry. I'll do it, I promise. I'll do what I came here for."

TWENTY-EIGHT

I SLIPPED QUIETLY AWAY FROM Tyra and tiptoed toward the stern of the longship. My back throbbed, but I ignored the familiar lash wound which I'd often received as a thrall.

Inside, I could feel it. I could feel every creak of the ship, every restless stir of a man, every chill breeze. Tonight was the night I'd been waiting for.

I wove a path through the sleeping men. Freyja lay on her side by Ragnar, her hands clutching his arm. I glanced at her fingers. One wore an opal signet ring, which I had not seen on her hand before. Maybe Ragnar had given her something from the Pictish raid.

He knew how to get what he wanted. Now, Freyja would become his sole delight, a pleasure to numb any feelings of regret, if he was even capable of such feelings.

I studied Freyja's contented, blissful face and watched her slow, steady breathing. I was certain she was the only woman who had ever loved Ragnar. When she awakened—no, I could not think of the loss of her loved one, of her emptiness, of her brokenness. The same feelings I felt about Mum.

It comforted me to know that any regret I had would all disappear when I killed myself.

I stood over my enemy and slipped off my cloak.

I rose my sword and pointed it at the jarl's heart, as I had faced a tree so many nights in Bergen, imagining my enemy's death. The luxurious weapon gleamed in the moonlight. Right there, the man I most hated was lying still and vulnerable, snoring like a fat hog.

I plunged the sword down toward Ragnar. A rapid jerk of a hand flung the weapon out of my grip.

"Stop it, lass!" Someone caught my wrists and drew me back. His hands were bitter cold, but strong.

I struggled with all my might to free myself from Erik's hold. He was restraining me from the only thing left for me to do.

Erik's nails bit into my arms, then he threw me with startling force into the water. I let myself sink below the surface, my heart pounding as I drank in the moment of heavy, cold darkness. My skin screamed from the icy water.

My blood boiled, and I felt on fire even though I was in the coldest place imaginable. Erik couldn't stop me. I'd do it anyway. I loved Mum, and I loved Tyra.

That was all that mattered.

I bobbed up above the water's surface again, gasping for air, Erik yanked me upward and over onto the longship deck. I lay on the wooden planks, coughing, my entire body numb with the frigid water.

I managed to sit, though my whole body was quaking. I avoided eye contact with Erik as he wrapped a thick quilt over my shoulders. Its warmth reminded me of Mum.

Mum.

I'd failed.

Again.

Erik hunched over some short stacks of hay with his hands clasped together. "I've been mighty wrong."

I groaned inwardly. What was he talking about? This was no time for conversation.

"I hated Ragnar, as ye do and as Tyra does now."

"Be quiet, Erik," I whispered sharply. "If it wasn't for you, I would finally have—just be quiet! Nothing you can say will change my mind."

"Don't hate, Sigrid. I know it's hard to believe, but God loves ye, and He doesn't want you to live like this." He leaned forward, his eyes blazing with hope in the darkness. "The Lord has shown me through Tyra that He wishes us to love everyone, even our enemies. He wants you to be free."

"He deserves to die," I said between clenched teeth. "Doesn't your God know anything about justice?"

I ought to try again, right before his eyes. I ought to risk it all.

"Aye, He will judge us all in the end," Erik said gravely. "Those who believe in Iosa will be saved, but those who are stubborn in their ways will burn forever in the depths." His intense, quiet voice urged me to believe him.

"This Iosa doesn't exist, and Ragnar deserved to burn a long time ago."

"What do ye have against the jarl?" Erik confronted me in a stern voice. "Ye hated him before Inge's death."

"You couldn't understand," I said in a strained voice.

"You don't have to tell me, but I want you to know you can trust me." He leaned his arms on his knees and bowed his head, which unnerved me, because now I couldn't see his eyes. "You know what I did to my father."

A chill shot through me like an arrow. Wrapping the blanket around me more tightly, I clenched my teeth to keep them from chattering. My heart ached, even as I wished my sympathy toward him would go away.

"Sigrid," he said, drawing my attention back to him. "I'm not sorry I stopped you, but I'm sorry I tossed you in the water. Are ye goin' to be all right?"

I lowered my gaze, wondering at the emotions overtaking me at his gentle words. I almost wanted to tell him everything. But I couldn't. He would never understand.

"What do you care?" I turned away from him and hugged my blanket closer to my chest. "Leave me alone, Erik. I'm tired of you and your stupid sermons about your stupid God and His stupid love. Love isn't real anyway, at least not the kind you babble on about." A sob caught in my throat. Only Mum's love was real. She had been the only one who truly understood me. I squeezed my eyes shut, but I could not erase the image of baby Inge and my mother drifting side by side, sinking deeper and deeper into the depths of the sea. I just wanted to finish bringing honor to Mum, so I could be with her again.

But I didn't know whom I was asking. I didn't know if any of the gods could hear me, let alone if they cared to help a thrall girl like me.

TWENTY-NINE

THE FOLLOWING MORNING, WE CAUGHT sight of lush green mountains through the dense fog. Hope rose through me like a breath of fresh air. *Ireland.* We were so close.

I turned to Tyra who lay in the hull.

Her black hair was a ragged mess. Her eyes darted wildly about, despair written all over her face. Inge's death had scarred her deeply, that was certain.

"Last night," I whispered in her ear, "Erik stopped me."

She murmured something and started crying again.

"I'll try again, sometime, when Erik isn't there."

Just then the Irishman came and offered a bowl of barley gruel to Tyra for breakfast. I smoothed down my tunic and tried to act normal.

Tyra refused the bowl. I offered it to her again, but she refused me as well. I handed it back to Erik, who set the bowl aside.

He stared at Tyra for a long, quiet moment. Then, enveloping his hands over her small, frail ones, he said, "God is with ye, Tyra." She started to sob again, pulling her hands from his and covering her face. Erik reached out his arms and embraced her. His voice broke. "I am so sorry."

I watched quietly. During these nine days, an intimacy had grown between them. They let go and looked at one another.

"The Lord is good." Erik's cheeks glowed. "May I pray for you?"

Tyra clutched his hands in hers. "I would like that." She bowed her head, and they murmured prayers for a few minutes.

When they had finished, Erik said, "With Iosa's help, ye will get through this. He has given you a strong faith. Don't let go of that."

Tears coursed down Tyra's pale cheeks. "I don't feel that I have any faith left. Ye are stronger than me because the Lord has given ye a humble spirit. Maybe God put us together on this ship so we would learn from one another."

I groaned inwardly but decided to shift my thoughts to making sure my poor friend put some food in her stomach. When I urged her once again to eat the barley stew, she received it quietly.

"I am sorry for how I acted last night." She grasped my hand, grief contorting her whole expression.

I hugged her tightly. "Oh, Tyra, I'm sorry for *you*!"

She squeezed me back then let go and studied me closely. She opened her mouth to say something, but Freyja stalked up to us.

"Ragnar has ordered us to clean the ship." She crossed her arms over her chest and tried to look stern, but I could see the compassion in her gaze when she looked toward Tyra.

Halfheartedly, Tyra and I grabbed cloth and a bucket of water and began scrubbing with Freyja.

Tyra wept as she scrubbed, but I left her alone, knowing that when Mum had died I wanted nothing more than to be by myself to grieve.

I mourned silently for her, for the baby. Why did Ragnar have to be so cruel? And if Tyra's *God* existed, and He was supposed to be loving, how could He let this happen to her precious child?

I watched Erik now, his muscles straining as he moved his paddle against the sea, with the steady pulse of the other men. His eyes were focused, alert, yet damp from crying with Tyra.

A humble spirit. Tyra had spoken of the idea as if bowing your head was a good—even strong—thing. But Mum had said to lift my head up, not bow down to a God that didn't exist. Not bow down to a God who would let Tyra's newborn baby die.

"The men mocked Him and put a crown of thorns on His head," Erik spoke in a low, earnest voice that night.

I munched on a slab of dried rabbit meat as I listened to his tale. Tyra and Freyja sat nearby, while Ragnar feasted with the men on another longship, their laughter and merriment ringing out for all to hear. He'd become weary of Erik's stories for now, but Tyra had insisted the Irishman entertain us ladies for tonight. This was supposed to be one of the most important tales: when Iosa is put to death.

"They divided His clothes among themselves by casting lots," he continued. "And on the cross, they hung a sign that said, 'This is the King of the Jews.' They did it to mock Him, since they did not believe His death was any kind of victory. They did not realize that He truly was king. The people even told Him that if He were the living Son of God, He should save Himself! And do ye know how Iosa responded?"

Freyja laughed. "I bet He said, 'You are all fools and I hate you!'"

I held back my laughter. That sure seemed like a natural response to me.

"Not at all," Erik declared. "Iosa turned His face to heaven and pleaded to God, 'Father, forgive them, for they do not know what they are doing.'"

Tyra watched as Ragnar drained a horn of mead on the nearby longship. Her look was filled with the brutal hurt that would never leave her. Forgiveness must be far from her mind.

"And ye know what else happened on that cross?" Erik's eyes sparkled with the passion that Tyra had often showed.

I leaned forward, curious as to why he and Tyra discussed their Iosa's death so often.

He turned to the scrolls and scanned the words intensely. Then he translated the Latin into Norse. "One of the criminals who hung there hurled insults at him: 'Aren't you the Messiah? Save yourself and us!' But the other criminal rebuked him. 'Don't you fear God,' he said, 'since you are under the same sentence? We are punished justly, for we are getting what our deeds deserve. But this man has done nothing wrong.' Then he said, 'remember me when you come into your kingdom.' Iosa answered him, 'Truly I tell you, today you will be with me in paradise.'"

I tilted my head and studied the wonder and joy on Erik's face. Paradise sounded beautiful. How could Iosa bring a criminal to such a place?

Tyra clasped her hands in her lap. "That's where my Inge is now. That's where even Ragnar could be if he only repented and asked God for forgiveness."

I swallowed the last bite of dried rabbit meat and then stood up and drew near her. I massaged her back with my palm, though my hand shook. Could she really have such kind thoughts toward him now?

"So, death," I said to Erik, in a determination to reign in my confusion. "Your god-man's death fixed up everything?"

He shook his head. "Oh, no—there's more to it than that. Three days after Iosa died, He came to life once more and soon after returned to heaven! When we believe in Him, His death defeats our sin, and His life gives us an eternal connection with God Himself."

I swallowed hard. "So, Inge is with this God?"

"Yes." Tyra's expression relaxed. "That's where she is."

I drew away from her, tightening my grip on the edge of the rowboat. Tyra was a sorry figure, pale and broken. I shuddered. It reminded me of my own grief over Mum, that even now cut deep inside me. How could she still believe in this Iosa?

In my mind, the facts were sure. Yesterday, Ragnar had destroyed the life of Tyra's little babe—and I wasn't about to let him get away with it.

THIRTY

A MAN HOLLERED, WAKING ME from sleep. "A ship! By the gods, it's four Irish ships."

"Prepare for battle," Ragnar roared.

I shot up from where I'd been lying down. In the distance, the Irish ships rowed swiftly away from us, but we flew faster. Our sails moved in wild playfulness like the raucous dancing of drunken men.

Ragnar stormed through his longship, jabbing the men with oars to wake them up. The Norsemen hurried to their feet and lost no time in obeying the jarl's orders. They took turns between rowing and preparing for battle. Soon each man gripped a weapon. Some carried sharp axes and swords, others long spears, and the skillful archers were armed with bows and arrows.

Ragnar plunked the tiny rowboat we'd taken with us in the sea. He shoved Erik, Freyja, Tyra, and me over the side of the longship into the boat. I gasped and clutched the side of the small boat to get my bearings.

He chucked an oar at Erik. "Protect the women!"

The four large Norse longships encircled the four small enemy ships. I caught my breath. Between two of Ragnar's longships, a broad-shouldered man was scrambling around a ship and ordering about dozens of Irish thralls. Lars.

My heart flipped over inside me, and I shook Erik's shoulder, pointing to our friend. "Look!"

As he turned to look where I pointed, his hand gripped the oar tightly. "No," he whispered.

But it was too late. Men began laying down planks and clambering over to one another's ships. They slashed at each other with spears and swords. Arrows flew about. Several of them overshot the Norse longships and sailed toward our small rowboat. I bit back a scream and ducked. One narrowly missed my back.

Erik rowed as far away from the scene as he could, just as he was ordered to do.

"What are you doing, Erik?" I yelled at him. "We have to help them!"

Erik gestured to Tyra and Freyja. "We can't put these two in danger."

He knew me too well. If I had no concern for my own life, I had ample concern for others. I clenched my jaw but nodded slowly. Tyra scooted close beside me. She clung to me like a child, her stamina thin and breakable.

"We'll be all right," I told her.

Then I surveyed the battle. Swords crossed. Spears and axes clanged. Arrows flew so wildly and so far that some landed in the water near us. I feared they could strike us if someone tried hard enough.

One Irish thrall dove into the water and swam toward our rowboat. Erik tried to paddle away, but the current was against him, and he had a much heavier load than the thrall. By the gods! I clutched Tyra's arm, as the man caught up to us.

Erik whacked him with his oar. The man keeled backward into the water. But a second later he pulled himself onto our rowboat. He slid out his sword from his sheath.

I punched him in the face. He recoiled but managed to stay in the boat.

I started forward, but the Irish thrall shoved me aside. I stumbled backwards and fell against the stern. The boat rocked sideways but managed to right itself.

The man cried out, raising his sword over me. I squeezed my eyes shut. This couldn't be how I died.

A harsh metallic sound shrieked through the air. I looked up to see Erik pushing a knife against the Irish thrall's sword.

The man stood his ground and pushed against Erik.

Don't! I dropped my hand down to the hilt of my sword.

Soon the thrall pinned Erik down against the side of the ship. His face was red and full of wrath.

I staggered to my feet. The small boat swayed back and forth precariously. I spread out my legs and my arms, fighting to remain balanced. As the rowboat steadied itself, I gripped the hilt at my side.

Before I could unsheathe my sword, Erik escaped the man's hold, grabbed his knife, and thrust it into the man's chest. The man groaned and slumped forward on top of Erik. Erik shoved the man into the water.

"Ye saved us!" Tyra breathed out, offering a grateful smile to Erik.

"The Lord is good." Then he grabbed his oar and began paddling as if nothing had happened.

That boy never ceased to astound me, to say the least. First knife-hunting a deer from a distance, then bowing before Niels to set me free, and now this? I couldn't help but be impressed by his courage. I had always thought he was weak, but I was beginning to see this bolder side of him more and more, and I knew it was real. I knew it was who he really was, deep inside.

I returned my attention to the sea battle and scanned the longships until I saw Lars. He stabbed a Norseman with a spear and hurled him into the water with a splash.

Ragnar stepped onto Lars's longship, his hand clenched at the hilt of his sword.

No, not Lars. Ragnar was too skilled a swordsman.

I dove into the sea and swam toward the longship in the rough waves, kicking my legs violently.

My friends called after me, but I ignored them and focused my energy on moving through the water. I dove downward, swimming underneath the longships, toward Lars and Ragnar. I bobbed my head out of the water and gasped for air. An oar whacked me in the face. My head swirled. The oar came at me again, and I grabbed it, my weight pulling it down. Soon someone released the oar into the water, likely in response to an attack aboard the ship. As I clutched onto the paddle and floated, I peered upward to see Ragnar swiping a sword at Lars.

Biting my lip, I took hold of the side of the longship. Gripping the ship's rim, I pulled my body upward and dragged myself aboard, soaking wet.

Just as I raised my head, Lars fell to the deck of the ship.

"Lars!" I cried out.

Ragnar sliced his sword in my direction. I flattened myself to the deck to avoid the sharp blade. Niels stood beside him, murmuring to him. When he had someone to guide him, Ragnar was a master sword fighter. He had practiced with the sword about every day since he was a twelve-year-old boy—just as Erik had.

Grim-faced, I pushed myself to my feet and met the jarl's gaze. It was just him, Niels, Lars, and me on this ship. Now was the time to show him who I was—in the chaos of battle with neither Tyra nor Erik to hinder me. I drew out the long, shimmering sword and thrust the weapon toward Ragnar, who swung his sword against mine in a natural reflex.

We stood frozen, our weapons pressed against each other, silent, determined. He looked at my sword. A glow ignited his eyes, an insatiable desire to destroy.

"Gerd, you fool!" Ragnar pushed me hard, and I tumbled backwards into the hull of the ship. Niels murmured to him directions, and Ragnar pointed his blood-stained sword at my face.

"Where did you get that sword?" he growled.

I rose to my feet, trying not to tremble as I clenched my hand over the jewel-decorated hilt. "I found it on a beach, sir." Then I thrust it upward at him, toward his face.

He blocked my attempt with a clang of his sword. "There's no other sword like it, and mine should be lost in the depths of the sea."

"Wouldn't it be with your father in Valhalla?" I asked. I hoped my words could hurt him just enough to keep his sword off me for a little longer.

"You know something about my father, and that sword." He widened his stance. "I would even say you look a lot like that thrall wench I sent to serve him in the afterlife—but what would these eyes of mine know about the looks of little wenches?"

"I'm not a wench."

And yet the shame of the funeral rituals burned inside me. Perhaps they had turned me into one.

An arrow whistled past me. I flinched, my gaze leaving Ragnar's for a moment. A man near us thrust an Irish thrall off the side of the longship to let the ocean take care of him.

"I know who you are." Ragnar grasped my wrist and drew his sword close to my neck, dragging my wide-eyed gaze to his face. "If you weren't that girl, how else would you know that this sword belongs to my dead father?"

"I was in Kaupang, sir, during the funeral."

"By the gods, how did you escape, thrall?"

I swallowed hard. "Sir, I've always known how to swim. My father taught me well."

He gritted his teeth. Niels spoke into his ear.

"You said you wanted to die. You took the place of Tyra." Ragnar shoved me backwards.

"I never said that, but I did—"

"Liar!" He swung his blade toward me.

I leaned backward and dodged most of the blow. "You are a murderer!" I screamed loudly. The mountain of wrath that had built up inside me over the past months finally exploded. "You killed my mother!"

"Your mother wanted to defy Norse tradition," Ragnar cried.

My stomach churned at the thought. Defiance against him and respect for our customs battled within me. I, too, understood the importance of tradition. But Mother's rebellion gave him no right to murder her.

Ragnar swung his sword and plunged it into my shoulder. I keeled backwards, shock reverberating through me and knocking any scream from my lungs.

He pressed me against the edge of the ship. "You stupid thrall. You have brought dishonor onto our entire village. The gods will curse us for it."

He lifted his sword above me. I felt so small and alone. "You stupid thrall!" The words rang in my ears over and over and in that moment a startling thought shook me: I deserved to die.

Ragnar's hold loosened, and he slumped to the side.

"Go, Sigrid," Lars shouted hoarsely.

I toppled over the side of the longship. Seawater rushed into my mouth and stung my wounded shoulder.

I struggled to swim toward the rowboat that bobbed away in the distance. Pain tore at my shoulder. Seawater sloshed over my face and mouth. I paused and floated on my back, gasping for air.

"I'm here, Sigrid," Erik called out to me.

I looked up to see the rowboat next to me.

Erik reached down and dragged me on board. He threw a blanket around me. "We've got to leave this place."

Good. I was done with killing for today. I was done with trying. All my efforts had been in vain. I flopped back against a sack.

Freyja brought out bandages and cleaned up my wound with a wet cloth. Then she wrapped my shoulder with a thin blanket, winding it about securely.

Tyra lay silently under some blankets, no doubt mourning over Inge or praying to that God of hers.

A wave of exhaustion threatened to drag me to sleep. My eyelids drooped close.

The rowboat lurched, startling me awake. The battle had become muffled echoes of terror, and the green mountains came into clear view. An expanse of white sand spread out before us, and further back, huge rocks protruded outward lining the shore. Beyond them, deep green pines and ferns flooded our view, while beyond that the mountains towered toward the heavens, surrounded by mist.

I sat up in the boat and breathed in the cool air. My shoulder fired with pain, reminding me of my fruitless endeavor not long ago.

Erik stared at the green peaks. "I think I recognize this place."

His face was not delighted though. He wore a slack expression, his eyes dull and wet.

"Aren't you glad to see your homeland?" I asked him. I had hoped he'd be. I had looked forward to the day he saw his country. Rather than him rejoicing as I expected, he seemed sad.

"Sigrid," he said, but he didn't say more. Sorrow penetrated his gentle expression. An ache burned my heart. Was he sad that his family was not waiting for him here in his homeland?

He rowed the boat to the sandy shore. Erik, Freyja, and I climbed out and pulled the boat up the long beach. No one was around, thank the gods, so we didn't need to worry about frightened Irish defending their beach from three scraggly-looking Norsewomen and one skinny red-haired fellow.

I turned to ask Tyra what she thought of her homeland, and I realized she wasn't here. "Where's Tyra?" I asked. I turned back to the rowboat. Swollen bags of supplies and rolled up blankets crammed together side by side met my gaze.

"We have something to tell you." Tears streamed down Erik's face.

Freyja cut her gaze toward the end of the rowboat. "She's under there."

My heart pounded. I flung the blankets off where Freyja had pointed. Tyra lay motionless on her stomach, an arrow in her back.

I fell onto the wooden planks of the hull and turned her over. "Tyra? Tyra!"

The arrow had gone straight through her back to her heart. Her empty sky-blue eyes that had once held so much joy and hope stared upward.

I pulled her head onto my lap and gently closed her eyelids.

"What happened?" I choked out.

Erik sank beside me and traced Tyra's gentle, serene face. She was so beautiful, even in death.

"The girl saved Ragnar's life." A smile played on Freyja's lips, baffling me with her frivolity about this painful moment. "When you swam off, Erik rowed the boat closer to the battle trying to find you. An Irish fool drew his sword to strike Ragnar, but Tyra flung her arms in the air, crying out. It caught the enemy's attention, distracting him from Ragnar. Unfortunately, she also caught the attention of an enemy archer." She stared off, toward the sea. "The arrow went right through her heart. If she ever even had one, that is."

I embraced Tyra's body. Tyra *did* have a heart. She had a heart so wide and deep that if I was honest, I'd say it was bigger than Mum's. After all Ragnar had done to her, Tyra still loved him enough to save his life.

Freyja sighed and said, "I am sorry for your loss, but I must leave now."

I shot a look at her. "You're not sorry. You're glad she's dead."

"I said I'm sorry," Freyja snapped. "It's a horrible thing that's happened. Now let me be."

I stood up and faced her, tightening my hands into fists. She had smiled at Tyra's death. Said Tyra had no heart. "Who do you think you are? You take pleasure in this moment. You're content to finally have the jarl to yourself. Am I right?"

Freyja turned her face away. "I know you are hurt, but I must leave."

"Fine, leave us." I narrowed my brows and gazed down at Tyra. Freyja was awful, but at least she would leave Erik and me to ourselves to mourn for our dear friend.

Erik cleared his throat. "Where are ye goin', Freyja?" he asked.

"Back to Ragnar," she said coolly. "You two will be fine here without the rowboat, won't ya? We'll show up in time for the raid."

I stared at her, my lip quivering. Would we get to the village in time?

Erik's pale face told me he was scared, too. "All right."

He drew Tyra's body from me and rested her on the sand then helped me out of the rowboat.

Freyja paddled away, back to the battle, her chin lifted high as if she'd already won it.

We turned to Tyra, staring at her for a long time. Memories of her warmth and grace gripped me. It was different than what I'd felt when Mum died, though I couldn't place the difference. Visions of Tyra playing and laughing with the children at Stellan's house enraptured my mind.

She'd tenderly cared for the cranky old woman who wanted a bath. She'd loved the lost children and broken mothers and poor thralls she'd never met before. I thought of her sweet laugh and her high-pitched song that soared through heights I never knew existed. My mind traced back to the day she'd offered herself to die in my place. Then, I remembered the way she spoke to the Irish, to Ragnar, to Erik, and to me, about her Mighty God, gently directing us to what she believed was true.

If Tyra's God loved her, why did her life end so quickly and brutally?

I sat beside her body, my wounded shoulder throbbing and fatigue weighing down on me. This land was green and beautiful, but empty, so empty like this feeling inside, this piece inside me that cried out in despair for the sweetest soul I had ever known.

THIRTY-ONE

ERIK CROUCHED DOWN AND STARED at the sand, misty-eyed. "She saved Jarl Ragnar's life."

Tyra rested on the beach to his left, alone and lost forever in an afterlife I hoped deserved her presence. Could she have gone to a good place if she hadn't believed in the Norse gods?

We stretched out our legs on the sand, our bare feet toward the ocean.

My shoulders shook, but I held the tears in. "She loved him," I stammered. "I don't know why."

"I can hardly believe it myself," Erik admitted. "Yet she was always so determined to love her enemies. 'Tis what she lived for and died for."

"But why? Ragnar only loved her body." I ground my teeth.

Erik stared intently at the growing tide. "Tyra had an everyday understanding of the love of God that reached into every person she came across and looked past the mistakes they made. For me, somedays I only fancy God in my head without heeding His ways, and that sure isn't right." He looked up at the sky, clenching his jaw. "Other days I hate my God with every piece o' me, and I just itch to yell and scream and walk right back to where I came from—the easy path of followin' yerself, and not the merciful Father who created ye.

But that only makes ye travel round and round in circles, chasin' yer tail like a mad hound."

He shook his head. "But Tyra had a love for God that went so deep every day, because she knew how deep He loved her. That's how she was able to love anyone she came across."

I clawed a handful of sand, then let it trickle through the cracks between my fingers.

"Do ye even care what I am sayin' to ye?" That old fear crept back into his face, his chin quivering so awfully that I worried he would cry and set me off bawling. Though my limbs felt heavy and weak, I hadn't shed a tear yet. I had to keep whatever pride I had left.

"I care," I murmured, not able to understand him or myself, not even knowing why I was lying. Why was he even talking about his God at a time like this anyway?

Erik brought his arm around my shoulders. I started to pull away from him, but his touch was so gentle that I relaxed into his shoulder. He wasn't like the Norsemen I'd met during the funeral rituals. He offered the comfort and strength I needed to keep me going. He even offered something I'd never understood before, something I longed for, though I couldn't place exactly what it was.

All I knew was I needed him. And if I didn't survive this, Ragnar would never be brought to justice. But Erik didn't believe in revenge. He didn't believe in killing for justice.

I slipped out of his arms and turned back to Tyra. Her sweet, loving face tore at something deep within me. Mum had died trying to save me, just as Tyra had died for Ragnar. But Mum had loved me because I belonged to her. Ragnar had offered nothing to Tyra. So why had she tried to save him?

I embraced my friend's cold, lifeless neck. "I don't love anyone as she did or you do. I never have. Oh, Erik, I don't even know if I love my own mother that much."

Erik shifted in the sand. "Ye speak of yer mother often."

I traced the soft lines in Tyra's face, ignoring his matter-of-fact remark.

A seabird began pecking at the sand nearby, curiously eyeing Tyra's corpse every now and then. A frosty wind swept right through my bones, so I curled closer to Tyra.

"Sigrid?"

I turned my neck sideways to look up at him.

Erik bent down and reached his hand out, touching my cheek. "I'm sorry," he whispered. "I know she was your friend for a long time before I met her."

I turned away from his gentle touch that, strangely, set my emotions into flames, rather than caused me fear. "I can't believe in a God who kills the kindest creatures alive."

"He didn't kill her, Sigrid, it was that blasted arrow—"

"Just as that blasted sword killed my mother." I grimaced. While he knew I wanted Ragnar dead, I didn't want to spill the entirety of my vengeful plan to him.

"Oh, Sigrid, I killed my own father, ye know. I understand." He rubbed the back of his neck, and I could sense his discomfort.

Yes, he could understand my grief. But he couldn't understand my desire to avenge my mother's death. How could he when he refused to let me slay Ragnar a few nights ago?

I held Tyra's limp hand tightly, tears clogging my throat and flooding my eyes. I swallowed hard, trying to push them away. "You can't, Erik. You can't understand."

He sighed wearily. I could sense his frustration, but his voice was mild when he spoke again: "We need to be goin'."

I looked up at him through my blurry vision. He jerked his head toward the white cliffs that hung over us, to the right of the sea.

I sucked back my tears in a valiant effort to maintain my pride.

"We came here to warn and defend the Irish," Erik said, "and I don't believe Lars has been able to warn them with the battle ragin' on out there. Might as well do it ourselves, shall we?"

I bit my bottom lip, wishing we could stay here longer. And yet, he did have a point.

"All right." I tried to heave myself off the ground, but I stumbled backwards. Erik reached out his hand, so tentatively, I let him pull me up.

When he didn't let go of my hand, my heart trembled. I tore my hand away and flattened down my rumpled tunic. I smoothed out my thick hair, but it kept bulging outward. I imagined my hair was in a hideous mess. If Tyra were here—were alive—she'd laugh.

But Erik stared at me, motionless. "Are ye all right?"

I dropped my gaze from his and fixed it on the grains of sand. "I'm fine."

"We best move Tyra, over past the rocks, so the waves don't carry her off."

We crouched down to Tyra's body and lifted her up. Erik held her head and shoulders, and I held her legs.

We carried her over toward the rocks, my heart sinking at the look on her peaceful face. She was stunning. The bloody stench of her wound was the only unlovely thing about her.

Water dripped onto my forehead, so I wiped it off with one hand. More rain fell, dampening me and all of nature. The pounding rain and Ragnar—I hated them both.

When we reached the rocks, we lowered Tyra's body to the ground. My chest ached. "We can't just leave her like this."

Erik stared out at the sea, where we could glimpse only a few ships in the distance. "The battle is likely going to go on out there for a few more hours. We have a bit of time. Let's dig up a hole. She deserves a proper burial."

We dug in the rich, Irish dirt a large hole, scraping and scraping till my knees and back ached. At last we had managed to create a ditch large enough to hold our dear friend. We lifted her body and lowered her in. The rain continued drenching us, so we quickly covered her body with dirt.

I found a white flat stone nearby and placed it on the newly formed grave. *Goodbye, Tyra.*

The rain pounded harder onto us. I wanted to stay with my friend, let the rain beat down on me, but Erik pulled me toward a crevice in a large rock for shelter.

I stared at the dirt-patched ground that covered our dear friend. My throat ached with emotion. I imagined the ocean swallowing up the tiny droplets of rain, morsels for the hungry waves to devour. The waves roared and swelled. I took comfort in them, as I had taken comfort in Tyra. The ocean had always been there for me, just as she had been there, as a hope, a reason to stay alive. When I observed the roiling waters or spent a day with Tyra, I felt at home. Now I had only the ocean.

"Why did Tyra have to die?" I asked. "Why did Inge have to and Gunnar and all those Irish and Norse who died in the battle out at sea? Why, Erik? Why did my mother have to . . . ?"

Tears freely coursed down his cheeks. "I don't know, Sigrid. I don't know."

My whole body quaked, but I kept my hands locked together, hugging my knees to my chest. I shifted my body away from the fellow sitting far too near me. Of course, he didn't know. Why did I search for answers from him?

His hand squeezed my shoulder gently. "Please, Sigrid, find peace with God. I can't bear to see ye suffer."

I rocked from side to side, holding back tears as hard as I could. I couldn't think about his God. I couldn't think about my unanswered questions. None of this should have happened.

"*I* should have died, not Tyra," I choked. "It should've been me."

"No, ye needn't say that."

Hesitantly, he laid an arm around my shoulder and drew me close to him. "Ye can cry now, Sigrid," he whispered in my ear. "She's worth it. She's with Iosa now."

I leaned into his chest and broke into deep, inconsolable sobs.

THIRTY-TWO

"HOW COULD SHE BE GONE?" I bawled into Erik's shoulder, every shard of dignity I had built up for weeks shattering inside me. My shoulder ached, but my heart ached more—more severely than it ever had before.

As the thunder roared, Erik wept with me. "She died much too soon," he said in a tight voice. "But God used her life to bring Him glory. She loved and served those widows and children in Bergen, and everyone else she knew."

"And Ragnar?" I spoke hoarsely, wanting him to say it all aloud, to understand everything.

"Aye," he whispered. "She loved him, too."

"That's what she did, huh? That was her purpose in life, to love."

"And to speak truth with that same love. God bless her soul."

There was a small hope in his voice, and suddenly, I wanted that same hope more than I could bear. Tyra had possessed that hope. I remembered her tender voice and her bright eyes as she spoke of her God. Her hope had sustained her through her horrid slavery to Ragnar. Her hope had made her radiant and strong in the face of his wrath.

The gods of my people had never given me hope. Instead, they'd cursed me with a life of slavery, binding me to chains even when my master wasn't around; the chains of fear, grief, and helplessness that seemed to define me.

Would I ever be truly free?

"I haven't done a chore in two weeks, and I still feel like a thrall."

Erik lowered his head to my face, so his lips almost touched my forehead. "Ye know what I'm goin' to say, Sigrid."

I slipped out of his arms and stepped out into the open air, pleasantly surprised by the sudden absence of rain. "Yes, I know. Iosa died to set me free." I relaxed a little as a breeze blew into my face. Iosa. Freedom. In my haste to make Mum and Ragnar my priority, I had buried the thoughts in the back of my mind. But they still intrigued me. "You know, Erik, that doesn't sound so bad anymore."

Could I give into a God who despised revenge? Could I give up my only reason to live?

Bending down to Tyra's grave, I tried to shift my mind back to the dear friend I had lost. But whenever I thought of her, I couldn't help thinking of her God as well. Erik was right. She'd had a purpose that defined her whole life: to serve and love Iosa.

I heard Erik step out of the shelter as well, and I felt his presence beside me.

"Please go away," I said stiffly, weakening at the sound of my tearful voice.

He didn't say a word, just left me, walking silently to the shoreline. He slipped his shoes off and let the tide wash over his big bare feet.

Without Ragnar I would have no purpose. The thought had continually surfaced in my mind these past few weeks, tugging at my conscience. What would it accomplish to kill him? Would taking revenge for my mother's death make me feel any better than before?

I stared at Tyra's grave in silence. I had never gotten to bury my mother. She was sinking in the depths of the sea, to nowhere, really. Had she gone through the golden gates of Valhalla, or was she all alone, frozen in the ice-cold underworld? Either way, she'd have no idea that I had made any attempt to enact vengeance for her. She was dead. My attempt to honor her would be like a mist in a wind: it would mean nothing.

Tyra had known exactly who she was, and what she lived for. But who was I? And what did *I* live for?

If I was being completely honest with myself, I wanted to please myself. I craved things for myself. Freedom. Joy. Love. I wanted to be free, but not only from the slavery I had already escaped or from the grief of Mother's death. I craved a deeper freedom, in my very soul.

The waves tumbled out in the sea. The ocean was as close to freedom I'd ever got. But even when I'd bathed in the waters, or scrubbed a chamber pot, or waded in it with Tyra, I had always wished for more. I longed for a freedom that surpassed my own knowledge. Tyra reminded me of it, and so did Erik, simply by being themselves. I wondered if Mum could wait a little longer in the afterlife after I killed Ragnar, until I found that freedom for myself.

The truth hurt. My whole life had been focused on only one person. It was not Mum's pride I had sought in my quest to kill Ragnar, it was my own. The thought of Ragnar writhing in pain for the evil he had done was so pleasing I had already attempted to kill him three times!

I stared at the cloudy horizon, clenching my teeth so hard I thought I'd lose them. I was a wandering fool living only to please myself, chasing my tail like a mad hound.

A memory of Erik at the babbling stream came to me. He was crying out toward the sky, distraught, as if he were truly nothing. Now he was like Tyra, bold and humble at the same time. Looking up—always looking up, like the little straw doll.

"I want to be something—I have to be something!" I cried out.

Pain struck my chest, and I trembled all over. I wanted to die, even though I felt it to my bones that Mum or even Tyra would not be there, wherever I went. I wanted to die, because I was nothing, and it was better to die than live on this wretched earth that did nothing but tear me apart, locking me in shackles of disillusionment.

As I knelt before Tyra's grave, a light warmed me. A light that I could not see. Presently, I heard a low, gentle, voice like a summer breeze.

"I died so you could live for Me, precious one. I died to make you something new. I died to take you out of darkness and to conquer the night. I rose again to claim victory over shame, fear, and pride. I am the reason you are alive, Siri; I am the reason why you should live." The warm voice paused, then whispered, *"You may be nothing to the world, but to Me, you are worth everything, even My very life."*

My heart jumped, and the light felt more certain on me, but I still couldn't see it. Somehow, I recognized His voice. This was Iosa. I was certain of it.

I drew out the doll from my satchel. I had long considered her a proud figure, with her head straight up. But now, as I studied her, I realized she was looking up at the sky. Looking up to Iosa, her whole being filled with wonder.

I raised my head toward the sky and cried out in desperation, "I am sorry for living for myself, Iosa!"

Once I tried out the words, I realized that it was true. I had been a complete fool this whole time.

And Erik? He was no fool. No pathetic creature. He was *not* nothing. I had beaten him, ridiculed him, hated him, when all he'd ever done was care for me.

I wanted to live for Iosa. I wanted to be with Him.

"I'm sorry," I whispered. "What a fool I've been, Iosa. You are the Son of God, the Savior of the world, everything Tyra said You were. She loved others because You loved her. I don't deserve You, God. I don't deserve You when I've hated You so much. But You *do* exist. I think I knew deep down inside this whole time. I was just too proud to admit it."

I bowed my head before the Almighty God, the Lord of the universe. Who was I compared to Him? I knew nothing. He knew everything. Why had I placed my trust in myself for so long? And how could He ever forgive me?

"I love you, Siri," He whispered tenderly. *"You are forgiven. Do you believe in Me, dear one?"*

It was so sudden, that it was hard to believe what had just happened. He forgave me; He wanted me; He loved me. Tears filled my eyes, but they were from a sudden burst of hope and joy in my heart. It felt similar to what I had seen blazing in Tyra and Erik's eyes. I didn't want this to go away.

"I believe in You, Iosa. I believe."

His kindness pulled at my heart, and I wanted to live for Him now more than ever.

When I opened my eyes, a bright light came pouring in through the clouds so fast I inhaled deeply in awe of its radiance.

Or maybe I hadn't been breathing this whole time.

THIRTY-THREE

I RAN TO ERIK ON the shore, letting my shoes fly off as my bare feet hit the soft sand. "You'll never believe what has happened to me," I exclaimed as I approached him.

But he didn't turn to me; he was staring at something out in the sea. One of Lars's ships was coming toward us. Flames engulfed the rest of the small ships behind it, the Norse longships circling the prey like vultures.

Lars stood aboard the ship, staring out toward the land. Overwhelmed with my new life, I ran through the low tide till the water sloshed over my hips. Then I dove in and swam to meet my friend and the Irish thralls. Soon, I pulled myself up onto the longship and stood up. Breathing heavily, water dripping down my skin, I gazed up at Lars's familiar scratchy beard. He was a brother to me, however cunning he could be at times. He had led Erik and I through a forest and over a mountain. He had shown us the way. And now, I had found *the* Way.

Lars frowned and backed away. "Sigrid, what are you doing here? You swam out here?"

My lungs were breathless. I clutched his hands. "Iosa saved me, Lars."

Tears ran down my cheeks, beautiful, endless tears that sprang from the depths of my heart. I wasn't ashamed of them anymore.

Lars raised a brow. "Sigrid?"

"All right." I laughed and wiped the tears from my face. "I was a little crazy swimming out here. But it's so good to see you again."

He nodded. "Nice to see you, too. Sorry for my mood, I'm just busy." He called out to the Irish slaves surrounding us. "Keep paddling—this girl isn't any danger to us. We're almost there." He turned to me again. "Did that redhead convince you?"

"No, Iosa *Himself* convinced me." I couldn't contain this joyous feeling within me. "I'm free now."

He furrowed his brow.

"I'm sorry, Lars. I hadn't been very thoughtful toward you back in Bergen. We really should have figured something else out." I bit my lip and paused. "But now, listen to me, Lars—Iosa saved me. Do you really think I would make something like this up?"

Lars slapped me on the side of my face.

I gasped and covered my tingling cheek. "Lars, what—"

"Where's Erik?" he snapped.

Erik? Oh, so now he cared about him? Thoughts fired through me, but the gentleness of God urged me to be calm.

"He's on the beach." I shot a glance at the beautiful white shores of Ireland where Erik was standing.

"What about Jarl Ragnar?" Lars demanded.

"I don't know," I answered. "We left Ragnar to get away from battle. Are all of you okay?"

Lars lifted his hand toward the Irish thralls then let it fall to his side. "You think we could survive against him? I've been a fool this whole time. I set out with thirty Irish thralls and these five remain with me. Three ships are sunk, supplies and all. You think we can warn and protect the Irish now?"

I smiled sadly. So many were lost at the hands of Ragnar. "Well, why not?"

"But why, Sigrid?" His voice was suddenly quiet, yet intense. "That's what we should be asking. Why?"

"You're half Irish, and we've come this far—"

"What's the point, Sigrid?" Lars pushed an oar against the current so fiercely I thought it'd take us to Kaupang with one stroke. "I never even met my Irish mum. My pa told me I'm a Norseman, so that's what I am."

"God loves them," I murmured.

"'Iosa saved me!' You say, 'God loves them!' I don't believe this," Lars growled.

"It's true, friend," I said. "I believe in Iosa now." Warmth radiated inside me, as I burst with love for him, for the Irish, for everyone I came in sight of. If only he could understand!

Lars steadied his gaze at the land ahead. "Good for you, I'm sure. Iosa will suit you fine, just as He did to the redhead." But he seemed to blink away tears, as if I had delivered the worst news. "What has Erik done to you?"

"He didn't do anything," I replied. "God sent Iosa to die for my sins, so I don't have to live in them anymore. I can be free, living for Him, instead of myself."

"By the gods, what is wrong with you?" Lars raised his paddle blade and lunged it toward me. "I heard this enough from Erik!"

I jumped out of the way then tumbled backward over the side of the ship into the hazy depths. I fought against the waves, choking in want of air. I flapped my arms until I regained control and found the surface of the water. My head popped out of the water, and I gasped for breath. Lars stood on the deck as if nothing had happened.

"Why am I saving the Irish?" Lars narrowed his eyes down at me in the water, threatening me, though I didn't know why.

"You chose to," I yelled. "You traveled all the way out here—I thought you wanted to." Kicking my legs, I bobbed up and down with the waves. "And, well, they are your *own* people!"

At that, his face blazed a wildberry red. Lars pushed the Irish thralls out of the longship, one by one. The thralls flailed their arms about in the water, but the water began to overwhelm them.

My heart raced. What was he thinking? I swam to one of the women and grabbed her arm. I struggled against her weight to keep her afloat.

"Come all this way, and then kill us, cap'n?" a man said above as he fought against Lars. "What is wrong with ye, sir? By all that is righteous, who do ye think ye are!?"

Lars flung a child into the waves nearby. Fighting off a scream, I caught the child with my other hand, while still grasping tightly to the woman. I swam toward the green mountains, striving to keep them above the water—the child was easy, but the woman kept panicking and trying to grab the child. My wounded shoulder seared with pain.

They clung to me and started dragging me down. The water sloshed over my face. I couldn't breathe. "Don't panic!" But water entered my mouth and soon was burning my lungs.

As their fighting bodies sank further into the sea, I sank with them. Why did God do this to me now?

I was tempted to let them go.

No, Iosa urged me. *Hold onto them. They are Mine.*

But—God, I am going to die; I am going to die.

I am with you, He assured me.

I clung to the woman and child, and they to me. *God*, I prayed, my arms aching, my head pounding, and everything in me weakening as water flooded into my mouth, nostrils, and lungs. *I need You to be my strength.*

Suddenly, I felt a staggering difference. I still had to fight against the ocean and struggle to uphold the woman and child, but the fight seemed not my own doing. It was not me who was grabbing hold of these Irish thralls, but it was the hand of God upholding the woman, the child, and myself.

My focus was blurry; I did not know where I was going. But I knew who held me; the One Who knew everything.

The waves swept us ashore, and I lay coughing in the sand as the tide rushed over us.

Erik sprinted to us, pulling each of us away from the tide. "Are ye all right?"

"Lars has lost his mind," I choked. My lungs craved air. I was soaked and dripping from the frigid seawater. And yet, somehow, I felt full and warm inside, alive in the presence of God.

I went to the woman lying limply in the sand and bent down to listen to her heart. Slow, but sure.

The boy gasped from where he lay in the sand. "Mum?"

Erik helped the weakened boy to his feet and pointed to the woman lying in the sand a few feet away. I backed off to let the child come to his mother. He wrapped his arms around her. "God is all around us, Mum! He made the waves carry us to shore."

I smiled. He realized who deserved the glory faster than I did.

The boy, about eight years old, had light blond wavy hair and vivid blue eyes that seemed to see right through a person. I recognized him as Colm, and his mother as Aine, the Irish thralls I had directed to Lars.

Erik smiled at me, but when he opened his mouth to speak, the boy cried out: "Mum! You can't do this! You can't!" His chin trembled. "Do you see me?"

She did not reply.

He turned to me, tears streaming down his pale cheeks. "Is she dead?"

I turned to the woman and laid my hands on her chest. I did the only thing I could do—what my own mother had taught me—and pushed on her chest to get the air pumping through her. *Iosa, please give her the breath of life. Please don't let her die now.*

Erik's brows pulled down in concentration as he placed a hand on the boy's shoulder. Then he muttered something I could not understand.

"Are you claiming her alive in the name of Iosa?" The boy's blue eyes glowed like the summer sky. I wondered that he could fear for his mother one moment and hope so violently the next.

I pushed on the woman's chest, over and over.

Erik smiled a little. "Somethin' like that."

"So am I," Colm said. "Are you doin' that, pretty lady?"

Erik had no clue I was a follower of Iosa now. What would he think if I told him? Would he forgive me for all that I had said and done against him? I stammered a reply: "No, I honestly didn't know you could order the Irish God around like that."

I pressed down on the woman's chest then released. I pressed again. Her eyelids were closed; her lips were parted. I prayed fervently as I pushed. *Please, Iosa, he's only a boy. He shouldn't ever have to know the same grief I do.*

The woman suddenly gasped and coughed out seawater. Her chest rose up and down, and seawater spewed from her mouth. Colm rushed to cradle his mother's head and embrace her. The woman sucked in deep breaths then reached up a shaking hand to trace her son's face from his ear to his chin.

A grin spread across the boy's face. "Mum, were you dead? Did you see the angels?"

The woman furrowed her brow and slightly shook her head, still gasping for breath.

As the two talked together, Erik spoke to me. "What happened with Lars?"

I shifted my thoughts back to my friend who'd murdered three Irish thralls in a fit of rage. "He's not warning the Irish anymore. We have to do it."

Erik raised a brow.

"He threw the three other thralls in the water and wouldn't let them get back on the ship. I couldn't save them all." Something tightened in my chest at that thought. I couldn't save them all. Could there have been a way?

"He drowned them?" Erik's mouth hung open.

"He's not on our side anymore," I whispered. "He hates us."

Erik stiffened. "He hates me."

I picked myself up from the ground and stared at him, his strong jaw, his concerned brow. "Oh, Erik, he hates me, too."

I tried to think of how to explain everything that had happened to me, but my thoughts halted at his penetrating gaze. His face was gentle and handsome, and, in this moment, my heart fluttered. Not only did I love Iosa now, but something within me was beginning to awaken toward Erik. I did not understand it, but it was a feeling, warm and sure, growing by the minute. Something had always been there, drawing me toward him, but I had been too blinded by my high walls of pride and shame to realize what was going on. I had thought I was a flower drooped in the darkness with nothing left in me to love a man. But now the walls had broken down, and a little bit of light had trickled in. Perhaps the petals would begin to grow again.

"We'll have to finish the quest ourselves," Erik pronounced, breaking me out of my thoughts. "We can find the village and warn them. I think I recognize this place."

His voice carried a quiet excitement. He was finally standing on his homeland after so many years. I ought to honor his anxiousness to find old friends—old family, if he had any left. And we ought to complete our mission. Ragnar planned to pillage the village tonight.

"You're right. Lars is in no position at all to finish what he started. We'd best get going quickly before Ragnar and the crew attack the village."

The woman chuckled lightly on the shore. "Who do I have to thank for helpin' us?"

"She helped God." Colm pointed at me.

"I'm Sigrid, remember me? I directed you to travel with Lars to Ireland. You're Aine, right?"

The woman smiled warmly, like my mother used to smile. "I remember ye. Thank ye, Sigrid. I am grateful to ye beyond measure."

After Erik introduced himself, we informed our new friends of our plan to warn the Irish. "Ragnar could be arriving any moment to ransack the village. We must hurry and warn them."

"You mean we get to be their heroes?" Colm asked.

"We get to be God's hands and feet," Erik corrected him gently. "For He has brought us here to keep the Irish from dying or being plundered from or being taken captive. Now, let's move quickly."

I sensed Erik's anxiety. The rain had stopped, and any moment Ragnar could come plunder the village. I realized that I truly cared about our noble quest. I wanted the Irish to have a better chance of survival.

Though I had been used to my people plundering and murdering others all my life, I understood now why I had always felt so guilty. God could not wish for anything against His love and grace. He wished to save all people, to love every one of His creations.

And because of that, I couldn't kill Ragnar. Though I had understood this before, the thought now hit me with a sudden coldness dropping to my core. I couldn't call myself forgiven if I refused to forgive those around me. I had to love my enemies as God had loved me even when I'd spat in His face. But did He really expect me to forgive *that* man?

The boy tugged at my arm impatiently. "Can we go be their heroes?"

Erik assisted Aine to a standing position then looped his arm through one of hers. I looped mine through her other arm, and Colm held tightly to my hand.

We helped Aine trudge through the sand toward the village Erik directed us toward. I glanced at Tyra's grave where the flat white stone sat in remembrance of my friend's pure heart. Sadness crept into me, but the reminder of heaven shone even brighter. The new assurance of an afterlife with Iosa overflowed me with joy. One day, I knew, I would see Tyra again.

THIRTY-FOUR

THATCHED HOUSES HID BEHIND A few trees, just on the outer edges of the shore. A narrow bluff towered above us, overhanging the ocean. A chilly breeze whipped past my white-blonde hair. We had reached civilization again.

The Irish villagers were standing about, staring at us.

Erik called out to them in their own language. At his message, a man ran to a nearby house. He retuned seconds later with a tall, well-built man with a red cloak and a black hat who appeared to be the chieftain. None of the other villagers were dressed so finely.

The chieftain greeted Erik warmly. He glanced at me, Aine, and Colm as Erik spoke, and then his focus shifted to the turbulent sea. His face turned white as snow.

He hollered toward a few nearby villagers. They shot up to their feet and ran to the village, shouting out to everyone in sight. The news spread, and throughout the village the Irishmen began collecting weapons. Some of the men began calling out, and women and children came to them.

Aine whispered to me, "They're goin' to a shelter. Let's follow."

"I can't, Aine," I said sternly. "I need to fight. I need to be a part of this."

Erik approached us. "Go along where it's safe. Quickly. The Vikings are coming soon."

Aine grabbed Colm's hand, but I stood still. "I want to fight the Vikings. I want to fight my own people."

Erik frowned and crossed his arms. "None of the women are fighting. It's best for you to go with them."

I pressed my lips together. Erik and Aine stared at me, slicing my stubborn rock of will. Maybe this was the best way. Maybe it was God's way. I wasn't sure.

Aine and Colm followed the crowd of women and children who were scurrying away from the village. I walked slowly behind them. Even though I glowed with a new love, I still hated Ragnar. And though I would have to spare his life for Iosa's sake, I wanted to fight in this battle. But whose side was I on? Whose side was God on?

Soon, we arrived at a large cave and everyone gathered inside.

I stayed outside the cave and faced the tall ferns that seemed to point up to the God who created them. "Iosa, tell me what to do."

No answer.

I prayed louder. "Please, tell me what to do."

Silence.

"Iosa, please, tell me," I cried out, my voice echoing into the endless green fern trees.

Why wouldn't He speak to me as He had always spoken to Tyra? Was there something wrong with me?

I sank to my knees and gripped the grass. "Lord, I'm stuck in between a people I've always known and a people I've come to love. I don't want to fight my own people, but I don't want to fight the Irish." I tore out a chunk of grass, which brought up a clump of rich brown dirt along with it. "What am I supposed to do?"

A child wailed from inside the cave. But the sound was soon drowned out by high voices, singing softly.

Come and see what the Lord has done,
the desolations He has brought on the earth.
He makes wars cease
to the ends of the earth.
He breaks the bow and shatters the spear;
he burns the shields with fire.
He says, "Be still, and know that I am God;
I will be exalted among the nations,
I will be exalted in the earth."
The Lord Almighty is with us;
the God of Jacob is our fortress.

He makes wars cease. The words of the song resonated inside me. God loved the Norse warriors? He wasn't only an Irish God, He was *the* God. He would be exalted among all the nations. So, why all this fighting?

I hustled away from the cave and out in the open glade of the forest. I followed the path that had taken us here, patting Valdemar's sword under my cloak to make sure it was still there. I'd have to find a shield.

When I reached the village on the shore, the sky cast dark shadows on the longhouses and the sea reflected the full moon. The bright moon was good fortune for Norse raiders wishing to plunder in the dark. Surely, they would strike tonight.

I had to stop this.

᛭᛭᛭

I stepped out on the open shore. The constant waves battered the sand without mercy. In the shadows on the outer edges of the village, I could see figures, hunched and ready to strike—the Irishmen awaiting the dreaded Vikings.

I gazed at the enchanting sea, my old friend, shimmering in the moonlight. Four longships sped toward the village like arrows hungry for a target.

I hadn't gotten a shield, but a voice whispered inside me to stand firm. I couldn't run away like a fool.

I stood my ground in the sand. I wouldn't move until He told me to. *Love your enemies.* Though my old self would hate me, I had to do it. It was God's way. But could I truly make peace between the Norse and the Irish, while making peace with the man I had hated for so long?

The ships landed on the beach.

The Norsemen clambered out and charged toward the village with swords and shields, bows and arrows, axes and clubs and spears. I had memorized plenty of their grim, hairy faces and some of their names during the nine days I had voyaged with them. Yet in this moment, these men looked like strangers, the angry faces, the hunger in their eyes, the greed.

Holding back a cry, I hugged myself tightly as the men stormed past me, their focus on the village ahead, and not on me, as if God hid me from their sight.

But then I saw him, the man who had tormented my dreams for so long.

He didn't follow the others into the fires of battle and the glories of plunder. He conversed with Niels for a moment, then Niels nodded and rushed off into battle without him. Perhaps Ragnar was so proud of his defeat of Lars' Irish thralls he thought he could do anything—bad eyes and all.

With a sword in his left hand, he faced me, a grin spreading across his face. "Who are you, and why are you standing there?" he snapped.

"Good sir, I have come to speak of peace." Aware of his bad eyesight and the dim light of the moon, I walked toward him slowly, extending my hand out to him.

He paused. "You fool of a thrall. Shall we continue our little fight?"

He grasped for me, but I easily dodged him. Then he drew out his sword and stabbed the air. Without someone guiding him, he wasn't half as good a swordfighter.

"Lars!" he cried out.

A man came running. A Norseman wearing a helmet the same as the rest of the men and clutching the same type of shield and sword.

"Lars, I'm not wasting my breath on the wench," Ragnar shouted. "Kill her."

The man stared at me incredulously. "Sigrid?"

My shoulders quaked, as I realized who this Norseman was. "Oh, Lars, what are you doing?"

His sword wavered in his hand. "Get your sword out, Sigrid. I'm not killing you unarmed."

Half-heartedly, I slid my sword out of its sheath and gripped the hilt with both hands.

He struck his sword toward my chest. I swung my blade against his, metal clashing metal. I felt sick to my stomach. I didn't even recognize this man, my former friend.

I pushed against him with all my might, even as my wounded shoulder ached. I clenched my teeth. I knew he was being easy on me. "Why are you doing this?"

He sliced the air inches away from my arm. "I'm Ragnar's new head servant. I entertain him, and I help him see both physically and mentally."

The missed strike was purposeful. He wasn't going to kill me. He merely wanted to hurt me, to play with my feelings. It bewildered me that he'd change our plan—his plan—when we'd been trying to stick to it for so long.

The hilt of his sword struck my head. Black spots burst in my vision, and I tumbled to the ground. My vision blurred as I clung to the sand. I raised my neck upward and blinked away the spots. Lars stood near me, looking down at me.

I stumbled to my feet again and faced him. I swung my sword toward him, although the weight almost knocked me back down to the ground, my head still swimming from the blow. Lars sounded his weapon against mine, then pushed me backwards halfway into the sea. The water sloshed over my hips and over Lars's knees.

Lars's sword swished dangerously near my cheek. I fell backward into the water, but the sword still pricked my ear.

Hands grasped my shoulders and pulled me upward. Lars held me like a babe.

I clutched my bleeding ear and still tighter to my sword. Lars carried me through the water and back to the shore. He plunked me on the sand, the sword dropping from my hands at the jarring impact.

Lars swung his sword near my chest. "I knew it wouldn't be any use trying to drown you, seeing as you have a reputation for escaping the antics of the sea."

I swallowed hard and said, "I can't fight you. You will always be my friend, whether I am to you or not."

Lars gritted his teeth and lowered his sword. I snatched my sword and ran away. To my relief, no footsteps followed me. He was letting me go.

I sprinted toward the village, looking about for Ragnar. I had to stop this fight.

A scream shot through the air.

I froze.

"Iosa save me!" Erik's voice rang out from somewhere above me.

I looked up. On the bluff overhanging the sea, two figures stood tall, one pushing the other toward the edge of the bluff.

Erik.

The other swordsman was skilled, striking his sword against Erik's and pushing Erik closer and closer to the edge of the precipice. Only one man was that proficient with a sword.

As arrows flew and swords clanged, I dashed toward the level ground that gradually sloped upward and formed the cliff. Focusing on Erik's cries ahead of me, I ran up the diagonal slant through the trees.

Something pierced my already-wounded shoulder. Pain shot through me. I cried out, slipped in the pine needles, and fell forward on the slope. I landed on my hands, and pain throbbed through my shoulder. Black spots clouded my vision. I felt for the arrow, grit my teeth, and pulled it out. Tears of anguish streamed down my face as I stared at the bloody weapon. The world spun, and my head dropped to the earth.

I blinked open my eyes, groaning at the intense pain in my shoulder. How long had it been? Was it too late?

My hand still gripped the arrow. I tossed it aside. Shaking, I inched up the rock face I had to climb.

Erik cried out again. I couldn't let him die.

I clung tightly to the sloped ground and clutched any protruding rock I could find. I tried to focus on my goal and not on my throbbing shoulder. I had to stop Ragnar from killing the friend I never deserved. It was the least I could do.

Oh, please, Iosa, don't let this happen. I have so much more I have to say to him. I dug my fingers into the ground, pushing and pulling, trembling at the strain of it. My shoulder felt like nails were digging deeper into it by the minute. Blood trickled down my arm.

Peering down through the trees, I sucked in my breath. Metal clanged against metal, sacks filled up with plunder. I peered toward the top again. I couldn't see anything yet, but I heard Ragnar yelling madly.

Finally, I grasped a rock at the top and heaved myself upward. Craning my neck, I searched desperately for the mop of red hair. Dust stung my eyes; the only thing I could see was Ragnar seated cross-legged on the ground, gazing out into the ocean. My breath stopped. He shouted orders down to the raiders in his rough, bellowing voice.

I cried weakly, "What did you do to him?"

THIRTY-FIVE

THE JARL OF KAUPANG LOOKED in my direction, his eyes narrowing in the dim light of the moon. "Sigrid? You're supposed to be dead."

I searched again for Erik, but the top of the cliff was empty. Blood stains marked the dirt inches from where the ground cut off into a steep overhang that peered above the sea. Erik wasn't in sight. My mind raged in confusion.

"Give me the sword, girl."

"Where is he?" I demanded, as if I, a mere thrall girl lying helpless in the dirt had any power over him.

Ragnar tossed his head back and laughed. "You didn't think I would let the lad get away with all he has done to me, did you?" He jumped to his feet and directed a sword at my face. This man could kill me before I could reach for the sword at my side. My shoulder was too weak and hurt too badly to move my arm in defense.

"Give me the sword," he demanded.

"What did you do to him?" I shot back, my voice filled with rage at the biting memory of him pushing Erik toward the edge of the cliff as my friend cried out in desperation.

Ragnar scowled down at me. "Hand me the sword, and I'll tell you."

"But then you'll kill me." I laughed harshly. "I may be a thrall, but I'm not stupid."

"It's *my* father's sword, and it belongs in the afterlife with him," Ragnar roared, fury contorting his face into familiar sharp lines. "Not to mention, my dear thrall, that you belong with him, too."

Before I could stop him, he'd snatched Jarl Valdemar's sword out of my sheath. Terror struck me. I understood well what he intended to do with it.

Iosa, help me! I pleaded. *Mum, Tyra, and now even Erik have died. I don't want to die, too.*

I swallowed hard, remembering what Ragnar had promised to tell me. "Master, where is my friend Erik?" I hoped my meekness would soothe his temper.

"Why do you care?" he growled.

"Because I love him, sir. I didn't use to." I half-laughed, half-scoffed at myself. "But Iosa changed me. Now I love him in a way so deep and real, like no love I've ever been able to have before. It's a love so evident that I know without a doubt that Iosa is real, and He died for me. He died for you, too, Ragnar. He loves you more than you know."

My heart pounded. I loved Erik more than I could express, and I had missed any last chance of asking for his forgiveness.

"I've kicked him off the cliff." He shoved me downward.

My wounded shoulder hit the rocky ground first. A cry from deep within me burst out from my dry throat. He hated me. The words bled within me like the open wound on my shoulder. Tears spilled over and ran down my cheeks. *I can't love him, Iosa. I'm not like Tyra; I'm not like Erik. I'm a fool of a thrall.*

Ragnar slid his own beautiful sword out of its sheath and tossed it aside. Then, he stepped toward me, raising his new luxurious weapon of plunder above me. My chest was tight; a tingling sensation spread through me at the knowledge of what he was going to do next.

He plunged the sword into my flesh. Pain tore through my already-wounded shoulder. He lifted his sword again, but a shout exploded from below.

"Bleed, thrall," he muttered. Ragnar lowered his sword and rushed closer to the edge of the cliff to shout orders at his men. His men shouted back. They couldn't seem to agree about something.

As quickly as I could manage, I shuffled toward his old sword that lay a few feet away on the ground. My shoulder raged in complaint as blood seeped out of the wound. I shifted my body sideways and forwards like a worm, to keep my injured shoulder from the crude earth.

A bitter voice cried out within me: *Wicked, horrible man.* Because of him, everyone I loved had died.

And yet another voice came, soft and gentle: *Because of Me, Ragnar has a chance to receive fullness of life. I love him, Sigrid.*

Love? How could You love a man like that, Iosa? I reached for the sword, my fingers barely touching the hilt. Exerting my aching body, I strained for the sword again, nudging the heavy weapon closer until I could grasp it and pull it to my side.

If I used the last of my strength, I could kill him. Then I could let myself bleed to death and return to my dear Mum. Fire burned within me, the same old hate swelling up inside me.

Ragnar was still leaning over the cliff and shouting orders at his men. I slowly pushed myself to my feet and lifted the sword above the man I hated most.

Love your enemies. The Voice pleaded. *Forgive no matter what. Love even when it hurts.*

I lowered my sword. What was I thinking? How could I hate so fully after being forgiven so much? I was acting purely out of revenge and hatred for this man.

"Ragnar, sir," I cried out and held out the sword, pointing the hilt toward him.

The man whirled around in surprise. He eyed the sword's hilt. Then he looked up to my face, a muscle jerking in his jaw. I dropped the sword, the strength in my fingers gone.

"You silly little thrall." He snatched the edge of my tunic and pulled me toward his face, so close my nose almost touched his filthy beard.

"Please," I whispered.

I need You, Iosa.

Ragnar shoved me to the ground and laughed. Rocks bit into my knees, spilling more of my blood onto the earth. I gasped in a sharp breath. He knew I was too weak to run away.

I remembered the forgiveness that had mended my shattered heart. I was redeemed and forgiven. If God could forgive me, I had to show Ragnar the hope I'd found—the truth. I couldn't give him salvation, but I could at least let go of my bitterness.

Shaking, I drew the doll out of my satchel and handed it up to him.

Ragnar's eyes widened. He grabbed his old sword and pointed it at me. "What are you doing, thrall?"

"Jarl Ragnar, I pray you will find peace like I have. If you only look up like this doll is looking up, you can find hope and forgiveness. You only need to look up and repent to God."

Ragnar took the doll out of my hand, his brow furrowed in intense confusion. Peace flooded into my empty, desperate parts, healing me.

Ragnar examined the doll and frowned. "A doll? What use do I have for a girl's plaything?"

"Jarl Ragnar," I said, "I'm giving you this to say . . . to say I forgive you." I breathed deeply, hoping he heard my heart, because I had long fought against these words. "And God will forgive you if you'll only ask Him."

As soon as I let the words out, I felt free, freer than I had ever felt before. I felt what Mum had wanted me to feel when she told me to lift my head up. But I'd done it not through holding onto my pride, but by letting go of it.

Ragnar perused me for a long moment, his dark eyes flickering. Then, he shook his head and sat down on a rock. His sword fell from his hand.

Change his heart, Iosa, I prayed.

Hunching over, Ragnar studied the doll, then he clutched the doll to his heart with one hand. "What have I done? Oh Inge, what have I done!" He covered his face with his other hand to muffle the sound of his weeping.

I lay there on that precipice, watching him cry uncontrollably. I didn't know what to do.

A man ran up to us and shouted, "Jarl Ragnar, sir, we must leave at once."

Ragnar howled, his face to the sky. "I've been the greatest fool of all."

Shaking, he stood and picked up his sword. Then he stretched his arm back and hurled the weapon off the bluff and out into the bottomless sea.

The man ran past me and grabbed Ragnar's arms. "Sir, we must leave at once—the Irish have rallied." The man gave me barely a glance then dragged Ragnar down the trail.

Before they were out of earshot, I called out, "God save you!"

And I prayed with all my heart that those words were coming true.

THIRTY-SIX

I ATTEMPTED TO PICK MYSELF up but staggered and fell to the ground, nearer to where the downward slope began. I inched my body toward the descending incline. Soon I was rolling down it like a bundle of hay. The rocks poked through my tunic, and I cried out.

I hit the bottom with a thud, pain shooting through my shoulder and ribcage and pressing the breath out of my lungs. I closed my eyes, tears dripping from the corners of my eyes, exhaustion keeping me from rising again.

When a low, gravelly voice spoke in Irish, my eyelids flitted open. A man lay his hands out and motioned them toward me and toward himself. He seemed to want to help me somehow.

I pointed to the empty shore, pleading to him with my eyes. All I wanted was to see my friend, the sea, one last time.

He frowned and shook his head. Then he pointed toward the longhouses.

I pointed toward the beach again. "Oceanus." I murmured, praying he could understand the one word Erik had taught me.

The man pursed his lips but carefully picked me up in his arms. I cringed at his touch but reminded myself that he was only trying to help me. He carried me to the shore and laid me down in the sand.

The Norsemen had likely headed off to sea not long ago. Ragnar, Freyja, Niels, Lars, and the rest of them. Farewell.

The Irishman peered down at me, tilting his head to the side.

"Just leave me be. Thank you."

He stood up, hesitated for a moment, then dashed away.

I heard loud cries in the distance, from somewhere out at sea.

A man was drowning.

I strained my neck upward and peered at the tide that rushed up to me, almost reaching me. The cry came again. I scooted my body forward. Iosa had still given me strength, and I would use that strength to save that man, even if it killed me.

I inched forward in the soft sand, pain ripping through my shoulder. I groaned, but kept wriggling my body forward. If I could just get in the water, I could begin to move more quickly. The tide rushed over my hands, then my face. Water filled my mouth. I gasped and coughed out, but I pushed myself further into the water, until the sand turned into rocks and the rocks scraped my knees. Waves splashed over me, and I moved my warms forward and back to paddle against them. A large wave hurled over me, then powerfully swept my weak body forward, back onto the beach.

Water choked my lungs, and I gasped for breath.

"Oh, Sigrid," a voice exclaimed.

I groaned. My right arm felt like it was going to break.

"Please, save the man out there in the water," I cried.

"We can't save you both at once." Aine's voice was firm. "Ye saved my life and my son's life. I will help ye."

"No, Aine," I pleaded. "Quick, get a boat and go out to him! I can last a little longer. I beg you, if it's my dying wish, save him."

Aine looked down at me and shook her head. "I'll save you." She ran off without another word.

Dawn broke through the dark clouds that covered the sky, glimmering in a faint light over the water. Thunder began to rumble, and rain gently showered the fertile earth.

I lay there, soaking in the rain like a dry plant. It felt good to my injured shoulder. While I had always considered the rain as evil, now it seemed as though God Himself were showering His love on me in this moment, reminding me He was with me and He cared.

I prayed for the man out in the sea and for Ragnar. Could it be true? Had the doll reminded him of Inge and triggered overwhelming shame? Was he crying out to Iosa when he said he was a fool? The questions came unceasingly. I knew, at least, his pride had been broken, and he had been deeply moved.

I drew in slow, deep breaths in an attempt to ease the pain that wore away at my shoulder like a constant plague. God had saved me, the greatest fool of all, and He may have saved Jarl Ragnar as well. I ought to be rejoicing, even in my pain.

Aine approached me with two Irishmen to assist her. The two men carried me to a house, Aine following close behind. I heard the weeping, murmurs, and hustling of the villagers as I was carried through the town. There was much to weep for. They had to find a way to live now with what little they had left.

We entered a small hut, and my rescuers laid me down on a straw mat. Aine began tending to my wounds while the two Irishmen departed.

"You should go to your son," I said hoarsely.

"Colm is safe with another woman. I can't leave ye. Not after all ye've done." Aine gently dabbed my shoulder with the cloth.

I winced and clutched my shoulder to try to ward off the pain. "I don't deserve any of this. I was once a fool, but Iosa opened my eyes. Erik told me about Him."

Aine kissed my forehead. "Don't think about yer love now."

"Oh, Aine, he and I were never—" My voice cracked.

I wished we had been. The thought was raw and inescapable. I wish we'd been more of friends, and I wish we'd also become more than friends. There was something in me that longed for Erik and me to have had the chance to love each other beyond friendship—to plan a future together. If only God had had more in store for us.

But what right did I have to wish for that? I hadn't deserved him. Erik could never have loved me like that, anyhow.

Aine patted my wet forehead with the cloth. "Be strong, Sigrid. Don't think of him. Think of yerself." She bound the cloth tightly around my shoulder. "Yer wound could have been fatal. Thank the Lord ye will live."

I winced and squeezed my eyes shut. *Oh, Iosa, please, help me! Help us all.*

I didn't know what I was praying, or why I was praying it. Maybe I truly wanted to stay alive after all. I wasn't sure what I wanted. Still, I desperately wanted things to change. I was terrified of living with these aching feelings of loneliness and loss. I was alone in the world with only a woman who felt obliged to repay me for rescuing her and her son from drowning.

Suddenly, a man rushed into the room, the same man who had gone to save the fellow out at sea. He spoke in a flurry of Irish, then ended with the word "Sigrid."

My body tensed at the sound of it.

Aine glanced from him to me. She asked him a question.

He pointed to himself. "Patrick." He asked Aine something.

She shook her head and directed him to me with a pointed finger. "Sigrid."

Patrick smiled at me then dashed out of the room without another word. "What did he say?" I asked.

"There's a man out there who wants to see ye. He saved the fellow who was drownin'" Her forehead creased.

I pushed myself off the mat, my shoulder burning like fire. "Where is he?"

"No, Sigrid!" Aine yelped. "He's a *Norse* man. He could kill ye!"

I stood and pulled my cloak snugly over my shoulders to hide the cloth wrapped around my wounded shoulder. The wound ached fiercely, but I grit my teeth. "I trust Iosa to go with me."

Aine pursed her lips and ducked her head. "Be on yer guard."

Outside, the sun rose above the sea. The dark clouds spread out a little, allowing hints of blue to peek through. When I reached the shore, armed Irishmen stood guard as the chieftain spoke with a tall, broad-shouldered fellow near a rowboat. I had seen that rowboat for nine days straight, tucked inside the longship ready for use. It was the boat Tyra had died in, and Freyja had sailed off in.

As I drew closer, my heart pounded within me. The man was shod in Viking dress like any Norseman, but he bore the face of one I knew too well.

I limped over to him. "Lars!" No matter what he did, he would always be my friend who had saved my life from the ocean and from a bear. I could not hate him even if he slayed me. God loved Lars, just as He loved me.

Lars greeted me with a small smile, then he studied me. "I have not been a good man," he murmured. "Will you forgive me?"

I nodded. "I already have."

"I murdered those Irish slaves." His voice tightened. "I drowned them in the ocean like a brainless lunatic."

"Your sins amounted to a great debt you owed God; but Iosa has released the debt of your sins on the cross. Turn away from your sin and trust in Iosa's work on the cross to set you free."

Lars pressed his lips together. "Maybe I will. Maybe the pathetic fellow was right all along."

I stared down at my hands. "I know it, Lars. But now it's too late to thank him."

Lars laughed. "What are you talking about?"

"Jarl Ragnar kicked him off that cliff over there." I turned to the cliff and pointed. Lars didn't respond. I turned back to him, but he was gone. "Lars?"

I surveyed my surroundings, the beach, the forest, and the village tucked right between them. He was nowhere in sight. I started toward the village then froze. Lars stepped out of a doorway, a ragged man thrown over his shoulder. He brought the redhead over to me and laid him at my feet.

My heart fluttered rapidly. Could it be true?

I leaned forward and examined Erik's face. His eyes were closed. His face was pale. I dropped to my knees and laid my head on his chest. His heartbeat pumped slow, but steady. Alive.

I stayed there, my ear against his chest, my arms around his neck for some time. When I finally looked up, I was alone with Erik on the beach.

I stared again at the Irishman. He was soaked and covered in thick, wet sand, but I noticed only his long jaw and gentle complexion. I clasped his cold hands tight between my fingers. *Wake up, Erik.*

"He is alive!" Aine's voice declared behind me.

I didn't answer and instead ran my fingers through Erik's red hair, emotions swelling within me. Emotions I did not know how to describe.

Aine crouched by me. "We need to get him back inside to tend to his wounds." I glanced up to see Patrick standing over Aine. Together, they lifted Erik up and away from me and carried him back to the house, leaving me alone on the shore. I stared out at the sea, my old friend. It hadn't taken Erik away from me but kept him alive to be rescued. *Thank you, Iosa.*

"I'm going home," Lars's gruff voice said from above me.

I jerked my head up at him. "You're not going to stay, even for a short time? Isn't this where your mother was born?"

He scowled. "My father never should have fancied that Irishwoman. And I never should have come here. Never."

I stood up and grabbed his sleeve. "You don't mean that."

His face hardened. "I do mean it. I mean it more than you know."

"Why?"

He studied me and then shook his head. "I have no reason to stay here."

"Neither do you have a reason to go."

"Yes, I do," he growled. "I must."

"Is it because Aine and Colm would be here to remind you . . . ?"

"Remind me of what?" A frown flickered on his brow.

"Of the Irish thralls you bought. Aine and Colm escaped when you tossed all those thralls into the sea." Inside I was scrambling for a reason for him to stay. If he stayed, maybe the Irish believers would inspire him to wholeheartedly follow Iosa.

"I didn't know any of them survived." His voice fell to a whisper. "God can't forgive me—how could He?"

"God forgives every sin, even Ragnar's—even my own," I insisted. "All He requires is for us to turn to Him and love Him instead of loving our sin. He forgives you, Lars. You're with Iosa now."

"Why do you suppose that?" he shot back.

I trembled under his chilling gaze. "I don't know. Are you?"

He folded his arms across his chest stiffly. "I suppose I am."

I touched his arm. "That's wonderful, Lars," I whispered. "Perhaps when you return to Bergen, you could meet Stellan. He is a good man my friend Tyra knew."

The ocean whispered across the horizon, the morning light dawning into its full strength. I continued to dream about Lars's future. "You could work with Stellan to tell the Norsemen about Christ. You could share your story, help the people of the north lands see the purest Light in the midst of great darkness."

Lars straightened. "Ragnar gave me Erik's scrolls, since I'm supposed to be his new servant. But I'm giving them back to Erik, the poor fellow. Maybe, when he's conscious again, you could ask him to let us take them back to the north lands. Paper is rare, and no doubt the ancient writings of the Holy Word of God are the rarest."

His statement brought my thoughts to an abrupt halt. Could God want me to go with him? I longed to stay here with Erik, yet I also knew God wanted me to place Him above anything else—including Erik. Did He want me to spread the news about Him to my own people?

The idea excited me, returning to the old land I knew so well. I ought to obey Him no matter what I might have to leave behind. After all, Erik wouldn't leave his homeland. Not after all the struggle of voyaging here, to the place he loved.

"When will we go?" I asked Lars.

Lars smiled at me and rubbed his chin. "We'll probably need a week to gather a crew and pack up supplies. Think of it! In a week, we shall leave on a grand adventure—an adventure like none we've ever had before!"

He reached out his hand to me, and I clasped it. We walked toward the house in which Erik was resting with a bounce in our step. When we entered the house, Lars's smile faded. Erik lay on a mat, his head resting on a pillow. A woman knelt over Erik, her hand resting on his forehead. She looked up as we entered.

Lars looked from me to Erik. "Do you think he may want to come back to the north lands with us after all?"

My cheeks burned. I had hated Erik for so long. Why would he want to come with us—with me? Maybe he cared about telling the good news, but I could remember well that sad wistfulness flickering across his face when he recounted stories about his homeland.

"He loves Ireland. This is where he belongs."

Lars nodded and squeezed my hand. "I'm going to gather whoever wishes to come on this adventure to spread the news of the Irish God!"

I smiled a little, but I couldn't pull my gaze away from Erik. "He's the Norse God too, Lars. In fact, He's the God of *all* people."

"I'll leave you be now," Lars whispered. He released my hand and hastened out of the house.

The woman still hunched over Erik, adjusting his pillow and the blankets over him.

"Will he live?" I whispered and shivered. With Lars's warmth gone, the cold air chilled me.

The woman bowed her head and did not answer.

I stepped over and pointed to myself. "Sigrid."

She looked up at me. "Marika," the woman replied in a thick Irish accent, a smile curling on her lips. "My brother be his father."

I remembered him mentioning his aunt and uncle before and his hope of seeing them again. So, he was not returning to his homeland without relations to take him in. That thought comforted me.

"Will he live?" I repeated.

Marika pressed her lips together then shrugged.

I paused in disbelief, then burst out: "Oh, for mercy's sake, tell me if he'll live."

Her sad, old eyes pierced me, reminding me of Erik's green-gray ones. Her silence spoke volumes: He'd been in the water for so long. Erik didn't have much of a chance.

I watched him as he breathed slowly, in and out. I was a girl who had needed help, a Savior, and he had told me about Him. He had done so much for me.

"Why isn't a fire lit?" I asked.

She frowned.

I limped around the room, moving slowly to avoid amplifying the pain in my shoulder. I salvaged a flint stone and a knife and rubbed them together in the fire pit. Then I picked up some dry twigs

I found around the earth floor and tossed them in, watching as they burst into flames.

I'd promised Lars I would return to our homeland with him. But could I really leave Erik like this?

THIRTY-SEVEN

COLM APPEARED BESIDE ME AS I sat next to Erik. He squeezed my hand. "He's going to live, ya know. I prayed that God would heal him."

"Where is your mother?" I asked.

"She found an old friend here in the village, and they are remembering together. She's got so much joy curved on her mouth."

I paused, not knowing what to do with this rambunctious child. "Why are you here then?"

"I'm supposed to curve joy on your mouth."

I tried to smile, never averting my gaze from Erik. It'd been a week and he'd still given no sign of consciousness. "That's very kind of you, Colm. You're a nice boy, just like he was."

Colm tugged on my arm. "Don't look at him like that. You know what God says? 'Ask for anything accordin' to My will, and it will be yours.' And why would He want Erik to die?"

His question pierced my heart, echoing over and over like the drumbeat during the funeral all those many weeks ago. Why *would* You want him to die, God?

Lars was still gathering men and preparing a ship to leave, but he'd be ready soon. *Should I return with him back home?*

"God wouldn't want Erik to die, would He?" Colm asked.

I looked blankly at the boy full of wonders. His big blue eyes seemed to be as wide as the ocean, swelling with a deep love for people. What joy God had when He created this child!

"I don't know, Colm. But it's the same as Tyra dying. I'm sure Erik prayed she wouldn't die, but she did."

"Who's Tyra?"

I shook my head, unwilling to speak for a minute as the memories hurled back at me. The boy waited in eager expectation. My voice was soft and barely audible when I finally spoke. "She was my best friend. She was beautiful, kind, and brave."

"She sounds like someone I know."

"Who?"

Colm laughed. "You, Siri!"

I straightened and shot a look at him. "Who said you could call me Siri?"

"My mum told me that it's the short form of Sigrid. I like it better. It's easier to say."

"Oh." I brushed a spare hair out of Erik's face.

"My mum said that if you know someone really well, you can call them by their shorter name."

"You don't know me that well."

Colm grinned and spread his hands apart. "Yes, I do—you're an ocean. Your heart's so deep and wide that you don't let any rain bother you. You just let it fall onto you and swallow it whole!"

I laughed at first, not knowing what to say. Then I brushed my hand fondly over Colm's hair. "That's beautiful, Colm."

Perhaps he was right. God had changed me last week with His power and love. I knew He was there, watching over me from high above the mountain peaks, yet He was within my heart as well, giving me a newfound grace toward even the hardest bites of rain—Ragnar.

Colm began singing, his voice carrying through the barren house like the fullness of the morning about us. I couldn't understand the Irish words, yet the tune sounded familiar.

"What are you singing?"

Colm held his head high. "'The Lord is my light and my salvation—whom shall I fear? The Lord is the stronghold of my life—of whom shall I be afraid?'"

I smiled at the familiar words and sang it in Norse, using the same tune. The first time I had heard this song I had hated God, rejected Him, refused to believe that He was good.

Now, I sang from my heart; I believed. Something opened inside me as I sang. Light poured into me, and peace overflowed my soul. Iosa was here, and I didn't need to be afraid. He was here, and I was here with Him. He was here, and I would live forever praising Him.

I squeezed Erik's hand. "Could you live again, just a little longer?"

Colm stopped singing. "Hey, they're singing, too."

The Irish were playing lively tunes on their pipes, people were singing, and laughter filled the crisp morning air. These people had lost so much, and yet were rejoicing. Iosa was still faithful and true.

"Can I join them?" Colm asked.

"Of course, you can. They're your people. And your mother will no doubt join them as well."

After the boy tore out of the room, I walked to Erik's sack of scrolls leaning against the wall. Lars had left them there.

The pages were full of the Word of God I had so stubbornly closed my ears to whenever he brought them out to read. If only I could read them now.

"Would you mind if I took them, so the people of the north lands could learn about your God?"

I was beginning to doubt I'd be able to see him wake up before I left with Lars. I would have to take them whether or not he was awake to give me permission. The souls of my people were at stake, and Erik had always longed to tell others about his God. Surely one of the Irish thralls back home could interpret the scrolls, and it would offer hope and encouragement for the believers, and good news for any of my people hungry for the truth.

Lars entered the house. The lighthearted music played clearly now, and I could hear the rhythmic pad of the Irish villagers dancing merrily.

"We might need to take his scrolls without his permission. Maybe we can tell Marika where they went off to—"

"His scrolls? What about you?"

"Me?" I laughed. "I think he'll be better off without me."

Lars swallowed hard, as if he didn't know what to say. "He's always had a soft spot towards you, Sigrid."

I looked up at him. The words melted inside me, giving me a strange hope, but then I stiffened. "He's soft towards everyone. That's what I love about him. He will be glad to be back in his homeland when he wakes up." I searched his eyes, feeling, in this moment, like I could tell him anything. "Lars, could you wait to go home until he wakes up, just so we can say goodbye?"

If he couldn't come with us, I wanted to at least see how he felt about being in his homeland at last. I wanted to see the joy ignite in his eyes.

Lars frowned. "But what if he never wakes up? What then?"

His question caught me by surprise and I couldn't form a response. I was counting on Iosa to wake him up.

Lars shrugged at my silence. "I'll hold off until tomorrow, so you'll have a little more time with him."

"Thank you," I said solemnly.

Lars gave me a sad smile and left the room.

I returned to Erik, grabbing his hand and enfolding it between my palms. It was different with him. He was the only man in the world I could trust.

My cheeks flushed as I realized he could wake up any moment and find my hands enfolding his palm. I released my hold.

Save Erik, Iosa—please, I prayed, over and over. Yet I knew that even if he were to wake up, I would have to leave him.

He didn't love me like I loved him.

THIRTY-EIGHT

I SPRANG UP FROM MY pallet in the morning, washed my face with fresh stream water, and brushed my hair with a bone comb Marika generously offered me. Then Marika filled a tub for me and, I assumed by her manner, ordered me to bathe. I had not bathed since I'd dove in the water to hide from Niels and his lust, if that even counted. I did not expect to have to scrub off so much grime. Not to mention I had scars and bruises everywhere.

When I finished, she handed me an old, green wool dress with golden trim that must have fit her when she was younger. It was the prettiest thing I had ever worn, and Aine declared it was most becoming on me.

I stared at myself in Marika's little silver mirror. I had never seen myself so clearly before, always used to gazing at my blurry reflection in puddles or streams. It struck me how my tan skin contrasted with my green dress. The sun had done its work throughout my many travels these past weeks. I examined the intricate braids Aine had woven that hung on either side of my face. I was only a thrall and a wench to the many Norsemen back home, but Aine and Marika treated me like a queen.

I put away the mirror and turned to pack my few belongings. I couldn't delay Lars for too long.

I came to the main room where Erik lay and grabbed the scrolls. His cheeks were flushed, and he breathed more deeply. He looked better than yesterday. When he returned to consciousness and good health, he would have his family to care for him. Besides, he was home in Ireland, his birthplace. And there were plenty of Christians here. He'd have everything he could wish for, every good thing he desired.

I released a long, shaky exhale, trying to rid the weariness that sank into my bones. But it lingered. I had put Erik and God to shame by the way I had treated the good fellow. To leave him would be difficult, but I had to do it. God was leading me to declare His good news to my people, and I couldn't back down from such an honorable task.

I needed to say goodbye.

I sat beside Erik. His face was full of gentleness and strength all at once. An ache gnawed at me so fiercely that I almost cried out.

"So long, Erik," I whispered. "I will always remember you. I will miss you with all my heart and soul. I never got the chance to tell you, but I love you. I love you so much, Erik."

I didn't know if he could hear me, but that didn't matter. His presence comforted me. He would be all right. Erik was the strongest man I'd ever known.

His eyes fluttered open. My heart leapt. But he didn't say a word. "Erik?"

His expression was empty. For a minute, silence hung over the morning air between us. I held onto his shoulders and stared at him.

"Erik, please stay alive," I whispered, however deaf to my words he still was. "Stay alive and marry a good Irish lass and live and love and care—just like you've always done. I have to go now." I studied Erik's face. I had never really tried to see him until now. For so many weeks, I hadn't even cared. "Always remember to be brave. Keep your head up, toward the sky."

His mouth slowly opened. "Pride," he choked out, his eyes glazing over in pain or indifference, I couldn't tell. He stared at the wall for a long moment, apparently too weak to turn or lift his head. Then his eyelids closed.

I stood up, my throat stiff with tears. "You're right. That's all I've ever cared about. I'm sorry, Erik. Please forgive me."

I grabbed my few things and headed out the door. I forced myself not to glance back at him but instead to fix my eyes on the ground, thinking of the God Who was the only One Who could forgive me for my hideous faults.

Iosa had saved me a week ago, and how my heart still beat with the new wonders of His love and mercy! That thought put a hope in my heart as I plodded to the wharf where Lars and the Irish Christians were packing their supplies on the ships.

I sat down on a large rock by the shore to await the boarding.

Aine sat down beside me. "I will always remember what ye did for me and my son, Sigrid."

"I will remember you, too, for getting me off that shore and bringing me to Marika's to heal. You saved my life as well." My wounded shoulder had indeed healed, only stinging now and then when I moved about.

She smiled, squeezed my hand, and sat there with me by the wharf where the ship awaited. The breeze blew tendrils of her auburn hair into her face.

Colm came running up to us, breaking our silence. "I'm going to miss you!"

"It was good meeting you, Colm."

"Good meeting ya, pretty lady!" Colm hugged me so hard I felt I'd burst. "Never stop singing, okay? Your voice is like the waves of the ocean."

"That's because it goes up and down on all the wrong notes." I chuckled and ruffled his hair. "Now go on and have a good life, Colm. Make sure Erik has one, too."

"Oh, he will," he said. "I prayed to God he would."

We set out, Irishmen rowing, women settling themselves in the hull, and the children in the women's laps. The Irish villagers waved goodbye to their friends and relations they might never see again.

Aine and Colm stood on the shore, and I waved back. The two beloved Irish God had spared. *Lord, bless them. Let Aine come to know You deep in her heart, not just her head, and grow Colm up to be a strong and courageous man for You. Thank You, Lord.*

The green, lush mountains of Ireland rose above us. Below lay the white open shores, where my dear friend now rested in peace.

Goodbye, Tyra. See you one day, in your Irish God's afterlife.

I smiled to myself. Iosa was now my God as well.

The ship rocked playfully on the salty sea. Once we had paddled far enough out into the ocean, the men stopped rowing and let the wind blow the sails and propel the ship onwards. This was yet another adventure. I let my eyelids droop close for a nap and felt the familiar lilt and pull of the ship, as the ocean current pushed us onward.

"A ship," one of the men called out. "It's coming toward us; it's the Vikings!"

THIRTY-NINE

LARS SHOUTED ORDERS IN IRISH, a great dread in his voice. Then he spat Norse words in my direction, "It's Ragnar's crew."

The Irishmen raised shouts of panic and rowed back in the direction we had come from. Water sprayed onto the deck and into my face as they paddled wildly. Mothers pulled their children closer to their chests, murmuring words of comfort. Within moments, the four Norse longships, twice as large as our small Irish ship, began circling us. I could feel the hatred burning on the Norsemen's faces. What hope did we have? I drew in a shuddering breath. They would kill us.

The Irishmen grabbed their weapons and shields, standing ready for attack.

Niels banged an axe against a pot, silencing the men's voices. Then he yelled. "Hold the arrows! Let me get what I want then I'll leave."

The longship drew alongside ours, so close I could begin to smell the Norsemen's stifling odor of sweat and grime. Niels slapped a plank between the ships and jumped up to cross to our ship.

The Irishmen held their weapons at the ready, but Lars raised a hand to stop them. If they made one wrong move toward this skilled swordsman, any one of them could die, too.

"What do you want?" Lars asked him.

Niels ignored him and approached me. I scrambled away from him, but he grabbed my wrist and struck my skull with the pot.

My head raged in protest. He heaved me up into his arms and stalked forward.

Colors flashed before me. I knew I should fight him, but I couldn't even tell which way was up. Niels released me, and I hit the deck, the jarring rattling even my bones. Niels kept a firm grip on my wrist, sending hot pangs of fear in my chest at the thought of what he planned to do with me.

My vision started to clear. Lars stood opposite Niels and me. We were on the Norse ship. Niels slashed a sword across Lars's cheek. "Don't even think of it."

Lars dropped his sword with a clang. His cheek trickled with blood, distress deepening his blue eyes into a dark and stormy sea. "Never crossed my mind, cap'n. You can have her." Lars bowed shortly and turned to sit among the other Norsemen as if he had belonged to this crew his whole life.

"Lars," I shouted at him, but Niels muffled my voice with his hand before I could say another word. I clawed at his hand, striving to pull it down, but it was no use.

Niels grinned at me then turned to his men. "Raise the sail. I have what I came for."

Iosa, help me. What would I do now? Live as Niels's concubine for the remainder of my days? There was no one to rescue me—not Erik, and now, not even Lars.

My stomach turned into a tight knot as I watched Lars dutifully obeying Niels's orders. What was he thinking? I thought his heart had changed, but maybe it was only on a whim he had decided to make this voyage. Maybe he came only because Norway was his home or because he wanted to please me with his supposed belief in Iosa, so he could one day secure me as his bride. But why wouldn't he even try to save me from Niels? He had betrayed both me and the Irish.

"Everyone, stop what you're doing," Ragnar roared. "*I* am the captain of this fleet, and I oppose Niels's orders."

It struck me that I hadn't heard a bellowing order from Ragnar today until this moment.

"Fools, help me tie him up again," Niels yelled

Some men pinned Ragnar down and fastened ropes around his wrists, as he struggled against them.

Questions clouded my mind. It baffled me that Ragnar's men felt they couldn't trust him.

"Sigrid, is that you?"

All the voices and chaos surrounding me seemed to stop as I gazed at the man on his knees across the ship. Ragnar's dark eyes pierced me with concern. He looked so subdued and afraid, like an ox prepared to be sold.

Freyja stood near him, smirking at me. The silver cross gleamed on her chest.

Ignoring Freyja, I watched Ragnar struggle against the men and grab something tied to his belt. My heart thudded heavily inside me when I saw the satchel he held out. The men yanked the satchel out of his hands.

I tried to reach for it, but Niels held me back. "What's going on, Master?" he drawled mockingly at Ragnar. "Forgot where your loyalties lie?"

I blinked. Why was Niels so cruel to the man who'd set him free? He, not Ragnar, was the one who knew nothing of loyalty.

"Let her go, my friend," Ragnar said sternly.

My mouth fell open. The Jarl of Kaupang was ordering for me to be let go?

Ragnar glanced at me. "I am a new man, thanks to you and your doll. No, really—thanks to your God."

Warmth flooded through me. "Thank You, Iosa," I mouthed to only Him who could hear me. And in that moment, I felt that I could not only forgive Ragnar but also begin to love him as a true brother in Christ.

"Let her go, I tell you," he demanded again.

Niels dragged me over to Ragnar. "What has happened to you?" he said between clenched teeth. "Why have you turned to the bloody side of the Irish?" He slid out his sword and stabbed it into Ragnar's shoulder. Ragnar cried out in pain, for the blade had sunk deep. But, strangely, I sensed he wept for Niels's soul as well.

Niels kept one hand gripped on my wrist and the other on the sword that was directed at Ragnar's throat.

Ragnar bowed his head lower. "I have done nothing but let Iosa come live inside me," he said hoarsely. "For so many years I have regretted my actions, but I didn't know how to change. Iosa has shown me how." He raised his head. "He can show you, too, my friend."

Niels spat on the boat deck. "Jarl Ragnar has betrayed us."

The Norsemen erupted into shouts and murmurs about why such a faithful leader would so suddenly betray them for a foreign God. Freyja herself stood motionless, and the pain in her expression broke my heart. She had loved him, I knew, and all I had ever wanted to do was to kill her lover.

The pang of regret was almost unbearable. Though I had confessed my sins to Ragnar on the cliff, I ought to make more proper amends with him to bond us in a new, healed relationship of brother and sister in Christ.

Niels spoke to Ragnar in a gruff voice. "If you hadn't been such a chap and set me free, I'd kill you, but since I have you to thank for getting me out of slavery, I'll toss you with the Irish dogs instead."

At Niels's command, the men heaved the wounded Ragnar onto the Irish ship. Immediately, the Irish backed away.

The jarl who was once vain and ruthless was now sitting among the people he had despised and plundered from his whole life. Would the Irish be able to forgive him for all he had done?

Patrick, one of the Irishmen, raised his voice, but I couldn't understand his Irish words, let alone hear it well enough above the sound of the waters lapping against the longship. He pointed to the Norse longships and shouted something else. In response, the Irish hurriedly began paddling away.

Niels gave a shout, and the Norse longship began its relentless pursuit after the Irish ships. So, he was not satisfied with kidnapping me. He wanted more.

Niels tightened his grip on my wrist. Even as I strained against him, I knew that nothing I tried could loosen his hold. I was caught up in a life of slavery once again.

The memory of his attempt to claim my body still bore into my mind like a jeering taunt at my helplessness. It was only a little over a week ago now since Erik had saved me with his humble words and a deep bow toward Niels. Erik had honored me. And in return, I had scoffed at him.

Now I stood alone in the fires of hell with no one to stop Niels. He would leave me vulnerable, weak.

But Erik's words whispered inside me, *Don't be the least bit afeard.* I belonged to God. I needed nothing else.

Nevertheless, the fear remained like a plant that could not be uprooted from the dry ground. Niels would take me for his own, and I had no power to stop him. He would kill the Irish whom I had come to love.

Even though the Irish had made good progress in rowing away, the Norsemen were catching up fast. Niels's face contorted into something so evil I could not look at him. "Aim your arrows and shoot," he commanded his men. "Shoot at them with every shard of anger inside you!"

The Norsemen from all four longships, including Lars, clambered about their ships to obey. The rowers maneuvered the ships to surround the one Irish ship, then the Norsemen aimed their arrows at the small ship. I tried to wrench my arm out of his grasp as he yelled at his men, but his hold was tight. Patrick scrambled into action aboard the Irish ship, ordering the Irishmen to set their arrows in place to defend themselves.

Norse arrows rained down upon the Irish faster than the Irish arrows flew toward them. An Irishman within my range of view was struck in the neck, and he keeled over onto the wooden planks of the ship. I bit my lip, holding back a cry. I was hopeless to do anything about it.

Then I saw Lars, on his knees shooting arrows near me.

I hastily took the opportunity as Niels gave commands. "Lars, please, you can't do this."

He continued firing arrows at the Irishmen without glancing at me. His eyes fixated on each arrow's flight, but not on where they landed. "I will do it, Sigrid."

The Christian Lars had vanished. I ached, feeling as I had when Tyra had told me to slay Ragnar after the death of her babe. If only people could stay the same, but I would not be here if I was the old, wretched fool of a Siri.

Niels gazed down at me, a droll grin spreading across his face. "Now, my love, everything will be as it should be. Ragnar and the bloody Irish will be destroyed, and I, Niels Leifson, will lead the valiant Norsemen. And you, my beloved Sigrid, you and me, together at last."

My heart thumped wildly inside me.

He traced my cheekbone, a triumphant smile curving his lips. "You are most beautiful, my dear."

Heat flushed through my cheeks. This was not love. Niels would take my body for his own. I prayed to God till tears sprang from my eyes. *Iosa, why would You bring me to such a dreadful fate?*

A cry rang out as the Norse battled against the Irish. But my view of the battle—and of Niels—soon blurred with my tears.

"Niels, you mustn't do this to me." I strained against his hold but wasn't able to move an inch. "And you mustn't fight the Irish. They desire only peace."

Niels's kind look evaporated, but his grip did not. "If that were so, then the Irish would not be firing arrows back at us right now."

My mind ran over all the things I could say. "It is only you—you and your pride that keeps us in this battle. If you set me free, as Ragnar told you to, we would not need to fight."

"My pride will lead us to victory."

I had to do something about this. But even if my hands were free enough, I did not have my sword. The luxurious weapon was now somewhere in the depths of the sea. As much as I wished for a weapon in this moment, I was relieved Ragnar had gotten rid of it on that cliff. I couldn't let myself be tempted to kill him ever again.

Niels dragged me to the hull of the ship and bound my wrists with some rope coiled nearby. My heart sank. I couldn't swim with the thick rope around my wrists. Niels turned to his crew and shouted more orders.

The Irish women and children panicked like wild hens, crying as they tried to shelter themselves under sacks of grain or behind barrels. An arrow pierced a woman, pregnant with child. I screamed in horror, but Niels clamped his hand over my mouth, muffling my cries.

Patrick commanded the Irishmen with loud incoherent words. The Irish rowers paddled closer to Niels's longship and the Irish fighters hastily gathered swords and donned helmets. Did Patrick really think they could better defeat the Viking warriors up close?

"Grab arms," Niels commanded. His desperate, guttural shout gave me a small hope. A small hope that he'd be on the losing side.

Once the Irish were close, they strapped the ships together with strong rope. Then they slapped down a board to scramble across to the Viking ship. Ragnar charged at Lars, their swords clashing: Ragnar's strikes careful; Lars's quick.

Ragnar hurled his sword toward Lars's chest, just as Lars stepped to the side and slashed Ragnar in the leg.

I squeezed my eyes shut, not wanting to watch the rest. I wanted neither of them to die. *Iosa, help me!*

Niels released me and started after an Irishman. I opened my eyes again. This was my chance. I could not wait any longer. Now that Niels had busied himself with attacking an Irishman, I edged myself toward the side of the longship, then flung myself into the sea.

Writhing my body back and forth, I struggled to keep to the surface of the water. Because of the ropes around my wrists, I couldn't move my arms how Pa taught me. It was only moments before I began to sink, the ropes incapacitating me from getting anywhere.

My lungs burned, desperate for air. Saltwater stung my throat. I flailed my bound wrists up and down, kicking my legs uselessly.

The more I struggled, the more the ocean submerged me in its beastly embrace. Bubbles flew out of my mouth as I cried out in vain in the deep waters. *Is this it, Iosa? Am I going to die?*

FORTY

SOMEONE GRABBED ME AND SCOOPED me up, swimming powerfully. My eyes were closed to keep the saltwater from stinging them, so I couldn't tell which direction he swam. He went fast, so we wouldn't get killed. Nevertheless, I shook with horror, struggling out of the man's grasp.

But then, the realization swept through me that this man had saved me. Without him I'd be drowning with these tight ropes about my wrists. I stopped struggling, and let my body fall limp in his firm hold. Whoever he was, he was saving me.

Soon my rescuer dragged me aboard. I coughed out seawater as the incessant rain chilled my already-soaked body. He lifted me up and laid me gingerly on a bed of hay.

"Comrades, I beg ye, do not hurt the Norsemen. Stop yer fightin', in the name of Iosa," a voice declared. A voice that carried a quiet strength and dignity. "Return to yer ship, good Irishmen."

I could not believe it. Even before I'd pushed up my aching body to look at him, his voice gave it all away.

Erik stood before me, his posture confident, his brow narrowed, his red hair and his clothes dripping with water. He was not only conscious, awake, and healthy—he was more alive than I'd ever seen him. And somehow, some way, he'd come all the way here.

Looking around at the Irish women and children, I realized he had brought me onto the Irish ship. The Irishmen who had been fighting on the Norse longship scrambled back across the plank to their wives and children.

"Will ye strike peace between us?" Erik called to the Norsemen. "If ye do not, we shall still not fight ye, for Iosa hast said: 'Do not resist an evil person. If anyone slaps you on the right cheek, turn to them the other cheek also. And if anyone wants to sue you and take your shirt, hand over your coat as well. If anyone forces you to go one mile, go with them two miles.'"

A radiance undeniably from Iosa glowed through his face for all to see. "We are at your service, just as we are at the service of our God. Our mission is only to spread the gospel of peace."

I stared at him. So Erik didn't want to fight, no matter what weapons were used? Now that I thought of it, his idea did make sense. God had called this congregation of Irish to spread the gospel to the Norsemen, not to instigate a fight. Peace was honorable.

Lars cried out from across the waters, "Erik, my old friend, there are two sides to a battle—the good side and the bad side. You can't be on both."

"Aye, Lars. The question is, which side is the good?"

Lars scoffed. "That is no question; that is your own opinion." He notched an arrow on his bow.

My spirits descended as the truth slapped me in the face: my friend Lars would never return.

But no matter what, I knew God was good. He was with me. He was with all of us.

A sweet, melodious song filled my being, and it rang out like a triumphant battle cry:

> *The Lord is my light and my salvation—whom shall I fear?*
> *The Lord is the stronghold of my life—of whom shall I be afraid?*
> *When the wicked advance against me to devour me,*
> *it is my enemies and my foes who will stumble and fall.*
> *Though an army besiege me, my heart will not fear;*
> *though war break out against me, even then I will be confident.*

I could not think of the dying, of each one of the Irish souls that was seeing Iosa today. I could not think of the hopelessness. I had to show faith that God would be the victor. We were strong because God was with us.

As I raised my song to a piercing high note, Erik turned his attention to me. He smiled at me, if only for a flicker of a moment.

How had he saved me? Did he know how to swim this whole time, just as he'd secretly known how to hunt?

I had so many questions, yet I kept on singing, my voice rising higher than ever. Soon Erik joined in my singing, and a few of the Irish who understood Norse. Our voices rose above the crashing waves, proclaiming a victory more powerful than arrows.

"We desire peace!" Ragnar declared from somewhere on the Irish ship.

I prayed to God that His will would be done, that His glory would shine in this utter darkness.

The Norsemen released their arrows. They aimed at the men, women, and children without mercy, stilling many of the singing voices forever. Then, every one of the Irish, young and old, laid down their weapons and knelt.

All around me Irish voices rose up in glorious harmony to a glorious God.

> *Lord, our Lord,*
> *how majestic is Your name in all the earth!*
> *You have set Your glory*
> *in the heavens.*
> *Through the praise of children and infants*
> *You have established a stronghold against Your enemies,*
> *to silence the foe and the avenger.*

The Norse stopped firing.

Niels made a fist and ground his teeth. Then he stepped across the plank and came aboard the Irish ship. He strode up to Ragnar, his chest only inches from his former jarl's. The Irish stopped their singing and shrank back, gripping their weapons tightly.

"Your God is nothing," Niels spat out. "You are nothing. You have made a fool of yourself, my dear jarl."

"I have found Someone worth more than a thousand years of plunder," Ragnar responded.

I watched Ragnar whose chest was thrust out, but not out of pride in himself. I, too, felt a pride surging through me—a pride in Iosa, the One I loved more than any riches found on earth.

"Let's speak of peace, my friend," Ragnar continued.

"What peace?" Niels drew his sword and sliced it through the air.

Ragnar stumbled backwards. His cheek dripped with blood. "I'm not the same man, Niels."

"I can see well enough to know that," Niels growled and raised his sword upwards. "But—"

Ragnar grabbed the sword's hilt and drove him backwards into the side of the ship. Niels winced as Ragnar pinned him down. He couldn't move.

My heart stopped.

"Yes, I know the same tricks," Ragnar said. "I'll just use them differently now."

With that, he grappled the sword out of Niels's hand and shoved him off the side of the ship with one thrust of the sword's hilt.

FORTY-ONE

A FEW NORSEMEN REACHED OUT oars in an attempt to rescue Niels flailing in the waters. But the rest just stared in astonishment at their old captain. No one raised a weapon or notched an arrow in a bow.

Patrick yelled orders, and the Irish rowed the ship away from the Norse fleet.

Erik pushed past men and women to reach the stern where I sat. "Sigrid, we won. Just like what your name means: victory."

A smile spread across my face as his familiar manner ignited joy in my soul. Victory. The idea struck me. Iosa had given me a name that carried through the rest of my life. He had given me a victory far greater than I could have ever imagined as a meager thrall, victory over my own selfish pride.

I watched as Niels's ship faded into the distance. "We certainly did win, Erik."

He stared at me and fumbled for words for a moment before finally saying, "I don't understand—why are you here?"

"I'm going home with these Irish Christians, who are planning to tell my people about your God." I calculated each of my words, hoping to not reveal any of my feelings toward him, which made me yearn to embrace him.

Erik dipped his head slightly in acknowledgment, then he glanced over at Ragnar who was fixing a patch in the ship nearby. He furrowed his brow. No doubt he was baffled at why the Jarl of Kaupang was helping a crew of Irishmen sail to his country to spread the news of Christ.

I grinned at my former enemy. "Ragnar, look here. It's my friend, Erik. He is not dead after all."

Ragnar stared at me, wordlessly, perhaps surprised I would talk so naturally to him after all that had happened. Then he approached Erik, whose face turned a sickly pale at the sight of him.

Jarl Ragnar did not seem to notice the fellow's fear. "My good sir," he cried, slapping him on the back. "I have changed, you see?"

Erik drew a deep, steady breath. "I can see it, Jarl Ragnar."

Ragnar pressed Erik's shoulder with a firm hand, then let it fall as his voice deepened. "I am sorry for everything. I don't have the words to say—would you forgive me?"

Erik lowered his chin. "Aye," he said. "If only Tyra were here to see ye like this."

Ragnar narrowed his brows. "Where is Tyra?"

"She—" I started, but the words caught in my throat, as images of my dear friend flooded my mind.

"She died in the battle against Lars's crew," Erik said.

That was all he needed to know for now. That she died for him was another story.

Ragnar's face grew pained and forlorn. Tears sprung from the corners of his eyes. "I always knew she was right. I should have listened to her."

Erik looked at Jarl Ragnar with awe and a new sense of compassion. "God forgives you, Ragnar, as surely as I do, as we all do. And

Tyra forgave you long ago, before you were sorry for it all. I'm sure of it."

Ragnar smiled at Erik, a genuine smile that reached his eyes which I had never seen on his face before. The creases in his forehead bore the hard lines of years of toughening up and choosing aggression rather than facing his pain. I had a sense that this was only the beginning of Ragnar's journey of healing.

Ragnar put his hands on his hips. "I'm coming with you all to spread the news about Iosa to the north lands, even though I don't know a scrap of Irish!"

Erik broke into laughter. "Ask me any time if you need a translator. I am at your service as always, sir. Only this time, much more gladly."

Ragnar laughed with him, a great bellow of a laugh. "You're a mighty fine lad. I feel like I can see you for the first time in my life, the way you really are—as if I had good eyes at last!"

I couldn't help but laugh with them, all the while wondering at it all. The man standing before Erik and me was an entirely different man than the one I had loathed for so long as a thrall. I watched him as he returned to fixing up the patch in the ship. The Irish around us smiled at him, and I knew they loved him.

"Sigrid," Erik whispered, drawing my attention back to him. He stepped closer to me, his forehead wrinkling. "I could hear every word ye said." He dropped his chin to his chest.

As I thought of what I had told him, my cheeks burned. I knew I had overstepped my bounds. I had never treated him like a proper friend. I couldn't expect him to love me.

"I'm sorry for being so cruel to you." My heart ached, and I ducked my head. "I was a cruel Norsewoman. Don't deny it."

"Cruel, indeed."

I pressed my hands to my face to hide my tears. "My pride was worse than your fear, Erik. Was that what you tried to tell me when you were drifting in and out of consciousness? Pride gets you nowhere, but fearing God is the beginning of wisdom—I think you said that once."

Erik hesitated. "Sometimes God uses our mistakes and makes somethin' beautiful from them. Back in my aunt's house, what I was tryin' to tell ye was that yer pride brought you to me. You were too proud to let your own people defeat you, so ye escaped your death on the longship. But God used that stubborn will of yours to bring ye to Tyra and me . . . and to Iosa?"

"Yes," I told him, figuring it was about time he knew.

His eyes widened, and he grasped my hand tightly. "Do ye know why I came here?"

"You wanted to say goodbye?" I murmured. "You wanted to make sure all was well with Lars and me, as any good friend would do."

His hand touched my shoulder, but he didn't reply.

"You know I used to hate you." I had to make him see I wasn't right for him. However much I longed for him, he needed a peaceful lass, not someone like me. "Will you forgive me, Erik?" I spoke in a small, frail voice, hopeful and doubtful all at once.

For a moment, he didn't speak. I held my breath, feeling the weakest I'd ever felt in my entire life—weaker than Erik had ever been. I'd laid my heart bare before the man I most loved.

"Yes, Sigrid," he said in a low, earnest voice. "I forgave ye a long while back."

I narrowed my eyes, containing the hope rising within me.

He could not repress a smile. "What right do I have to hold a grudge against ye when God has already done everythin' to call ye His own? Even if He had not, He has given myself too much grace for me to hold anything against ye."

"Thank you," I whispered and stared at him across from me, wondering at it all. "Call me Siri, won't you?"

"Siri Finnsdatter . . . " He drew nearer to me, his warm breath mingled with my shivering exhales. "When I was kicked off that cliff, and I was flailin' me arms about in the water, I saw ye, in a vision. Ye held my hand and told me that the ocean was a good place, if ye embraced it. So I asked God to help me, and I stopped cryin' and started actually tryin' to swim. Ye helped me through it, Siri."

"God helped ye," I said, confident and steady. "As He has helped me."

Emotions whirled within me. He wasn't looking at me as a sister. But still, how could he love *me*? I was a mess, and I didn't want to weigh him down with all that I was.

"Don't think about it, please." I hardened my expression. "You don't know anything that's happened to me. You have no idea what's been done to me."

His lips formed in a grim line. "I'm so sorry for all you had to go through during that funeral. No one should ever go through such things. If you don't want to be so near me, I understand. We can be distant. I can leave now on the rowboat, if you wish. But if you'd allow me to stay, I'd like that very much."

I rose to my feet and embraced him. A full, fresh breath of hope entered my lungs. He understood what had happened to me. That was all I needed to know. "I want you to stay, more than anything.

But don't stay for me, Erik. I want you to be happy. I want you to have a girl who deserves you."

"Siri, I'm the one who doesn't deserve ye, after what I did to my father and let happen to my family and after all my weakness—"

"Killing your pa was an accident," I broke in. "And we're all weak, Erik, every one of us. Only God is strong."

Thoughtfulness resided in his green-gray eyes. "Would you consider going home with me, Siri?"

A deep, overwhelming feeling awakened inside me at his words. He had truly forgiven me. "Which way is home?" I glanced northeast, where we were headed, then southwest, where we'd left his homeland behind.

"To the people of the north lands, where we will spread the good news and love of Christ to all."

"But what of your own home and people?" I lowered my gaze, too overcome to say another word. I longed to tell him everything—the feelings spinning inside me, the love I had for him. But the words were stuck in my throat, even as my heart overflowed.

Tears rolled freely down his cheeks. He didn't hide them, like I did. "I love ye, Siri," he said huskily, cupping my chin. Before I could reply, he bowed his head so low that his lips touched my freezing hands. "I've waited so long for the day ye would choose to believe that Iosa is God, He is real, and He has died for ye. Ah, Siri, God is so good, and I wish to know Him a plenty more." His knees dropped to the ground, stilling my breath. "Please, will ye learn with me? For the rest of our lives?"

Laughter bubbled through my throat. "Aye, Eamon."

For a moment, I was unsure if I had crossed a boundary in saying his beloved Irish name. I'd stored his true name within me ever since he'd mentioned it.

But love ignited in his eyes, truer and sweeter than any love I'd ever seen. He gazed at me for a long, quiet moment, then he cupped the back of my head and kissed me.

My heart rejoiced, and I thanked God from the deepest part of my being. He had poured out His blessing upon me, wave upon wave, over and over, crashing down till He'd consumed my pride. He'd given me a reason to live, a reason to swim stronger than I ever had before.

Erik held me to his chest. I was amazed he would love me, one who had scorned his every word and deed. Together we'd journey through life, with our heads straight up and our knees down in surrender.

"Who is a God like You,

Who pardons sin

And forgives the transgression of the remnant of his inheritance?

You do not stay angry forever,

But delight to show mercy.

You will again have compassion on us;

You will tread our sins underfoot

And hurl all our iniquities

Into the depths of the sea."

—Micah 7:18-19

ABOUT THE AUTHOR

Grace Caylor is a college student at the University of Arizona double-majoring in English and Creative Writing with a minor in the Persian language. *The Thrall's Sword* is her first published book. She is a Jesus-follower, word-lover, and song-bird, and to combine these interests she likes writing songs to sing for her Lord and Savior. More than anything, she loves God, and she craves time spent with Him in nature with her Bible, pen, and her beloved journal. Her author blog for *The Thrall's Sword* is www.gracecaylor.com. As she adores Jesus more and more each day, she blogs her insights about God's grace at: graceabounds00.wordpress.com.

For more information about
Grace Caylor
and
The Thrall's Sword
please visit:

www.gracecaylor.com

For more information about
AMBASSADOR INTERNATIONAL
please visit:

www.ambassador-international.com

Thank you for reading this book. Please consider leaving us a review on your social media, favorite retailer's website, Goodreads or Bookbub, or our website.

When high school teacher Myles Bradford wins the Powerball lottery, he decides to do something truly unexpected: run for President of the United States. Thrust into the spotlight, he faces attacks and false accusations from political enemies while striving to climb the ladder of success. As his attention is pulled farther away from the things that matter most, Bradford may learn that even success has its price.

Real estate tycoon Rachael Carson knows what's coming when a mob of radical government leaders threaten to take over the world's financial system. Abandoning her New York penthouse and moving to her mansion at Irish Hills, she plots to save her wealth and rescue homeless victims who fall prey to the evil dictates of an advancing world takeover. Will they survive in a world gone mad?

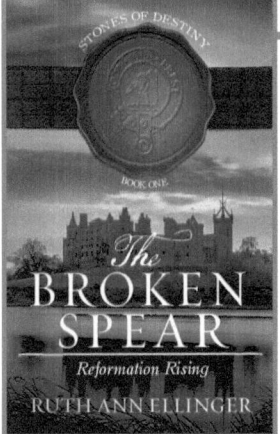

The Carmichael Clan—the men of The Broken Spear—lead an uprising against the Roman Catholic Church in a quest to reveal the truth of God's Word to all, thanks to William Tyndale's translation of the Bible into English. Against the backdrop of Papal inquisitions, where seekers of Truth are burned at the stake, one family defends the cause of Christ – against all odds.